Emma and the
WHITE RAJAHS
OF DARTMOOR

First published in 2001 by Halsgrove
© 2001 Pauline Hemery

ISBN 1 84114 099 6

British Library Cataloguing-in-Publication-Data
A CIP data record for this book is available from the British Library

HALSGROVE
Halsgrove House
Lower Moor Way
Tiverton EX16 6SS
T: 01884 243242
F: 01884 243325
www.halsgrove.com

Printed and bound in Great Britain
by The Cromwell Press, Trowbridge.

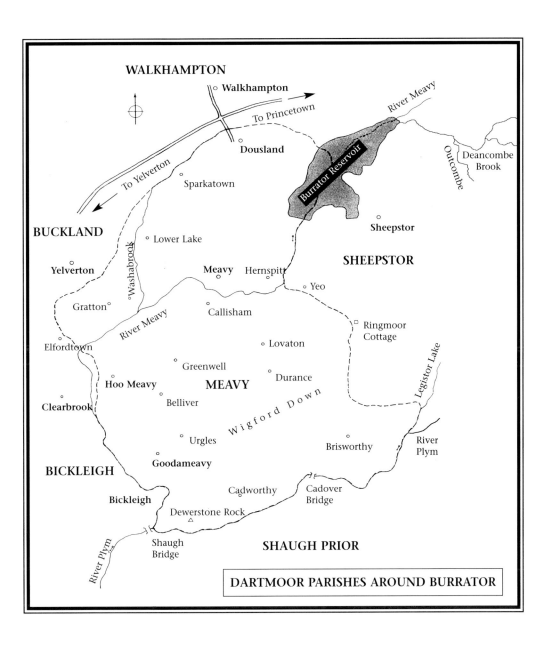

WALKHAMPTON

● Walkhampton

To Princetown

● Dousland

To Yelverton

○ Sparkatown

River Meavy

Burrator Reservoir

Outcombe

Deancombe Brook

○ Sheepstor

SHEEPSTOR

BUCKLAND

○ Lower Lake

● Yelverton

Washabrook

● Meavy Hernspitt

○ Yeo

Gratton ○

River Meavy

○ Callisham

Ringmoor Cottage

Elfordtown

○ Lovaton

Legistor Lake

○ Greenwell

○ Durance

Hoo Meavy

MEAVY

Belliver

Wigford Down

Clearbrook

○ Urgles

Brisworthy

River Plym

BICKLEIGH

Goodameavy

Bickleigh

Cadworthy

Cadover Bridge

Dewerstone Rock △

SHAUGH PRIOR

River Plym

Shaugh Bridge

DARTMOOR PARISHES AROUND BURRATOR

5

INTRODUCTION

SHEEPSTOR village on Dartmoor nestles under the massive tor of that name and a century and a half ago it was far from the world, a moorland solitude. There was only one road to the village until the Plymouth Water Corporation created Burrator reservoir. Now it is one of the most popular beauty spots in Devonshire. Amongst the granite walls and moorland turf, the peace of long ago can still be found.

In this historical novel the Shepherd family are purely fictitious, from Sam and Sarah to their great, great, great grandchild Emma. Outhome Farm and the Deancombe valley, however, are as real as Maple Ridge in Canada, as Sheepstor village, Burrator and the Dartmoor countryside in Devonshire. Here there are more hidden secrets than I am able to imagine – if only stones could talk.

I have tried to enter the lives of real people who affected the lives of Dartmoor folk, long since forgotten. In my vision, the inhabitants of Sheepstor parish were influenced by the actions and authority of the affluent and famous in their midst, a reality in the nineteenth century. Lives of these real people have been drawn from their autobiographies, personal letters and other original source material, such as census returns, documents and church and parish registers. Writing this story was like piecing a jigsaw together – I hope the result is a complete picture.

I am grateful to those listed in my acknowledgements and to the authors in my bibliography. They made the story possible. It remains my hope that the reader will visit the Deancombe valley on Dartmoor, the village and church of Sheepstor, the Brooke tombs in the churchyard, the tor itself and Burrator House. The English dynasty of the three White Rajahs of Sarawak, which lasted for a hundred years, is still remembered today in Sarawak 160 years after its inception. In England there is a thriving Sarawak Association where the life and adventures of James Brooke are celebrated. Many people all over the world become infected with Brooke fever.

Pauline Hemery,
Clearbrook.

To Peter, with my deep love and admiration

I

'DON'T do it Emma. Let sleeping dogs lie.' Tom Shepherd sat in his customary chair talking to his favourite granddaughter.

'I *have* to Grandpa. Who am I? Where do I come from? Didn't you ever wonder about the past?' Emma went to sit by Tom's knees.

'Oh yes I did, my love. When we came out here to Canada from Dartmoor I was only nine years old and all through my teenage years I was at my mum and dad to tell me about our family. They were either very good actors or they really didn't know.'

'Well, I want to know and I intend to find out.' Emma smiled up at her grandfather. 'We come from the same stock you and I.'

'Yes, I'll give you that,' Tom said, beaming at Emma. 'You are what you are, my love. You are like no other.'

The old man sat forward in his chair. 'In 1924 when our family left Dartmoor, life was hard and we all had to muck in to make a living. There just wasn't any time for dreaming.'

'Tell me again all you can remember, Grandpa. You used to tell me things when I was little.'

'You're a grown woman now Emma and you'll see through an old man's romanticising. I'm eighty six years old and those years as a lad belong to another time, another person.'

'That's what I mean,' Emma declared. 'I feel I don't know who I really am. I'm twenty seven with a failed marriage already. I need to know where I come from. Every time I look in the mirror I see I'm different from my friends. I've always felt the difference, when I was a child I felt so isolated. Trying to research our branch of the Shepherd family out here in Canada has been terribly difficult. I've studied the internet, read all the books I can find in the library and made investigations at the Record Office but I really need to go back to my roots. Can't you see that, Grandpa?' Emma pleaded.

'Yes, you know I can, my love, and it's something you'll have to do for yourself. What do your mum and dad and your sister say?' Tom asked.

'They agree. They can see I'm restless. Hester is happily settled with her husband and children and wants me to be happy, too. So, I've given up my teaching job and I'm selling the flat. The flight from Vancouver to London is booked for May.'

'My, you are organised,' Tom smiled at her. 'Well, you have my blessing. I wish I was young enough to come with you.'

Emma got up off the floor and hugged the old man. 'I'll keep in touch by phone to Mum so she can keep you up to date. Did you remember anything about your old home just now?' Emma prompted.

'Only that our school closed down in Sheepstor the year before we came out here. I walked down to Meavy school with the other lads and lasses from around the village for a few weeks. As I recall we walked through fields and along lanes and really enjoyed ourselves.'

Emma pulled up a chair and sat by her grandfather. Tom became lost in thought. When he spoke again he had moved on to his family's arrival in Maple Ridge in Western Canada.

'The journey by steamship was long and hazardous, and mother was quite sick.' Tom put his head back on his chair and Emma could see that he had drifted back to those times nearly eighty years ago when her great-grandparents had arrived in a new country to make a life for their family.

'Many families sailed from England in the 1920s,' Tom went on, almost to himself. 'My father's family had passed on, we were thrown out of our farm by the Water Corporation, so where were we to go? Others in the valley who had to leave their farms went to other parts of the moor or emigrated like us but we never kept in touch. We had a little compensation from the Water Corporation, sold our animals and bought our passage out here.'

Emma regarded her grandfather. He had worked hard all his life and his parents had been pioneers in this district of Canada. Life for her and her generation had been comfortable because of their labours and foresight.

'How brave your mum and dad were, Grandpa. Your father must have felt such responsibility for you and your mother.' Emma felt a rush of pride for the ancestors she had never known. 'You must have been such a comfort to your mother.'

Tom wiped a tear from his eye and looked at Emma. 'Yes, she had a harsh life and I know she would have given anything to have had a daughter but the journey out here put paid to that. She told me she couldn't endure childbirth a second time after that voyage, and then the years just slipped by.'

'Mother used to talk about the beautiful land she saw when we first arrived,' Tom resumed. 'The ridge of lovely maple trees stretched for two miles along the river. Father was impressed by the good soil, the rivers and the mountains in the Fraser valley. The forests had already been cleared for farming by earlier settlers and each little community had its own church and minister. The municipality of Maple Ridge grew up in the 1880s after the completion of the railroad. It was a new country and all the folk we met were pioneers. Dartmoor was the only land Father had ever known.'

'When you get there, Emma,' Tom said smiling to his granddaughter, 'you'll find the history on Dartmoor goes back for centuries. The first settlers to British Columbia came only about one hundred and fifty years ago. Still, you know all that with your education.'

'Grandpa, I never quite understood why you settled in the Yennadon district of Maple Ridge. I know there's some connection between Yennadon and Devon.'

'Well, that was a remarkable thing, Emma.'

Tom sat up, flushed with excitement. 'Not far from our old home on Dartmoor, about a mile down the railway line, there was a house called

Yennadon. Father knew old Albert Prowse who had built his home on the edge of that part of the moor called Yenna Down. The railtrack crossed the lane near his house and we all called it Prowse's Crossing. Mr Prowse, so father told me, was an accountant on the old South Devon and East Cornwall Railway and had worked with the great engineer Isambard Kingdom Brunel. His son's marriage had failed, a terrible disgrace in those days, and this son, ASW Prowse decided to come to Canada, along with his own grown-up son Ernest. Am I boring you?'

'Oh no, Grandpa, please go on. I might find the Prowse family living near Sheepstor in my researches,' Emma said.

'I bet you will, or people that remember them. Anyhow, Albert Prowse's grandson Ernest went to work for a Mr Spinks who was editor of a daily newspaper in Vancouver. Spinks and his family lived in this district of Maple Ridge, then called Lillooet after the river. Well, Ernest married Spinks's daughter, Jessie, in June 1909 on his twenty-sixth birthday soon after they got here and became the first postmaster of the district. The neighbouring district was called South Lillooet, so to save confusion with the names...'

'I know this part so well, Grandpa. The children at school loved to hear this in my local history lessons. Ernest Prowse had the privilege of naming the district and called it Yennadon after his old home on Dartmoor in England. It reminded him of his family home, this sparsely populated little community of Yennadon, sloping down to the river with woods and meadows in the shadow of blue hills and mountains. But I didn't realise Yennadon was so near to your old family home in England, Grandpa. Ernest Prowse and his family later moved to the city and he became Lord Mayor of Vernon six times. I've always felt proud of that, as though coming from Dartmoor we were somehow connected.'

'So have I, my love,' said Tom. 'And that's why Father settled here. Ernest and Jessie Prowse's daughter, Bonita, went to school with your grandmother.'

'Did your father ever get to know Ernest Prowse?'

'No, father told me he heard him speak once but he was of a different class, you see.

'Does the district remind you of Dartmoor, Grandpa?'

'Well, in all seasons, come rain or shine, you're aware of the hills, just as you are on Dartmoor. It is more mountainous here but Father always said Dartmoor was special, nevertheless. Old Mr Prowse owned the land in Dousland on which they built the branch line to Princetown, right near the Sheepstor and Burrator Halt – that became a new station in the year we left. I only travelled on the line once, with mother. We went to Princetown from Dousland for a picnic with friends and on our return journey one carriage of the train was full of convicts being escorted from Princetown to Plymouth by their warders. Where was I?'

Emma said, 'Tell me about when you first arrived here.'

'Oh yes,' Tom recalled, 'Father and mother were made to feel at home here and Father soon got work on Mr Trethewey's farm. Joe Trethewey was beginning to establish a large sheep and cattle ranch and he welcomed Father with open arms. He put him in charge of the sheep, the job he had done on Dartmoor all his life. Joe gave us a working sheepdog which Father trained and he was content. He called it Shep after a dog he had back home on Dartmoor. Funny thing was, there were lots of Japanese families living and working here between the wars and some thought that father, because of his looks, was one of them.'

'Then came the depression of the 1930s,' Tom went on, 'but it didn't affect us greatly. There were hard times but I remember Maple Ridge Park opening up and I rode my pony along the old logging trails. Mail was delivered to individual boxes by the time we arrived here and Yennadon Post Office had closed. I went to the old school here.'

'What a lot of changes there have been in your lifetime, Grandpa.'

'Cor, that's for sure, Emma, but the beauty of the scenery remains for people to enjoy. Folk here enjoy life in the countryside, away from the bustle of the city. I expect you'll find the same in Sheepstor, my love. After I married Beth, your grandmother, God bless her soul, we bought a place where we grew strawberries and raspberries and that's where your mum was born. We called her Alice after my mother's mother. Beth adored her little daughter. Thank goodness it's still very rural and peaceful here in Yennadon. Yes, I remember her talking about Bonnie Prowse.'

When he spoke again it was about his time in the war and any memory of those years when he lived on the moor in Devon as a small boy seemed to have completely vanished. Emma kissed the top of her grandfather's head and promised to call in to see him again before leaving Canada.

'I hope I haven't tired you, Grandpa. I'll have such things to tell you when I get back. I'm taking my camera so I'll post you some photos as soon as I can.'

'That'll be good. Give my love to your mum and dad, Emma. It's about time they paid me a visit.'

'I'll tell them, Grandpa. Take care,' and Emma headed out into the sunlight.

2

ON HER final night in the flat, Emma looked around her. Not much to show for twenty seven years on this earth. Her former husband, Neil, had told her she was too righteous and teased about her prudishness. Then he announced he was off to South America, with someone much younger and prettier than Emma. It did nothing for her self-esteem. Neil had been an out-of-work artist when they married, much to her parents' disapproval and it took only a couple of months for Emma, to realise they had been right; the marriage was a huge mistake. Neil expected her to teach all day, cook when she arrived home and be an exciting and willing wife.

'Your peculiarities fascinate me,' was one of his regular statements.

Though she had been determined to carry on teaching once he had gone, stress took its toll on her health and the previous year she had decided to take her counsellor's advice and resign. But something was needed to fill the hours and going back to live with her parents was the last thing she wanted, so Emma rented a flat and threw herself into making it homely. For the first time in her life, she felt in charge of her destiny. As slowly, slowly, her self-respect was returned, so the compulsion grew to get to the truth about her family history.

Her father had always told her that she and her mother had Chinese or Malaysian blood in their veins. But it never seemed to bother her mother who always changed the subject by insisting that her own father Tom had come from farming stock on Dartmoor. Then everyone would laugh about Tom's connection with Dartmoor – the convict prison, that is, not the moor.

Out of the county of Devon, the name of Dartmoor is synonymous with the place where some of Britain's worst criminals have been incarcerated. The country's bleakest prison stands at Princetown in the centre of Dartmoor, a high moorland region of great beauty, the last wilderness in England.

Tom was delighted to see Emma again the evening before her journey to England. He knew it was her obvious ethnic origin that was gnawing at her.

'How long will you be staying, Emma?'

'Six months or so I hope, Grandpa. It's my dream that I shall have found out all I want to know by then. But it all depends on how my money lasts,' Emma added with a smile.

'Go to my desk and open the right-hand drawer, my love. That's right. Take out the brown envelope on the top.'

She withdrew the large envelope with her name written in her grandfather's small, neat handwriting and took it to him.

'This is for you, my love. I'd like you to have it now.' Emma began to protest when she saw the amount of cash but Tom interrupted her. 'Hester has had her share and I have made provision for her children.'

'I shouldn't have mentioned money. I don't want to take this, Grandpa. Spend it on yourself, please.'

'There's nothing I need, my love. I'm comfortable, happy and blessed with many friends. I put it by for you before I knew you were travelling to England. Anyhow, you will be going to Dartmoor on my behalf as well as your own. It's my family, too, remember.'

'Oh, Grandpa, this is so kind. I can't pretend I'm not grateful. I know it will make my time in England much easier. I don't know how to thank you.'

'Yes you do,' Tom said through his tears, holding her tightly. 'Find our roots, then maybe you can look forward to the future. To me, that's worth more than all the money I'm able to give you.'

Tom looked at Emma seriously. 'I'll admit, I didn't want you to go at first. Hunting up our family's history felt like prying into family secrets. But now I can see that understanding the past will help you to find yourself, Emma. I hope you will find out the truth. It can't harm our forebears now.'

'Your mother's family came from the same area of Dartmoor, didn't they Grandpa?'

'Yes, mother used to talk of her parents when I was a lad. Brown was her family name, a large family, I believe, but mother had only one brother.'

'I may find it pretty easy to look them up but it's your *father's* side of the family I'm more interested in, as you know.'

'I'm sorry you never met him, nor your grandmother. I've only this one photo of my parents taken on their ruby wedding anniversary, shortly before they both died.'

Emma studied with renewed interest the snapshot she had seen many times before. That grave looking man, William Shepherd, held the key to her past.

'Dear Grandpa. If I start to despair of my quest, I'll gain new strength from thinking that I'm helping you.'

'You know you've always been special to me,' Tom went on, unusually emotional. 'Hester is, and looks, like your father's side of the family. Go to Dartmoor and discover our origins, you're a brave young woman. God bless you, my love. May your angels guard you.'

They hugged. Tom had not said that anything like this to her since she was a little girl. Yennadon, deep in the heart of British Columbia, had been the only home Tom knew since he was nine years old. Like Dartmoor, it could be a place of immense beauty and solitude, its mountain range and rushing rivers a magnet for harassed city dwellers. But for those who lived there, life focussed on tending their animals and gardens. For Tom's parents, William and Ella Shepherd, leisure was unknown either in Sheepstor or Yennadon; there was little time left over for looking back.

Emma took a last look around her flat. There was no sadness, only intense excitement and anticipation. Her boxes of teaching materials were stacked by the door to be collected by her father and stored in her parents' attic, and a large holdall with a small bag stood ready for the journey. Emma sensed her life was about to be taken over by a spirit deep within her; a fearlessness that permeated her being – the journey to London, travelling down to Dartmoor, looking for evidence of the Shepherd family – it was out of her hands. Lying in bed that night she thought, no she knew, that she was being guided to the most power-ful move she would ever make.

Emma longed for the hours of darkness to pass and for the dawn to come in at her windows. At last, her father arrived on the dot to take her to Vancouver Airport.

Emma was bright with beautiful eyes. She wore no wedding ring and looked much younger than her years. Her long dark hair was tied at the nape of her neck and her slender figure made heads turn as she moved with easy grace.

'Keep us in the picture, Em,' her father was saying behind her as she headed for the gate in the airport when her flight was announced. 'You know your mother will talk of nothing else but how you're getting on while you're away.'

'She'll be far too busy with her clubs and meetings to bother about me, Dad. But I promise to ring when I reach London. Contacting you from Dartmoor mightn't be that easy.'

Turning to give her father an uneasy hug, she followed her fellow passengers onto the London flight.

Ben Rose stood watching her but she gave no backward glance. Emma already felt her life had been taken over and an inner peace filled her. 'Sheepstor here I come,' she said to herself. 'Please let me find out who I am. My name is Emma Rose. I am a daughter, sister and granddaughter. I was a wife but where I come from is a mystery.'

She hummed to herself as she boarded the plane and exchanged smiles with her fellow passengers.

3

EMMA planned to spend a few days in London before starting her investigation in earnest in Devonshire. All alone in the teeming capital, she determined to forget the grief and unhappiness of Canada and enjoy being a light-hearted tourist.

By day she wandered through the famous streets and markets, taking in museums and art galleries. Standing at the gates of Downing Street, she was delighted to be caught up in the historic moment of the birth of a son to the Prime Minister and his wife on Sunday 21 May 2000. The parents of Leo Blair, the first baby to be born to a serving prime minister for over one hundred and fifty years, were both in their mid-forties. Emma tried to imagine those Victorian times and wondered if her quest would steer her back there.

'There's hope for me to have a family of my own,' Emma thought to herself, wishing she had a husband who truly loved her. Maybe my search will shepherd me,' Emma smiled to herself. Her search was for the Shepherd family and although she had never been called Shepherd, she had always been close to her grandfather, Tom Shepherd. She had reverted to her maiden name of Rose after her divorce.

She toured London on the top deck of an open-air bus and travelled from the Embankment to Greenwich by boat on the Thames. Emma was fascinated by the knowledge of the tour guides and enjoyed the vast amount of history as each one of them pointed out and described prominent buildings and landmarks. Much of one day was spent at the Millennium Dome on the bank of the Thames and as dusk fell she viewed the great city from the gigantic ferris wheel known as the London Eye at Westminster.

Evenings were taken care of with a cinema or theatre trip. Her time in the big city had sped by in a whirlwind of fun. Postcards were despatched to family and friends in Canada and now Emma felt her old self again, with an excitement she had never imagined. She looked forward to the future with a warm rush of anticipation as at last she drew out of London's Paddington Station bound for Plymouth on a mid-afternoon train.

As she sank gratefully back in her reserved seat on the crowded train, Emma had a chance to reflect, her thoughts only mildly disturbed by the clashing tones and tunes of mobile phones. So this was England. London had been a wonderful distraction to help her forget the past, but she had always lived in the country and took pleasure in gazing out on the green, tranquil countryside. A canal with colourful barges, fields dotted with cattle and sheep with gambolling lambs, vivid fields of acid-yellow oilseed rape, ancient church towers, villages and modern housing estates, all rushed past the carriage window of the Great Western train. On leaving Exeter Station, she saw the twin towers of the cathedral recede as she looked happily down on the coastline, the sea dotted with sailing boats, water birds feeding in the wet sand and men carrying buckets, wading in the estuary mud. Thatched roofs of cottages, fields of amazingly red soil and the brooding outline of Dartmoor, this was Devon – just as Emma had pictured it. She could not help wishing she had a friend to meet her at Plymouth station.

'It's your search, my girl,' she said to herself sternly. 'The project you want to do on your own. Take one step at a time and keep your mind on the mission. No time for doubts now.'

Emma knew she was going to be guided. That inner presence she had felt when she made the big decision to come to England, to seek her family roots, had never left her.

From her hotel near Plymouth Hoe, booked for two weeks, she looked out across the English Channel. Now there was no time for doubts, her days filled with studying in the city's Central Library, Record Office and Family History Centre. She pored over census returns, parish records and directories containing details of the parish of Sheepstor.

'Shepherd. I'm researching the Shepherd family in Sheepstor,' she explained at each visit. Everyone was delighted to help this pretty young woman with a Canadian accent and guide her in the right direction.

On returning to the hotel each evening, as the sun set behind the Cornish hills, she carefully logged her new findings in her file and planned her work for the following day. Strolling around on the Hoe and Barbican she looked down on the timeless scene of ships and boats bobbing on the water. In this part of Plymouth the sense of history was palpable; and so was her excitement. In her allotted two weeks she had traced her great, great, great grandparents who had both been born, married and buried in Sheepstor. They had a son and a daughter, both born in the year of 1860.

Living in Sheepstor at this time, she learned, was the White Rajah of Sarawak. Emma, hardly daring to believe in such a coincidence, realised the number of Malay visitors who would have visited the Rajah in Sheepstor. It must have been unusual at this time for a tiny Dartmoor village to be linked with Borneo. Surely more than a coincidence that her family lived in this parish.

Even better, the old home of the Rajah was now run as a guest house, she discovered. Booking herself in for a week, she left Plymouth and travelled to Sheepstor, a journey of only some ten miles but to another world. A world of remoteness and beauty, with a tranquil lake and trees, surrounded by rugged Dartmoor hills. Standing in front of Burrator House, she could not hold back the tears. A plaque on the wall stated clearly that indeed Sir James Brooke, first White Rajah of Sarawak, had lived here.

'I've come home,' she thought as she rang the bell. 'I know I'll find myself here – at this house, in the village and on the moor. Thank you, thank you,' she said aloud.

She was smiling through her tears as the door opened to welcome her into the warmth of the house.

'You must be Miss Rose. Welcome to Burrator House,' John Flint said smiling. 'Come in and meet Elizabeth, my wife.'

Emma felt instantly that the house was welcoming yet full of secrets that could only be imagined. In the following weeks she walked and walked, in the magnificent garden, around Burrator Reservoir which was a local beauty spot, and around the tiny village. The week she had booked stretched into months. In her mind she placed families, their names noted from census returns, who had lived here in the nineteenth century. As she speculated on the way of life in this moorland village and Victorian fashions, it was not hard to imagine the hardships of those times.

A strong Malaysian link was much in evidence in Sheepstor. Sitting in the garden or by the lake in front of the house, Emma wrote down her story. Piece by piece the events and people fitted together making the picture whole and very real. So strong was her imagination that facts became blurred with fiction.

One mission remained. She needed to find the Deancombe valley and the ruins of the home where her ancestors had lived and toiled. The Local History Society at Yelverton had given Emma a few names of those who knew the area well. Any one of them would be able to guide her to the valley, she was told.

'The final piece in the jigsaw,' Emma thought. 'Then I shall return to Canada and make a fresh start to my life.'

Her final investigation was to link her past to the present and future in a way she could not have foreseen. She wrote letters to her parents, feeling closer to her mother than she had done for years who, after all, was a vital link in the chain. To grandfather Tom she described the village, the church, the moor and the countryside. She gave him the names of people who still lived in Sheepstor, hoping some of the names would jog his memory. A few folk had heard of the Shepherd family from Sheepstor, but they were old and, sure enough, could only tell her that the family had left the area when farmers around the reservoir received notices to quit, nearly eighty years earlier.

She visited the old family home of the Prowse family, Yennadon House in Dousland. The doctors who lived there now were fascinated to hear of the Yennadon connection with her home in Canada and added a piece to the jigsaw by telling her that relatives of the Prowse family lived in nearby Yelverton.

The months of May, June and July were wet and cold. As she zipped up her anorak and donned sensible shoes, she thanked John and Elizabeth Flint for their kindness. She always told them where she was making for each day, a rule people have on the moor in case they are late in returning and a search party has to be called. Arriving back at the house at the end of the day was like coming home for Emma.

'I'm travelling with a man I've met a few times at the Royal Oak Inn in Meavy,' she told them early one morning. 'We get on really well together and he says I've inspired him to delve into the history of the deserted farmsteads. His name is Dan and he seems to know Dartmoor like the back of his hand.'

'Bring him back here for an evening meal, Emma. That is if you'd like to,'

Elizabeth Flint added quickly catching Emma's sharp look. The Flints had genuinely enjoyed Emma staying with them.

'Thank you. It's most kind of you. I was suddenly back home and my mother asking to vet my boyfriend,' Emma smiled apologetically. 'I'd love to bring him to meet you both.'

Emma set off briskly down the drive of Burrator House to wait for Dan, his dog and his Land Rover. He was driving them to the end of the road in Sheepstor, below Gutter Tor. From here they would walk over the moor as her family had done many, many years ago.

4

EMMA began her story in 1859, the year in which her great-great-great grand-parents, both born and bred in Sheepstor, married in the little granite church. Emma lived through the generations sensing their joys and sorrows and yearning to share their way of life in another era. She rejoiced in her connection with the large and established Dartmoor family, the Crebers.

Sarah Creber had worked at Burrator in Sheepstor for Mr and Mrs Henry Terrell since she was thirteen and a half. Harry Terrell was a fine huntsman and rode over Dartmoor much of the day, when not seeing to his stock on his farm. A jovial man, of ruddy complexion, he was known to his friends as the Dartmoor Philosopher. He had bought Burrator in October 1850 from Rob Andrew who had inherited the farm from his father William. They had run it as a working farm, filled with both animals and children. Terrell liked to think of himself as a gentleman which meant he employed many folk from Sheepstor village, Sarah being one of them. She lived with her parents in the cottage next to the church, officially named East Hellingtown.

Sarah liked Mrs Terrell. Her jobs included the laundry, scrubbing the flag-stone floors and helping to prepare the vegetables for the meals. Mrs Terrell was equally fond of Sarah who, according to Grace Thorn, the elderly house-keeper, was hard-working and worth her weight in gold. After eight years at Burrator, Sarah confided in her mistress that she was to marry Sam Shepherd and live with him in his farm cottage up in the Deancombe valley, way out on the moor.

'It will be lonely for you up there, Sarah,' Margaret Terrell said fondly when Sarah told her a few weeks before the wedding. 'It's a lonely spot and a good hour's walk from the village whichever way you go.'

'I know Mrs T,' Sarah said addressing her employer in her friendly way. 'But I'd still like to keep working for you.'

'Well, my dear, we don't want to lose you. If you think you can walk here and back every day, we shall be delighted to keep you on.'

In her youthful exuberance Sarah saw no reason why she wouldn't be able to walk, probably run, down the valley to work every day. When Margaret Terrell told her husband Harry Sarah's news later, he burst out in amazement.

'Good God, poor girl! Whatever is a pretty young maid shutting herself up there for? Sam's a decent chap, but he's let his cottage run to rack and ruin since his parents died.'

'Well, it's a good job she's staying on with us then,' his wife retorted.

Harry Terrell knew and was known to every family in the Deancombe valley and neighbouring valleys. Hailed wherever he went, he frequently found himself holding court with his wit and humour, leaving men rolling on the grass in mirth. As an expert horseman, he enjoyed hunting with fox-hounds and often rode with his friend Jack Russell from north Devon. But wherever he was at the end of the day, he always rode home to his wife who grew used to being woken at two in the morning by Harry throwing pebbles at her bedroom window.

The Deancombe brook tumbled down through the valley off the moor, providing the farms on its banks with clear, fresh water and dividing two Dartmoor parishes, Sheepstor and Walkhampton. Sam's farm, Outcombe, pronounced Outhome, had been his parents' home before him and was the remotest in the coombe. It was mainly a sheep farm, surrounded by the hills of Dartmoor. Other farms in that little valley were Combeshead, Deancombe, Middleworth and Narrator farms. The latter and Outhome were on the left bank, in Sheepstor. Four times a year on the quarter days in March, June, September and December, Sam paid his rent to the landowners, the Lopes family. His cottage was small but the farm's twenty or so fields had served the Shepherds well. Sam grew corn and potatoes in the small fields while the larger pasture fields were grazed by his cattle, sheep and ponies.

As Harry Terrell rode up over Eylesburrow, the hill beyond Sheepstor, he would often see Sam with his flock of sheep and pass the time of day. After his wife had given him Sarah's news he rode over to Sam, to congratulate him.

'I'm that pleased for 'ee Sam. Sarah's a good worker and a comely maid.'

'That she be, Sir,' Sam said touching his cap. He was a private man, brought up to know his place in society. 'I didn't think she'd have me,' he stammered, 'but it's put a spring in my step.'

The two men laughed. It was perhaps as well that Sam did not hear what Terrell said as he turned his horse. The Terrells were being kind to Sarah, and Sam was grateful for that.

The wedding day dawned clear and bright. The little church of Sheepstor was packed with well-wishers as Sarah walked up the aisle on her father's arm. It was Easter Monday afternoon and the church was prettily bedecked with primroses from the hedgerows. The woodland scent of flowers, and of the moss wrapped around the little jars that held them, thankfully masked that of mould and damp on the church walls. The church was not in good repair.

'What a shame the church is in such a dilapidated condition,' one of Sarah's aunts whispered to her neighbour. 'The parish is so poor we need someone to live here with pots of money.'

The musicians stopped playing and the church was hushed. Sam did not look at Sarah as she reached his side. He looked awkward in his shirt, tie and dark suit. Sam, not only Shepherd in name but also in occupation, was more used to caring for many hundreds of sheep that roamed the moor.

Maggie Terrell, Harry's daughter, was Sarah's best friend and bridesmaid. Maggie stepped forward to take Sarah's bouquet from her, before Sam and Sarah made their vows to each other.

'Samuel William,' boomed the vicar, Reverend Joseph Cork. 'Wilt thou have this woman to thy wedded wife, to live together after God's ordinance in the holy estate of Matrimony? Wilt thou love her, comfort her, honour, and keep her in sickness and in health; and, forsaking all others, keep thee only unto her, so long as ye both shall live?'

'I will,' stated Sam quietly, looking at Sarah with tears in his eyes.

The vicar repeated the words to the smiling young woman.

'Sarah Victoria, wilt thou have this man to thy wedded husband?'

Sarah hardly heard the words. She was overcome with happiness and never could remember replying to Mr Cork's question.

After the couple were pronounced man and wife, the five bells in the tower pealed out, proclaiming to the villagers, who were nearly all in the church, that Sam and Sarah were to begin their life together. Harry Terrell had provided the pony and trap, gaily decorated with ribbons by his stable boys, to take them the short distance to Burrator. There, Mrs Terrell and Mrs Thorn had set out tea, scones and cream with homemade jam, and a fruit cake.

'It was so kind of you to invite everyone back to Burrator,' Sarah told Mr and Mrs Terrell. 'There wouldn't have been room in mam and dad's cottage for all this lot.'

'It's a pleasure my dear,' shouted Harry Terrell. 'And may I say how lovely you look today, Sarah.'

'Thank you, sir. I am feeling very happy. Sam, come and thank Mr and Mrs Terrell,' Sarah called. Sam tried to hide his piece of fruit cake in his hand.

'Thank you both,' he stammered. 'You've been most kind to us.'

'Think nothing of it, nothing of it,' Harry said, slapping Sam on the back, causing him to choke on a cake crumb. 'I'm glad we've got the room for it.'

Sam was a shy man, small in stature, with a stammer. He felt ill at ease in company, much favouring to walk the hills and valleys of Dartmoor minding his sheep. Outhome farm cottage was tiny, one room above the other, with an outside stone shed and a privy in the garden. This was a small stone shed containing a bench with a hole which held a bucket. The contents were put on the manure heap in a corner of a nearby field. None of this, or the remoteness of the cottage, perturbed Sarah. She was the maternal sort of girl who wanted a home of her own. And Sam had been the only man who had shown much interest in her.

The pony and trap from Burrator took Sam and Sarah down the drive after the wedding party then on to a rough track, out on to the village road, past Park Cottage, Essery and Redstone farms and Longstone Manor. Passing Narrator Farm, they crossed the brook and stopped at the narrow stony track which led to the farmsteads in the Deancombe valley.

'Thank you,' Sam shouted to the young lad driving the pony. 'You've saved us a tidy step.'

'Thank you, Bob,' called Sarah as she jumped to the ground. 'And thank Mr and Mrs T again for us.'

'Yes, I'll do that. Bye then,' grinned Bob as he turned the pony and trap in the lane and went off at a trot, back to Burrator.

'There's going to be cider for the lads in the stables. Bob's pleased to be getting back,' Sarah put her arm through Sam's. 'I'm so happy, Sam,' she said, 'I've been longing to be alone with you. Good job the sun's shining down on us, with us in our glad rags.'

5

ARM-IN-ARM Sam and Sarah walked up the track. An embarrassed silence suddenly hung between them as they both realised that this was the first time they had ever been really alone together.

''Tis hot, Sam. I must undo the ribbons on my bonnet.'

''Tis that,' Sam chuckled, loosening his tie. 'The east wind's a bit nippy, though. Let's get home and light the fire.'

Dogs barked at Deancombe farm as they made their way to their new home together. Crossing Deancombe Brook by the ford, Sam lifted Sarah across the water.

'You'm as light as a feather, Sarah. We'll have to fatten you up a bit,' Sam said putting her gently on the track.

'Go on with you Sam. I'm as fit as a fiddle. Talking of fiddles, didn't old William play lovely s'afternoon? It was good of the missus to ask him along.'

'Yes, it was a good turn out.'

'Here we are then,' Sam said pushing open his cottage door. 'I'm afraid you'll see this place needs a woman's touch.'

Sarah had been in the cottage before, when she and her mother had walked over the moor to call on Sam. It was dark and dreary inside. The furniture, too, was dark and heavy-looking and no curtains hung at the windows. The bits and pieces of furniture had belonged to Sam's parents who had lived here the whole of their married lives.

'Would you mind if I moved things about a bit, Sam?' Sarah asked, hoping she would not embarrass him. 'You know, so that it feels like our home.'

'Do what you like, Sarah my dear. It's your home now and I'm only thankful you've come to share it with me. I ain't touched it lately, 'cept for giving it a sweep through.'

Sarah kissed Sam. He held her tightly and kissed her lips.

'I've got to get out to the ewes and the lambs, Sarah, t'otherwise they won't be pleased I've brought a wife along up here with me.'

'I'll light the fire and get the kettle on Sam. Don't be long,' she said, giving him a hug.

Sarah was happy and still felt exhilarated. It had been a lovely wedding day. Sam was twenty years older than she was and set in his ways. Sarah, twenty-one years of age, was unaffected and natural in all her habits. Her only excursions out of Sheepstor had been to Shaugh Bridge for the annual church picnic, a beauty spot where River Mew meets the River Plym below Dewerstone Rocks off the moor. This craggy hill above the confluence is covered in trees, mostly oaks, and is the foot of south-west Dartmoor. A lovely place for picnics and games. Sam had not even been this far.

Sarah busied herself downstairs, planning how she could make it more cheerful. Then she went upstairs. The room consisted of a large bed with feather mattress, covered in a faded patchwork counterpane, and a chair. On a table to one side of the bed stood a new candle in a white china candlestick. Sarah could see the effort that Sam had taken to make it clean and tidy. An old mirror hung on the wall next to a faded sampler, worked by Sam's mother, bearing the words *The Lord is my Shepherd*.

'I'm a Shepherd now,' Sarah giggled to herself. She took off her bonnet, gloves and coat, laying them on the chair. She went to the window, smiling happily.

'Sarah Shepherd, Mrs Sam Shepherd,' she said aloud.

The view made Sarah clasp her arms across her chest and hug herself. The sun shone on the moor and white clouds scurried across a blue sky. Sheep and ponies dotted the landscape. Oak and beech trees swayed in the wind and the sound of the tumbling brook reached her.

'Mam and Dad are only t'other side of Sheeps Tor,' Sarah thought, 'and I'll have a long walk to the village and back six days a week. There won't be much time for brooding.'

Sarah went downstairs into the living room and, taking a jug, went out to the yard to collect water from the brook. The April day was cool now but the sticks soon crackled in the fireplace. The room felt cosier very quickly and Sarah looked in the cupboard. Her mother had sent provisions up by Sam the previous day so Sarah set about preparing the first meal she and Sam would eat alone together in the cottage. The room smelt of burning wood, ash and oak, instead of the old musty odours. Sarah sang. She noticed the clouds racing across the sky through the window and delighted in the sound of the brook bubbling over granite boulders. She was at home.

When Sam came in he hardly recognised the only home he had ever known. The aroma of wood smoke mingled with hot delicious food. The furniture had been shifted and the Dartmoor breeze blew in through the open door. He stood in silence in the doorway. Sarah was beaming at him and they held each other in enfolding arms.

'Do you approve of what I've done, Sam?' Sarah asked, not needing an answer.

'I've only been gone a couple of hours, maid. You're a wonder.'

'Do you have to go out again, Sam?'

'No. I'm in for the night.'

Sam closed the cottage door.

Sheeps Tor, a massive granite tor, looks like a giant slumbering animal on a grassy hill. Seen from miles away, the tor gave its name to the village and the common land around it. Towering over the farms and cottages in the valleys below, it seems to be holding the secrets of thousands of years, the secrets of man's labours and loves. Man lived and worked on these hills thousands of years before the time of Christ. Granite relics of their homes, the hut circles, and graves are part of the landscape of the moor.

Massey Lopes was the landowner of the valley farms in this area and lived at Maristow House off the moor. Succeeding his father Ralph five years earlier, Massey had made himself known to his tenants, gaining their respect and talking easily to them. Sarah hoped he would make improvements to their cottage.

Less than three months after their wedding day, Sam and Sarah walked to the village of Horrabridge to watch the first steam locomotive pass along the newly constructed railway line from Plymouth to Tavistock. It was Sarah's twenty-second birthday. There was much jubilation in the area at the coming of the railway and many Sheepstor villagers joined Sam and Sarah in the walk over the moor.

The platform at Horrabridge station was full of people and Sarah grabbed hold of Sam as the monstrous engine passed over the road bridge, whistle blowing, and puffed into the station. Tavistock and Plymouth were now within easy reach of Sheepstor. As the train made its way to the market town on the sunny June day, the Sheepstor folk walked back the four miles to their village, feeling they were at last in touch with the world.

Sam and Sarah were very happy. They loved it when they were at home together and Sarah was usually at Sam's side out in the fields when not working at Burrator. Sam often walked to meet her when he expected her home but today she was going to be late. Maggie Terrell was taking her for a picnic in the grounds of Burrator.

It was mid-July and Sarah ran towards Sam when she saw him on the moor near Yellowmead Farm on her way home later that afternoon.

'Oh Sam,' she said as he hugged her. 'You know you don't want me to go out to work, well you may get your way.'

'What's happened, Sarah?' Sam asked, one eye on the moor for any sheep of his that may have strayed. 'Don't they want you anymore?'

'Bain't that, Sam. The Terrells have sold Burrator, the house and the estate,' Sarah explained. 'And you'll never guess who bought it. It's a king. A king from the East! Maggie told me, so I know it's true.'

'Go on!' Sam chuckled. 'You'll be telling me next there's three of them, all bearing gifts. And a baby in a stable!'

'I seed him with me own eyes, Sam Shepherd. He came to the house this morning. He is very tall and looks important.'

Sam smiled fondly at his wife.

'It's true, I tell'ee,' Sarah said, giving Sam a push. 'You just wait and see. As for the baby...'

6

SARAH left Burrator at lunchtime each day and called in at her parents' cottage on the way home to Outhome. Her mother usually had a bit of bread and dripping ready to give Sarah which she ate as she walked home. Sometimes her father, who was a sick man, walked part of the way with her, as far as the track beneath the tor.

'I'll be later tomorrow, Mam,' Sarah said as she left the cottage on the day before the planned picnic. 'Maggie and me are going to have a chat and something to eat by the brook when I've finished my jobs, so don't try fattening me up.'

'Right oh, my love,' her mother called down the path. 'Give Sam my best wishes.'

'See you tomorrow,' Sarah called and began her long journey home.

Harry Terrell returned home to Burrator just in time for his evening meal on the day when events were to change their lives. The house, a grey building, was sheltered from the winds and half-hidden from sight.

'Oh, Papa,' Maggie called after him as he rode up to the stables. 'Mama wondered where you had got to.'

'I'm sorry, I didn't reckon on being so late… please go and tell your Mama that I shall be with her directly. As soon as I've cleaned myself up a bit,' called her father.

'Give her extra fodder, Bob, and a good rub down,' Harry said to his stable lad. 'Us 'ave had a long ride across the moor.'

'Right you are, Sir,' Bob said as his master dismounted.

'See you in the morning, Bob,' Terrell said, disappearing into the house.

After washing and changing, he strode into the dining room. 'I could do with a drink,' he said to his wife. 'I reckon I've got some startling news for you both.'

He sat down at the table and smiled at his wife and daughter. They had named their daughter Margaret after her mother but they called her Maggie. She had a lonely life at Burrator. Walking into the village she spoke to everyone she met but her only friend was Sarah Creber, the girl who worked in their kitchen. Now Sarah was married, and to Maggie, Sarah Shepherd was not the same. She was always in a rush to get home and talked of little else but of Sam and life on their farm.

Only that morning, she had told Sarah how badly she missed their chats and walks in the garden.

'You're always so tired these days, Sarah,' Maggie had complained. 'And you're always in a hurry to get straight off home, too.'

'Yes, I do feel tired, Maggie, and I've been feeling sick lately. I do love to see you, honest, but I've got Sam's meal to cook when I get home.'

'Yes I see that,' Maggie said. 'I'll ask Mama to let you off early tomorrow and we'll have a picnic by the brook before your long walk home.'

'Oh, *that* would be lovely. I'll make sure to tell Sam I may be a bit late home. And I'll tell Mam not to feed me up,' Sarah laughed.

Maggie had watched Sarah run down the shady carriage drive to the road and returned her wave as Sarah turned the corner then headed straight into the house to find her mother.

The three Terrells settled down to dinner and Harry Terrell said grace.

'I hope it's a good meal tonight,' Harry beamed at his wife. 'We have something to celebrate.'

'Do tell us your news at once, Papa,' urged Maggie. 'I've got something to tell you, too.' She was longing to tell her father about the picnic she was to have with Sarah the next day.

'It's been such a hot day, Harry,' Margaret Terrell answered her husband, 'but we have three courses to eat and I've cooked the woodcock.'

'Oh good. Good,' Harry said, his complexion looking more ruddy than usual.

As they ate the trout he said, 'You'll be shocked at my news. Shocked, I say. I don't know where to begin.'

'It's certainly not like you to be lost for words, Harry,' Margaret said smiling at her husband.

'Oh, please just tell us, Papa, I'm bursting to know.'

'Well, my dears,' he said, putting down his knife and fork. 'I've sold this house – well, what I mean is, I've sold the whole estate. What do you think of that, eh?'

The two women looked at him open mouthed.

'Good God, say something,' he said after a long pause. 'What do you think?'

Margaret Terrell, whose serene temperament was completely opposite to that of her extrovert husband, merely asked quietly, 'Who have you sold it to? And where are we to go?'

'I don't know yet where we will go, but I'll tell you this, I'm to get double the price that I paid for it.'

'Oh Papa,' cried Maggie. 'Tell us the story from the beginning. I shan't eat another thing until you do.'

But the meal was eaten and the two women listened patiently while Harry told them of the day's events. It had been a lovely sunny day and Harry Terrell had had business to attend to in Totnes. He left Burrator at daybreak and rode across the moor on his hunter. As he rode through Totnes town his agent saw him ride past the office. Harry heard his name called.

'Harry, Harry, can you call in for a few minutes?'

Harry looked back over his shoulder then turned his horse to retrace his steps.

'I've someone with me who wants to meet you, do come in a minute,' pleaded his agent.

Harry dismounted and tethered his horse. As he entered the dim office from the bright sunshine it took at least half a minute for his eyes to become accustomed to the dimness of the room. He saw before him a tall gentleman, very tall with receding hair and kindly blue eyes shining from a face pitted with pox marks.

'Harry Terrell, this is Sir James Brooke. He'd like to buy your house.'

'Would you now, sir, well it bain't for sale.'

'I took the liberty of telling Sir James what a beautiful spot you live in, Harry. Sir James has been very ill and ordered to live on Dartmoor. It would suit him most admirably.'

'Pleased to meet you, Mr Terrell,' Sir James said, in a most educated accent. 'I can see from your healthy countenance that your home would be the place for me. Are you certain you can't be persuaded to sell?'

'Think about it, Harry,' his agent spoke kindly. 'It would give you capital and money to buy a neighbouring property.'

'Why don't we talk about it over a drink and something to eat?' suggested Sir James. 'Shall we say the hostelry at one of the clock?'

'I'll be there,' Harry said taking his leave of the two gentlemen. ''Til one o'clock then.'

The agent had indeed told Sir James Brooke all about Burrator and made it known that Harry Terrell was not a wealthy man, spending any money he had on his staff and the upkeep of his estate.

'Burrator estate lies on the edge of the village of Sheepstor in the south-west of the county,' he told Sir James, 'where the brook of that name rushes down the valley and through Burrator gardens to join the River Mew. A tor on Dartmoor is a pile of granite, tor being a corruption of tower and nearby the house is Beara Tor, a small pile of rocks, which means tor in the woods. Much of the estate is woodland, running down to the Mew, a bright clear river which joins the Plym off the moor. Over the years, Bearator has become Burrator.'

The agent warmed to his theme. 'The River Mew has cut a deep natural gorge, dividing the parishes of Sheepstor and Meavy, with Walkhampton parish to the north. The whole estate is a haven for wild animals and flora. In the valley below Burrator is the headweir of a leat, that is a water course, engineered by Sir Francis Drake in the sixteenth century to carry fresh water by gravity from Dartmoor to Plymouth. It is an area full of beauty and history, with bracing air and pure water but for all that secluded – the nearby villagers will be glad of employment. Most of your neighbours will be from the farming community.'

'Without even seeing it,' said Sir James, 'I feel it's the place for me. But will Terrell sell?'

'For the right price, sir, I think he will,' the agent replied. He was not finished yet. 'The estate is triangular, two sides bordered by streams and the third by the lane leading to the tiny village of Sheepstor. Woodland and water birds nest in the gardens, even Canada geese, and wild flowers abound everywhere. It is a romantic parish spreading well beyond the village to encompass wild moorland. Terrell has a pony and a hunter, three large dogs and a terrier and a few game-cocks he puts up for fighting. He has a fine herd of dairy cows which I'm sure he'd be persuaded to sell along with the estate.'

'You know it well, it seems,' Sir James said. 'You make it sound mighty attractive and soothing.'

'Well, it is that,' the agent said. 'Harry and Margaret Terrell are most hospitable and I've spent many happy hours there. I don't know of any other place that will restore you to health so quickly, Sir. I hope Terrell sees sense. Could you ride over there tomorrow? I could meet you there if you want.'

'I'd like that. Let's go and see if we can persuade Mr Henry Terrell to sell his home to me.'

7

Harry Terrell completed his business transactions in the town, with the usual hearty greetings from all who recognised him. Whatever position in life a person held, Harry treated all alike. His speech was of true Devonshire dialect and as rustic as his appearance. Although rough and ready in his ways he had a kindly nature and helped anyone in need. Harry Terrell considered himself to be a pillar of society and was proud to be a churchwarden of Sheepstor church.

The nearest town to Sheepstor was Tavistock, his birthplace, judged a very sporting town. Hunting, horse-racing on Whitchurch Down and cock-fighting were the favourite pastimes of most of the inhabitants and Harry had a name in the district as a good critic of ponies and farm animals. The largest village nearby was Horrabridge from where the post was delivered daily to Sheepstor.

Terrell and Brooke were strikingly different not only in character but also in appearance. Though of the same age, Terrell was sturdy and fit with black hair, piercing dark eyes and an aquiline nose; the impression made by Brooke was of a refined gentleman; tall with a lean upright figure, scanty grey hair and a high bald forehead. His once handsome face was scarred but he spoke in a soft mild voice choosing his words carefully.

At the inn in the centre of Totnes, the three men got down to discussing Terrell's estate.

'I'll give you twice what you paid for it,' Sir James Brooke declared. 'And more if you want.'

'Perhaps we could come to Burrator tomorrow morning, Harry?' his agent enquired. 'The day will suit us both if it is convenient for you.'

'By Jove, it will be a shock for Mrs Terrell and Maggie. A real shock, I say. But yes, if you can meet with Sir James tomorrow you can certainly bring him over.' Harry beamed at his friend. 'I shall be at home all day.'

'Good, we shall see you at about eleven o'clock, Harry. You won't regret it.'

'It is most gracious of you, Mr Terrell,' Sir James added. 'And I thank you.'

'Give my regards to Mrs Terrell,' the agent said at their parting. 'Also to Maggie.'

'I will that. Until tomorrow, then. Good-day to you both.'

Terrell liked a long ride, and on his journey home across country, had plenty of time to think about the events of the day. Here was an opportunity that surely would not be repeated. A Rajah from an eastern country offering a high price for his home. He was too poor not to consider this offer, indeed he began to believe this chance meeting was a signal he must not ignore.

As Harry Terrell was relating the events to his wife and daughter he became more flushed and excited.

'That's what he said, my dears, twice what I paid and more.'

'But he hasn't seen the place. Has he ever called here?' enquired Margaret Terrell quietly.

'No, never. He's staying at the Dousland Barn Hotel and because of ill-health he's been ordered to live on our side of Dartmoor. Now let me get on with the story.' Harry looked at his wife with a happy expression.

'Sir James paid the bill at the inn and was very persuasive. The bottom of it is, I've said he can come over here at eleven o'clock tomorrow afore noon, and if he likes the estate he can have it.'

'Who did you say the man was, Papa?' Maggie asked. 'I know he's Sir James Brooke, but…'

'I didn't understand either, my love,' her father said interrupting her. 'He's a Rajah, he reckons. He told me it's a sort of eastern king, and sure enough, he looks every inch a king to me.'

'Of which country, my dear?' his wife enquired.

'Somewhere in the East. Borneo, I think he said. It's all a bit much to take in.'

'Oh my goodness,' exclaimed Margaret Terrell. 'This house isn't fit for a king!'

'Oh yes it is,' Harry shouted. 'It's served us well and we've been happy. What else can a man ask for of a home? Eh?'

Leaving the dining room, they sat in the drawing room mulling over this bolt from the blue, each with their own concerns over such a sudden jolt to their settled life.

'I nearly forgot, Papa,' Maggie said. 'I've asked Sarah to come for a picnic down by the brook tomorrow. Is that all right?'

'Yes, of course, my dear. But I would like you here to greet Sir James in the morning. He's been quite ill, so I did feel sorry for him. Must be from living in the tropics, I suppose.'

Maggie went to bed, thinking excitedly of the secret she would reveal to Sarah at the picnic the next day.

Margaret Terrell began to reflect on life beyond Burrator.

'We should move nearer to a town for Maggie, my dear. She has a lonely life here.'

'I'm glad you consider the move, my dear. Riding home across the moor I had time to think. It's a wonderful place, is Dartmoor, for getting your thoughts in order.'

Talking more to himself than to his wife, Harry went on, 'I could sell Brooke my stock – keep my horse, of course – and we could live at Leaford until we find a suitable home for ourselves.'

As a temporary measure, Margaret thought this was a good plan. Leaford was also Terrell's land, not far from the gate leading to Burrator, where two cottages for the poor had once stood. The converted cottage would be comfortable for a few months, while they looked for a suitable residence. Sheepstor was a special village and community where folk cared for each other but kept themselves to themselves.

It was a lonely place for a young woman like Maggie who ought to be mixing with society of her own age and quality. They had lived there for nearly nine years and Maggie had been a schoolgirl when they bought Burrator as a farm. Her closest friend, Sarah Shepherd, was a sweet girl but not of their class. Much of their money went on improving the property... yes, selling the house at this time might not be such a bad thing.

The day of the picnic was warm and sunny. In their dresses, aprons and bonnets, Maggie and Sarah walked along the path to the west of the house. Passing the orchard and the stroll where Harry had planted young trees, they walked down towards the sound of the Sheepstor Brook. Crossing Homer Meadow and Western Park fields they reached the wood, shouting to make themselves heard above the noise of the falling brook. The brook was on its final journey before it joined the River Mew in the valley below. In a short distance it fell steeply, one hundred feet below Beara Tor, the granite pile in the wood which gave its name to the estate.

In the bed of the brook were enormous granite boulders from the clitter, or fallen rocks, of the tor which had been moved by the force of the current over the winters of many centuries. The brook came from a mire near Ware's Warren and in winter time was a raging torrent.

The two young women sat under the shade of an old beech tree and opened their picnic basket. Spray from the falling brook splashed on their aprons. Shadows of the leaves danced on the pools. Over the noise of the water, birds sang from the tops of the trees.

'How lovely it would be to sit in one of those pools on such a hot day, Sarah. We have to wear so many clothes.'

'I suppose we could remove our bonnets, Maggie. No one comes this way, only the wild creatures in the wood.'

Laughing, and each with exciting news to reveal that they had told no one else, the girls ate the food and drank the cordial. After nearly two hours had flown by, Sarah packed the picnic basket.

'I've had such a lovely time, Maggie. But now I must get back to Sam.'

'I shall never forget this day, Sarah. Let's put our bonnets on and follow the brook upstream to our garden.'

Sarah and Maggie walked through Puckery Meadow and crossed over the brook on one of the rustic bridges. They both knew their lives were to change forever.

'I shall miss you, Maggie.'

'Don't forget you'll be working for a king, until your baby is born. I hope the Rajah appreciates the beauties of Burrator. I can't believe it is any more beautiful in the East.'

Sarah made a hasty visit to her parents' cottage, to let them into the secret she had just revealed to Maggie – that they were to be grandparents.

'Well, I'd already guessed, Sarah, didn't I, Father?' said her mother. 'We're fair delighted, and that's a fact.'

Mother and daughter hugged and Sarah hurried home at last to Sam, on the moor waiting for her as usual. It was on this summer's day when she told him about Rajah Brooke coming to live at Burrator and gave him the pleasurable tidings that he was to become a father.

8

BURRATOR was all that Brooke imagined it would be, and more. He delighted in the proportions of the house and declared the gardens more beautiful than he could have visualised. The Terrells welcomed him warmly and at once he fell in love with everything about the place though in that year of 1859 it must have been a modest dwelling for a ruling sovereign. The purchase was made possible by a generous friend of Sir James, Miss Angela Burdett-Coutts. She was the richest woman in Great Britain and according to Edward, Prince of Wales, the most remarkable woman in the kingdom after his mother, Queen Victoria.

The agent, Charles Mortimore, told Sir James that the £2,800 he had offered Terrell for the estate was, if anything, lower than the value of the land because of the development of the coming railway. Miss Coutts was a benefactor of the other country connected with Sir James in Borneo, and it was while staying near her residence, Meadfoot House, in Torquay in Devonshire, that doctors had advised him to find a house on Dartmoor.

'It was all your doing,' Sir James told Miss Coutts. 'If you hadn't sent me to that agent in Totnes, I should never have found such a retreat. I shall have a minimum of work done on the house and move there in the autumn.'

'I'm so pleased. When we come down here we shall meet often, I hope. The hedgerows in Devonshire are particularly beautiful in the months from April to July, don't you think? Are the hedges on Dartmoor so lovely at this time?'

'Indeed they are. The lane leading down to the village of Sheepstor from the highway is filled with wild flowers and luscious green summer foliage. I thank you and the trustees most sincerely for consenting to buy the estate for me. I shall be for ever in your debt for all the funds you are sending to Sarawak.'

'It is nothing to me,' Miss Coutts replied. 'You know how I came by my great wealth, and I am only too delighted to help your causes as well as my own.'

Miss Coutts hoped to have raised £20,000 from friends to mark appreciation of the Rajah's public work but the fund realised less than £9,000. From this sum the Rajah purchased Burrator estate. Sir James always addressed her as Miss Coutts.

Angela Georgina Burdett-Coutts, youngest daughter of Sir Francis Burdett, was born in London in 1814. Youngest of the twelve grandchildren of Sir Thomas Coutts, she took the name of Coutts in 1837 when she inherited the entire family banking fortune. Her grandfather had left his estate to his second wife, a former actress, who in turn bequeathed it to Angela on condition that she assumed the additional surname of Coutts. Angela was determined to help the poor in London and the fallen girls, as she called the ladies she saw on the street beneath her windows in Piccadilly at night. Poor and neglected children were always her particular care.

Two of the greatest influences on Miss Coutts were her great friends, Charles

Dickens and the Duke of Wellington who had at one time been the love of her life. She had even proposed marriage to him but being forty five years older than her he declined, fearing she was throwing away her young life on an old man. People still cheered the Duke wherever he went in London and he was never forgotten as the hero of Waterloo, indeed Queen Victoria and Prince Albert had named one of their four sons, Arthur in his honour. The Duke's funeral was a great occasion attended by vast crowds; on its way to St Paul's Cathedral, where the Duke was to be buried, the funeral procession passed by the London home of Miss Coutts in Piccadilly. Now her greatest cause was Sarawak and Sir James Brooke. She was eleven years his junior and they had taken to writing to each other on a regular basis since he had come to England after suffering a slight stroke.

'You are Queen of the poor, my dear lady. I find it difficult to express my thanks.'

'Please Sir James, say no more. Tell me about your life, you are such an adventurer.'

'I was born in India fifty six years ago. My family came from Somerset but Papa was a judge in the East India Company. What atrocities the Indians have committed on women and children in the mutiny in the last two years! That is now gladly at an end. I remember it as such a magnificent country. Fortunately, all the administration of India has been taken from the East India Company and is now with the British Crown.'

'Well,' Sir James continued, 'I was fifth of the six children of my parents, Thomas and Anna, the only surviving son, and when I was twelve years of age I was sent as a boarder to a school in England.'

'Did you enjoy that?' Miss Coutts enquired.

'No I did not,' Sir James replied vehemently. 'I was sent to Norwich Grammar School and I ran away to my grandmama who lived in Reigate in Surrey, quite a few times.'

Miss Coutts laughed. 'You were an adventurer even then. Did your grandmama return you to school?'

'Each time I arrived at her house she contacted my guardian who lived in Bath and he had to travel to her house and escort me back to Norwich. She was always kind, I remember, and gave me wonderful meals. I must have been a problem to them both but I was not aware of it much at the time.' He laughed with her.

'So when I eventually left school, or perhaps I had run away, I'm not quite sure now, I joined the armed forces of the East India Company. I was sent down to Devonport then sailed for India. I knew this was the life for me; I felt exhilarated and fearless. Nevertheless, I was shot and became seriously ill. The bullet could have killed me but it lodged in my body, in a most inappropriate place, and had to be removed. I was sent home to England again to convalesce and Mama kept that Burmese musket-ball in a jar on her mantleshelf for as long as I can remember.'

James Brooke spoke fondly of his mother all his life. When later he sent his sword to his nephew the enclosed note read: *'Take care of my sword, it was given me by a mother as tender as the world ever saw, and no speck must rest upon its blade.'*

'Papa and Mama retired to the West Country and I resigned my Commission. Not long after, Papa died leaving me a small fortune – enough to buy my yacht, a 142-ton schooner, named the *Royalist*. So, loaded with provisions and weapons and carefully chosen friends, I set sail for the Far East.'

'Why the Far East?' the lady enquired.

'I had always been fascinated by it, Borneo in particular. I set sail just before Christmas in '38 and arrived in Singapore five months later. We sailed on after a short stay, headed for Borneo and the *Royalist* dropped anchor off the coast of Sarawak in the mouth of the river beneath the mountain of Santubong. It was indescribably beautiful.'

There was a companionable silence before he continued.

'In those early years I had only four assistants; a doctor, an illiterate servant, a shipwrecked Irishman and an interpreter I could not trust. But as events turned out, I was soon to end up governing the country which took every last penny I had. All I have is seventy pounds a year as a pension.'

Miss Coutts delighted in the company of her brave adventurer. They talked easily together and when their eyes met there was an obvious tenderness for each other. If she was to give large sums of money to this Eastern country she wanted to know all about it. The welfare of Sarawak was still uppermost in Sir James' mind but he found peace in this moorland solitude, enjoying the attention of the villagers and the company of friends he invited to Burrator.

Writing to an old school friend about Sheepstor village James Brooke stated:

'I have determined to stick up my staff at the foot of Dartmoor and am in treaty for the purchase of a small property with a house which is to become my home. Here or in Sarawak, as may be, my bones shall rest and my few years of life be passed after the turmoil of a troubled life.

"The knights are dust,
Their good swords rust,
Their souls are with the saints we trust."'

9

As the richest heiress in England, Miss Burdett-Coutts was second only to Queen Victoria as the lady of the land. Her presence at Queen Victoria's coronation in June 1838 inevitably stirred up considerable speculation as to who she would marry. It would almost certainly have stunned those present to know that at the age of sixty-six she would marry a man of twenty-nine, following the death of her beloved companion Hannah Brown. Mrs Brown had been her former governess when she was Hannah Meredith, and on the death of her husband Dr Brown in 1855, Hannah remained the inseparable friend and chief companion of Miss Burdett-Coutts.

Many honours were bestowed on Angela in her lifetime, most of them never before awarded to a woman. Possessed of excellent business sense, she managed her own vast wealth and personally aided the enterprise of Sir James Brooke in Sarawak, taking a detailed interest in his affairs.

'We have good trade with Borneo now I believe?' Miss Coutts enquired.

'Excellent, dear lady, trade prospers but it did not so, of course, twenty years ago. When I first arrived I greeted the Malay ruler who gave me permission to explore the country. As there was a rebellion much in evidence, we sailed away after a few weeks to plan our next strategy but the ruler, Rajah Muda Hassim, requested we return and help him to quell the revolt. He was the heir to the country and brother of the Sultan of Brunei. We, that is my men and I, sent the natives fleeing into the jungle. Hassim wanted to pursue these men and kill them as he was not able to restore law and order.'

'What did you do?'

'I persuaded Hassim to spare their lives and let me deal with the situation. He thought to bring peace here among the savages an impossible task and promised all the trade I requested and the title of Rajah if I succeeded. I, of course, accepted the challenge and Hassim pleaded with me on many occasions not to desert him. Over the next months we travelled throughout the country encouraging the natives to abolish slavery and the awful custom of head-hunting. These severed heads, a symbol of manhood, hung outside the houses and were used for bartering. Piracy was also widespread but my crew and I began to bring peace in the country.'

'The Rajah Muda honoured his promise to you, though?'

'Yes, eventually. It took a couple of years. Over the months the people of Sarawak, of which there were perhaps thirteen tribes, offered their allegiance to me. Their affection was moving. I became governor of a large part of the country but there were still separate provinces with their own governors.'

Sir James produced a small document from his papers given to him by the Sultan of Brunei when he had sailed there for the approval of the Sultan who was head of state. The deed was sealed and signed in September 1841:

The country and government of Sarawak is made over to Mr Brooke, to be held under the crown of Brunei, with all its revenues and dependencies, on the yearly payment of 2,500 dollars. That Mr Brooke is not to infringe upon the customs or religion of the people; and in return, that no person is to interfere with him in the management of the country.

'The people must have thought you a very special person. A young white Englishman leading their country.'

'There were problems. Five years of uprising, turmoil and piracy followed but I began to gain the respect of the Malays as I travelled up the rivers. At last the day came when the Sultan granted Sarawak completely to me and my heirs. I was a true Rajah of my own kingdom owing allegiance to no one. But I have to say, the British Government were none too happy.'

'The affairs of Sarawak were discussed in the House, that is true. It was reported in the press that you wanted the British Government involved.'

'Of course I did. They were trading in my country and I needed revenues, as I told them. The people there treated me like a god and I think ministers were jealous. It was highly irritating. My only aim was to introduce a better system of government and to develop new sources of commerce. Then I started to suffer bouts of fever and had to come to England to recover.'

'And to a hero's welcome!' Miss Coutts was recalling the time twelve years ago when she had renewed her acquaintance with Sir James. 'You were showered with honours both in Southampton and in London.'

'It was an honour to renew your friendship, dear lady. It was a wonderful honour, too, to be invited to Windsor Castle. That, I have realised since, was of your doing.'

Sir James smiled affectionately at his friend. 'I enjoyed my stay there immensely. The Queen and the Prince Consort loved to talk about their children – Vicky, Bertie, Alice, Alfie and Lenchen, their name for baby Helena. Her Majesty was pregnant at the time – she had another four children after my visit to Windsor, I think.'

'Yes, little Princess Beatrice, the youngest, is two years old now. They are devoted to their children.'

'That was very obvious on my visit to Windsor. Prince Albert talked always of Vicky and of her fine accomplishments. It was an amazing whirlwind of thrills and engagements when I was in England at that time,' Sir James went on. 'I was even presented with the Freedom of the City of London, a great honour, but you, dear lady, are more worthy of that honour than I.'

'It is kind of you to say so, but no lady has yet ever received that honour,' Miss Coutts replied smiling up at Sir James.

The friendship between Sir James and Miss Coutts was well recognised. Queen Victoria, if not the British Government, appreciated the good work Brooke had accomplished in Sarawak.

'I received the Knight Commander of the Bath in Singapore. Her Majesty's representative, William Napier who was Lieutenant-General of Labuan, performed the ceremony at Government House.'

'At last, the belated knighthood!' Miss Coutts exclaimed.

Fascinated by this Rajah from an eastern country, Miss Coutts had invited him to stay with her and her companion at Stratton Street in London. Their next few weeks were spent entertaining and being entertained by her circle of titled friends.

As Sir James Brooke, he sailed once more from Singapore on to Sarawak, in his possession a sealed letter. Sir James had vowed never to marry; to be tied down to any one place or person or family responsibilities had never been his nature, he was an adventurer. But this letter contained the name of a lady proposing marriage, to be opened and revealed only if he should change his mind. It was duly thrown into the fire, unopened. Many of his friends believed the identity of the letter-writer to be Angela Burdett-Coutts.

Years of bouts of malaria, smallpox, strenuous work in a tropical climate and the many revolts and attacks by pirates inevitably took their toll on his body and his mind, the final straw coming in a murderous attack by a gang of Chinese who had been digging for gold inland. Determined to kill the Rajah, they set fire to the English houses in and around the main town of Kuching. He narrowly escaped with his life by plunging in the Sungei Bedil River under cover of darkness and swimming across to summon help from local Malay chieftains. His house of four bedrooms with a large sitting room in the centre, was burnt to the ground by the Chinese. This house, known as 'Mr Brooke's Residence', had been filled with all the Rajah's beloved books.

They spared the house of Francis McDougall, the first bishop of Labuan and Sarawak, and his wife Hariette. McDougall had founded the Anglican church in Borneo in 1855 and won the respect of the Chinese where somehow Brooke failed. Tragically, their eldest son Charlie died at school in England at this time, just nine years old. His distraught mother published the letters she had written to him whilst he was at school, as *Letters from Sarawak Addressed to a Child*. Poor Hariette who suffered many miscarriages and still-births in Sarawak poured out her grief at the loss of her first-born who had died thousands of miles away from her:

> Charlie, Charlie art thou gone?
> Torn from mother's fond embrace.
> Can it be that ne'er again
> I shall kiss that smiling face.
> Oh Charlie it is hard to bear
> So early with my child to part.
> I thought that thou throughout my life
> Would be the solace of my heart.

Eventually the Chinese were defeated but outbreaks of pirate revolts continued. Increasingly despondent and ill, Brooke was advised by worried friends like McDougall and Spenser St John to leave Sarawak, the country to which he had brought peace in place of disorder, and good government in place of oppression. There were signs that long years of absolute power in a kingdom so near the equator had damaged the Rajah's mind; Bishop McDougall attributed it to smallpox.

It was at this moment and in this state of mind that Brooke announced he had an illegitimate son who had been his groom some years before in England. He was Reuben Walker, now in the Indian army. He changed the young man's name to Reuben George Brooke and asked his family to accept George and to make him welcome into the Brooke family. James believed Reuben was his son and the family had to accept him.

His sisters and nephews presumed that James must have had an affair with a housemaid whilst convalescing with his parents at Bath. If James thought this young man of twenty-three was his son then there could be no doubt in his own mind that he had had an affair and had fathered a child.

Two stories told about James Brooke were now thrown into doubt. One was that he was impotent because the bullet had entered his genitals, the reason why he never married. The other was that he had secretly married a Malay woman in Sarawak who bore him this son. Twenty-three years ago, however, James had never set foot in Borneo.

The story of George Brooke was confused but most disturbing to his nephews who were his heirs. They believed it to be the delusion of a sick and lonely man but James was proud to have a son and granted him an annual sum of money from the revenues of Sarawak.

Back in England, Sir James suffered a stroke and was advised to convalesce in Devonshire, bringing him once more into the orbit of his long-standing friend and benefactor, Miss Angela Burdett-Coutts.

He stayed at the Dousland Barn Hotel not far from Sheepstor for a week, riding around his estate, learning all he could from Harry Terrell. Southern Dartmoor was superb; this wonderful countryside was now his home; the springy turf, the heathers and gorse, the hills and tors all as they had been for centuries. He fell instantly in love with this unchanging landscape. As they rode up the Eylesburrow mine track, the hill beyond Sheepstor that led to central Dartmoor, Terrell pointed out, across to his left, the Deancombe valley.

'One of the maids at Burrator lives over yonder. Her's bin a good friend to me daughter Maggie, so I hope you'll take care of her. She got married to one of the farmers out over last spring. Her name is Sarah. Sarah Shepherd.'

10

JAMES Brooke looked upon himself as a dreamer of dreams. He imagined living in a small cottage on Dartmoor where he would end his days but with enough quiet interests to employ his time.

In a letter he wrote to Miss Coutts on 25 July from Dousland, he described Burrator as the cottage of his dreams. He wrote:

'My little Box – that is to be – is snugly situated under Dartmoor – a stream babbles close at hand – wood is plenty and in all it boasts 72 acres of land. I might have searched for ten years without meeting a place within my limits so retired, so near the world and so suited in all respects to my tastes. I have in a week's stay derived great benefit from the bracing and elastic air and I take my daily ride, and walk, to distances I little thought ever to have accomplished again. Yesterday I was five hours on pony back on the moor!'

Harry Terrell showed Sir James the part of Dartmoor around Sheepstor. The staff at Burrator were going to stay on and work for him. In this tranquil village he had found his retreat, where he could drop anchor and enjoy home life. The Terrells were moving out of Burrator into a much smaller place nearby and on one of his visits to the house they told Sir James they were going to sell their furniture.

'List everything in the house,' Sir James told them. 'Put a price on each and I will take what I want.'

After looking at the Terrell's list, and not wishing to displease the couple, Sir James told them he'd take the lot.

'You bain't going to have my bed I was married in,' said Harry. 'But if you're willing to pay what I ask you can have the rest.'

After taking possession of the house and furniture the Rajah wrote to his nephew John Brooke Brooke (who had changed his last name from Johnson to Brooke) on the day the Terrells moved out. He wrote:

'The former owner has just left us. The valuation of everything in the house was £180 so you may fancy how dilapidated is a great part of the furniture. I have written to Mr Sheen about the beds and couch. There is no reason for money to be delayed but you see how the cat jumps. To make the beds and couch very comfortable I shall require blankets and quilts. Also six pairs of nice cotton sheets and six pillowcases for each pillow. Choose a pretty chintzy pattern. It should be light with small patterns, cottage style. This is my refuge.'

One day when they were out riding together, Harry asked Sir James, 'How do you say that foreign country of yours? I can't get it right.'

'We say Sur-ah-wak,' Brooke said, stressing the middle syllable. 'But in the Dyak language out there the letter k is silent. Other English people pronounce it Sara*wack*.'

'Well,' whatever 'tis, I doubt I shall ever get to see it.'

Sir James took possession of Burrator on 18 August 1859 and the Terrells moved out two days later. Feeling the importance of buying the estate in this tiny village in Devon, he had written to his other nephew Charlie in the previous week, of his pleasure of the beauty of Sheepstor and of its situation:

'My name will be enrolled amongst the landed gentry. I shall become Lord of Burrator and a squire of Devon. Burrator is situate in the parish of Sheepstor – a snug valley at the foot of Dartmoor. The house is small but a fresh stream runs before it and a cascade falls from one hundred feet close by in the grounds. It makes music. The property consists of 72 acres of pasture and woodland, some fine beeches and sycamores are about the house. There is the opportunity of pasturing ponies and cattle over hundreds of thousands of acres of moor and you can ride twenty miles as the crow flies. Hunting is excellent – woodcock shooting and shooting is to be had over six thousand acres.'

The move gave him a new lease of life. In letters he wrote from the seaside resorts of Dawlish and Torquay, before his purchase of Burrator, he had written phrases such as, 'I shall soon go the way of all flesh before long, Jubilate.' Such sentiments he scrawled on top and across his finished letter.

To Brooke on 17 August, from Plymouth, he wrote:

'My dear Brooke,

This is to say the purchase money of Burrator has been paid and that tomorrow morning I take possession. Address me Burrator near Tavistock. I wish to see whether it will come safely. If important – Burrator, Meavy near Tavistock.

Ever your, J Brooke.'

To Charlie on the day of purchase he wrote: *'I am in the agony of purchasing a sweet little property which today is to be mine.'*

In the *Plymouth, Devonport and Stonehouse Herald*, dated Saturday, 10 September 1859, the following appeared in a column on the back page:

'We understand that Sir James Brooke, the Rajah of Sarawak, has purchased the estate of Henry Terrell Esq at Sheepstor and will shortly reside there.'

One of his first letters to Miss Coutts from Burrator was dated 15 October 1859 in which he delighted in his home. He wrote that he forgot a great deal about the outer world from his little home in Sheepstor:

'It is wild and lonely and with much of natural beauty in its scenery which endears it to me.'

This was just the retreat Sir James needed in England, a haven to come back to after his travels abroad. The staff at Burrator honoured him and attended to his every need and those of his many guests, including, of course, Miss Coutts and her companion Mrs Brown.

Sir James appointed a new groom, John Sauls, a young man he had met on his travels. Officials came from Sarawak, too, and Sheepstor folk were amazed by the society they met, some having travelled thousands of miles to their tiny village.

In early November Sir James was advised by his doctor to spend a month at Bath. He wrote to Miss Coutts:

'I commence the use of the baths, not a disagreeable remedy, and I hope a month's use will prove the doctor's wisdom in recommending them.'

He was still in constant contact with Sarawak, where he had left Brooke Johnson in command.

While Sir James was away, Sarah Shepherd told the housekeeper Mrs Thorn that she would be leaving the service at Burrator when it was convenient.

'I'm expecting a baby in March and I have to take more rest,' she told her.

'Congratulations, Sarah. If your mother could look after the baby perhaps you may like to help us out next summer, when we've got a houseful.'

'I should like that, I'm sure,' Sarah said smiling. ' I shall miss it here with the comings and goings, but it hasn't been the same for me since Maggie Terrell left. It's certainly a contrast from Outhome.'

Winter was very beautiful on Dartmoor and when snow fell it was a fairy wonderland. Sheepstor village was cut off from civilisation almost every winter and Sarah felt pleased that her late pregnancy was occurring at this season. She was young and healthy but the walk to Burrator was not easy in driving wind and rain, and impossible in thick snow.

Sam was excited at becoming a father and Sarah delighted at feeling the new life moving within her.

'You're a picture of health, Sarah,' Mrs Thorn smiled. 'I wish to God the master had some of your fitness. Only this morning he told me that he wished his shattered body could back his spirit.'

'Did he enjoy his stay in Torquay?' Sarah asked.

'Yes, he enjoys being in the company of that lady. He always looks a bit down though on his return. He misses the company.'

Grace Thorn put the gooseberry tart she was making into the stove oven.

'Miss Coutts and Mrs Brown are coming to Saltram next month so that will cheer him. She's a real lady, is Miss Coutts, and a true friend to the Rajah.'

'Do you think he'll go out East again?'

'I shouldn't be at all surprised, Sarah. It's his life, he's always been used to sailing on the high seas.'

'He's a kind gentleman, but not friendly like Mr Terrell.'

'Well, you'd known the Terrells since you were a girl, and you were close to Maggie. It's bound to be different. Come on now, we'd better get some work done.'

'Mind you,' she said to Sarah as they cleared the kitchen table. 'I often wonder how the Terrells are getting along. They're as different as chalk and cheese. Mr Terrell was an outspoken man but he told me himself that the Rajah would *do* ten times more for the place than he ever did. Sir James has quickly gained respect in the village for his kind acts and he has visited all the families.'

The Rajah was not aware of Sarah's condition. Sarah knew it would have been different had her previous employers still been at Burrator.

II

WINTER was grudgingly giving way to spring when Sarah went into labour. The day was wet and misty with little visibility on the moor. It was Lady Day and Sam had walked to the next village of Meavy to pay his quarter's rent. This was usually a grand time for meeting friends and neighbours in the Royal Oak Inn where the land agent collected the money but Sam was not in the mood to linger today.

'Sorry I can't abide here,' he said waving his stick in the air as a farewell, 'I have to get back to Sarah. Her's overdue now, and the babby could come anytime.'

The other tenants discussed Sam when he had gone and talked of the great change in him in the last twelve months. 'He's a changed man, to be sure. Petticoat rule, I should say, but he's a pleasure to know these days,' said one laughing.

When Sam reached home he found Sarah in pain and distress. 'I'm going down for mother, I can't bear to see you like this.'

Sarah smiled weakly. 'You've only just come in, Sam. Have a bite to eat first. It's thick mist out there.'

'No, sooner I go, sooner I'll be back. You'll be able to hold on, will 'ee?' Sam said, sounding very concerned.

'Yes. Tell mam not to worry,' she called as Sam went up over the moor.

Her mother stayed at the cottage for two nights. On 27 March the mist had lifted, the sun shone and Sam and Sarah's baby was born in the upstairs room at Outhome. Sam was out in the yard filling the feeding troughs when he heard the lusty cry and dashed up the stone stairs, bursting into the bedroom.

'Oh my love, what a time you've had. How are they, mother?' Sam was full of compassion and much agitated. 'Is everything all right?'

'Yes, all is fine, Sam,' his mother-in-law said kindly. 'Sarah is very tired. You have a fine son, Sam. Here, take him.'

Sam took the bundle from Mrs Creber and looked down on the yelling infant, his son. He sat on the bed by his wife.

''Twas worth it, Sam,' Sarah smiled. 'We've got a son. Our own baby.'

Sam passed the baby to Sarah and her mother helped her to put the crying child to her breast. After a few moments of bewilderment, the baby latched on to Sarah's nipple and there was silence.

'Peace at last. Thank you mother, we couldn't have done without 'ee.' Sam kissed her which much surprised his mother-in-law, then he kissed the top of Sarah's head.

'Go on with 'ee, Sam. It's my first grandchild, you know. I'll clean up here and come back in the morning if you're sure you can cope,' his mother-in-law said.

Sarah smiled at them both. 'I feel tired but so happy. We're going to call him William Samuel, Mam, Will for short. What do you think?'

'Will, a manly name,' her mother declared. 'Will Shepherd. Yes, I like it.'

'You get on, mother. Father will have missed 'ee.'

Sam felt the pride swell in him as he saw his young wife and baby. Could this be true? Sarah had given him a new lease of life, someone to work for, now he had a son as well. Sam was never far from his cottage these days, if he could help it.

'She'll want for nothing, mother,' Sam said at the door. 'I won't leave her till you get back tomorrow. The ewes that are ready to lamb are in Little Field near the house. You and father come up for dinner, I've got a couple of rabbits ready for the oven and lots of tiddies.'

'I don't know about father but I'll be back bright and early, Sam. Bye for now,' Lily Creber called. 'Let them both have a good sleep.'

Mrs Creber climbed up the hill out of the coombe and made her way home across the moor in the evening sunshine. She took Sarah's usual route to the village. Up to Outcombe Corner on Leedon, across Outcombe Waste and the ford below the mire, over the moor to Yellowmead farm and down Tor Lane. The way then to the Creber's cottage was through the east church gate by the well, through the churchyard and out by the west church gate next to East Hellingtown's garden gate. Anyone she saw was stopped and told about her being a grandmother and the news of the birth quickly spread around Sheepstor. Sarah and her baby were fast asleep even before her mother had lost sight of Outhome.

The baby gained in weight and grew rapidly. Sarah loved her new life, caring for Sam and Will. The Terrells meanwhile had found another home in Tavistock and Harry was not seen so frequently in the Sheepstor valleys.

Meanwhile Sir James at Burrator gave the impression to the villagers that he was a contented man. This was, at times, far from the truth. He wrote to his nephew Charlie:

'You ask, hope, that I am happy!! How is it possible? I have a satisfaction that I have a hole where I can retire and suffer unwatched, but betrayed by my country. I am doubtful of the future so, how can I be happy? My mind however is master of my body and I am prepared that I might be able to pass the dregs of my life in peace, but Sarawak must be secure before that can be. George sends his love. Stuart also, who is here for a little recreation before study for the marines.'

Outwardly, he continued to portray himself as lord of the manor, happy, kind and compassionate. The village benefactor.

Just as Mrs Thorn had suggested, Sarah left Will with her mother at the cottage when the Rajah was entertaining and extra help was required in the house. Not only family and friends of the Rajah stayed at Burrator but many young men he met on his travels and officers from the Sarawak Government. Sam was amazed to hear the tales Sarah told him, when she returned home, of the goings-on at the house. Sarah enjoyed helping out and her wages were a welcome boost to their meagre existence. Mrs Creber doted on Will and the baby thrived on the attention he was given by mother and grandmother. But when autumn came and Sarah was not needed at Burrator, she did not regret staying home in the valley where she assisted Sam and looked in on her neighbours.

On the afternoon of 1 October 1860, Sir James Brooke laid the foundation stone for the new Sheepstor village school at Leaford where the cottages for the poor had once stood, and not far from the entrance to Burrator. Here the Terrells had lived for a short while before moving away from Sheepstor. Until now there had been only a small Dame school, near the church.

After the ceremony, the sponsors of the school, who included Sir Massey Lopes, the managers and the villagers were all invited to tea at the Rajah's home.

Sir James wrote to Mrs Brown:

'Today we have a fuss upon the laying the first stone of our school – I have opened my house for a Tea and cakes, for all comers – I don't like it, but I hope some of them may. This is a duty I owe to Society.'

The school opened the following year with Mrs Rebecca Williams as schoolmistress. Soon after, Sir James travelled to London where he appealed to the Queen and nation for generosity towards Sarawak. Once again he sailed to his Eastern country from Southampton, in confident mood. Dartmoor air had revived his spirits and travelling through Egypt, he reached Singapore on New Year's Day. Miss Coutts sent him £5,000 and more funds later after he had landed at his destination in February.

While he was away, officers from the Brooke's government in Sarawak arrived to stay at the house at his invitation, intrigued to see the home of their Rajah in England. For them it was like a pilgrimage to his retreat after reading in letters his glowing reports of the surrounding countryside and healthy air:

'Come and settle on Dartmoor,' he wrote to many friends. *'There is nothing in England to be compared to it. You are the free denizen of wild country, riding as the bird flies and with rights of pasture of hundreds of thousands of acres for your herds and ponies.'*

Thus the Rajah's years at Burrator were far from lonely. He always had friends staying at the house, or was off visiting them all over the country.

He enjoyed the company of his sister Emma, the mother of the nephews he corresponded with so often. He wrote to her in that year that Stuart, one of her sons, might go to Canada with George. He invited the boy to stay with him at Burrator until something was settled.

'He'd be happy here and the shooting should employ him.'

As he left for Sarawak at the end of the year, he invited Emma to come to Burrator.

'My retreat will always welcome you. You will be well cared for. I leave Sauls, the two maids and villagers come in daily.'

November was windy and bitterly cold. As the month ended, the wind blew from the north bringing the first snowfall of the winter. The visitors from the East had never seen snow and were fascinated but found the climate too cold to endure. Warned by the Burrator staff that the weather was worsening and Sheepstor was usually cut off from civilisation by drifting snow, the party decided to get off the moor guided by John Sauls and the stable lads. Snow fell silently and thickly. In an amazingly short space of time the settled snow covered the carriage drive and gardens of Burrator with visibility down to a few yards.

The ladies in the party were much distressed, especially those with children. Fascination turned to panic. They all travelled on horseback as the wagons could not be pulled through the snow. Large flakes whirled from the dark clouds, shrouding the countryside and blinding the travellers. With heads bent in the driving snow, holding their children in front of them with babies strapped to the horses behind them, John Sauls and the lads led the company across the valley off the moor on to the highway. The snow settled, making it impossible to see the track ahead. Behind them their tracks were quickly obscured. The travellers could only concentrate on keeping John Sauls and the rest of their party in view. Leaving Sheepstor was an alarming ordeal.

12

SARAH, up at Outhome, watched the snow falling on the moor. The wind whipped the snow into drifts right up to the lower mullion window sills. Will was asleep in his basket in front of the fire, and as Sarah watched mesmerised, the flakes fell in their millions. Amusing herself she tried to keep her eyes on one flake at a time as it fell from the sky to the ground. It was getting dark and somewhere out on the moor Sam was searching for a sheep that had wandered down the valley.

Suddenly the door was blown open and Sam almost fell into the room barely recognisable under his blanket of snow. He thrust the door shut behind him against the wind.

'Oh, thank goodness you've come home, Sam. I've been so worried about 'ee. Give me that and get your coat off.' Sarah took a bundle out of Sam's arms and, supposing it was a lamb, lay it carefully in front of the fire next to Will's basket.'

Helping Sam to take the sacking off his shoulders, she undid the buttons of his coat.

'Come and sit by the fire, Sam, and get yourself warm.'

'I'll do it, my love. You take a mind at what I've brought home.'

Sam unlaced his hobnail boots as Sarah knelt on the floor and undid the bundle. Her face turned as white as the snow outside the cottage.

'Good Lord 'ave mercy,' Sarah gasped in a whisper. 'What's this, Sam?'

Sam looked all in. 'I only hope it's still alive, Sarah. It was wrapped up tightly but I heard a muffled cry, down on the banks of the River Mew.'

Sarah stared. There on the floor by her baby was, not the orphan lamb she fully expected to see, but another baby! A tiny, newborn baby, wrapped in the most exquisite blankets and shawls. Its large brown eyes were wide open, the only visible part of its body.

'Come to the fire, Sam,' Sarah said making room by her. 'I've got some broth on the heat for 'ee. Talk when you're warmed up a bit. I want to know every detail.'

The baby began to whimper. Sarah slowly undid the outer blanket and rubbed its chest.

'Can't 'ee give it some of your milk, Sarah? You've got plenty enough for Will. You've always said you could feed two babies. It looks very new.' Sam put a log on the fire and went to light another candle.

'It must only be a few weeks old.' Sarah was agitated but undid her buttons and put the baby to her breast. Gently and slowly, in great contrast to Will who pulled and sucked hard, the baby took some milk and fell asleep in Sarah's arms. Sarah's heart melted. 'This is no ordinary baby, Sam. Just see its clothes.'

Sarah lay the baby next to Will in his basket to give it warmth and poured Sam's broth into a bowl. 'Now, Sam, tell me from the beginning 'afore Will wakes.'

Sam sipped the hot broth slowly and in whispers told Sarah how he had walked right past the baby who was lying almost covered in snow by a granite rock that was jutting out.

'It might have been there a couple of hours,' Sam said. 'The snow only started drifting when I'd turned for home after the wind got up. There were no tracks at all and no sign that anyone had passed by.'

'Good job you passed that way, Sam. Go on.'

'I took the sack off from around me waist, wrapped it up and tucked it under me arm. Gyp sniffed around a bit but I got her to drive the sheep home. Nightfall was coming on. I couldn't have left it there, could I?'

'Oh, no, my love. You've done the right thing. We'll go down to Burrator tomorrow, I expect the visitors there are going frantic. It's definitely a baby from Borneo. We'll care for it tonight. When it wakes I'll make it clean and we'll see what it is. I think it must be a girl with such dainty features. Our Will was never as small as this.'

They hugged each other and looked down on the sleeping babies. Will was eight months old now, with two lower teeth and already trying to crawl around the cottage, putting everything he was able to pick up into his mouth.

Sam had been down on the banks of the Mew with his dog Gyp, looking for a sheep he knew had wandered down the valley. He was scrambling up the steep bank near Sheepstor Bridge when he spotted the animal covered in snow and ice. Using his crook to pull the sheep towards him, he caught sight of the bundle of blankets peeking out under an overhanging granite rock. Slipping and sliding on the bank, with driving snow stinging his face, he pulled the bundle towards him and heard the weak cry like that of a kitten. Driving the dog and sheep before him he climbed onto the bridge now in deep snow.

Sam trudged home, along the track towards Middleworth farm and up the comparative shelter of the Deancombe valley. The track up the valley was strewn with granite boulders and difficult even in clear visibility. Sam found his journey home formidable, the terrain in snow and ice treacherous, but he kept his eye on his dog which was intent on driving the sheep in front of him. At the sight of Deancombe farm, Sam's spirits lifted and crossing the brook he saw the candle glow in his cottage window. He put the sheep in the pen with the rest of the flock and shut Gyp in the shed, giving her a large meaty bone. To his wonder and concern there had been no sound from the bundle he had carefully borne from deep in the river valley. He was much relieved when Sarah undid the bundle.

The snow fell all night making it impossible for even Sam to go further than his barn to feed the sheep he had sheltered the day before. Still the snow fell, for days on end so that not even the nearest of neighbours could call or visit. When eventually they did make contact, they could not make it out of the valley. Sarah stayed out of sight in the house and Sam made no attempt to take his neighbours indoors. They were all snowed in until mid-December.

The baby girl was placid, almost serene, and Sarah had to watch over Will in case he smothered her. The longer they were all shut up in the house, the more onerous it was to think of giving her up.

'This baby has become part of our family, Sam,' Sarah said. 'You saved her life. I just can't believe her parents haven't come looking for her, whatever the weather.'

'What do you intend to do, my love?'

'Can't I say she's mine? We'll keep your finding her a secret. I've fed her my milk and she's like a sister for Will. I love her, Sam.'

The first person to know about the new arrival was Mrs Creber when at last she was able to get out to Outhome. Sarah's mother told her that there had been no mention of a baby going missing from Burrator – or from anywhere else. She also knew that the visitors had left the house on the day the blizzard began. The servants were all alone there now and were not expecting any more guests. The staff on the estate talked of joining in the Christmas celebrations in the village.

At length, Sarah confided her plan to keep the baby and claim it as her own.

'Look at it, Sarah,' her mother protested. 'Anyone can see it's a foreign baby. How are you going to explain that?'

Sarah and Sam had gone over and over this question, and Sarah, without too much difficulty, had persuaded Sam to go along with her plan. He just wanted to please her in every way.

'I've been often enough at Burrator,' Sarah said to her mother. 'I'll say it's my child, that I had an affair with one of the visitors. Sam's agreed to this. He doesn't want to lose her either.'

Mrs Creber did not like this at all. She was not a gossip and kept most of her own thoughts to herself, but felt sure in her heart of hearts that this idea, Sarah's plan, was not right.

'As long as they don't come back for her, Mam, it'll be all right. I won't come down the village for a bit, we've been shut up here for nearly two months. You can tell anyone who asks that we've had another baby, and that she was born early.'

Her mother could see Sarah had it all worked out. 'I suppose those who lost her will think she perished in such weather. I wonder when they first found her gone? She wouldn't have survived the night if Sam hadn't found her, would she?'

'No, Mam, that's true, you can see she's very tiny.'

'The sooner you take her down the village, the sooner they'll accept her. Come to a service after Christmas in church. You can wrap her up so that she'll be hardly seen. Good gracious, Sarah, how did you get me to go along with your scheme?'

'Thanks, Mam, I couldn't give her up now, she's ours – mine, Sam's and Will's.' Sarah hugged her mother.

'Has she got a name? Was there anything on her clothes?' Mrs Creber stood up and slowly buttoned up her coat. She felt reluctant to leave her daughter and the babies, it was such a homely scene and Sarah had never looked so happy.

'No, Mam, nothing. Just look at the blankets,' Sarah said showing her mother. 'I'll never be able to give her such riches, but she'll be rich in love here with us. I've called her Annie. As long as no one comes to claim her, she'll be Annie Shepherd.'

13

A MORE out-of-the-world village than Sheepstor would be almost impossible to imagine. Only one road led to it, leaving the highway from Plymouth to Prince's Town, the village later to become known as Princetown. A steep lane, flowing with water in the winter, led down to a bridge over the River Mew into the secluded valley. Carts and wagons were in use now, but not long before the only means of transporting goods had been by pack-horse and the town of Tavistock, a day's journey away.

The village was isolated, its families closely united by marriage. It was a little world to itself. Dances were held at Park Cottage, the beer house, and villagers sang in the church choir, played instruments to lead the church music or pealed the bells in the church tower. William Andrew was a great violinist.

The churchyard wall was by way of a ringside seat for villagers gathered to watch bull-baiting, wrestling and cockfighting which took place in the field south of the churchyard. Dwelling in the tiny village clustered round the church were the inhabitants of the old vicarage, the curate and his family across the road in Brook Cottage, and families in two or three cottages and a farm. Burrator was nearby, as were the school, beer house and Longstone Manor, the other parishioners living in farms scattered out on the moor.

Mr Bowden lived in the run-down old Vicarage, Thomas Reed in Park Cottage and Mrs Rebecca Williams lived at the school. Most of the families had lived in the parish for generations, handing down names such as Elford, Legassick, Ware, Northmore, Andrew, Stanbury, Bayly, Jackman, Creber, Shepherd, Bowden, Palmer, Willcocks, Luscombe and Shillibeer. The parish boundary ran from Yeo Farm in Meavy village to the Old Mine House out on Eylesburrow, and Ditsworthy Warren out on the moor in the upper Plym valley. Longstone Manor had been home to the wealthy Elfords for centuries but was now run as a farm by the Crebers.

Many of the farms, secluded in the river valleys, were medieval settlements. Sir Massey Lopes was restoring the buildings to make life more comfortable for his tenants, leaving his inscribed mark and the date, ML 1858, on door lintels of the barns in the Deancombe valley for future generations to see. Burrator was not so old, having been built as a farm in about 1780.

Most of the land was moorland, watered by numerous streams and rivers. A survey a few years before stated that Sheepstor parish had 127 souls and 3,469 acres of land; but though the tiny village was so hidden away, the massive granite hulk of Sheeps Tor itself that gave the village its name, was a landmark that could be seen by sailors entering Plymouth harbour from out in the English Channel.

The snow had thawed at long last after Christmas so that the curate was able to hold a service in the old granite church one Sunday afternoon in January. This time of day enabled the farming families to return home before dark.

John Sauls, the coachman at Burrator, greeted the curate at the old oak door. 'A contrast to the weather my master is having,' he said to the curate. 'He's probably too hot and we're too cold.'

'I don't know where he gets his stamina from to travel as he does,' the curate replied. 'Will he be out there for long?'

'We hope not,' Sauls answered. 'Home some time in the year, I expect.'

The little church was packed with parishioners, all greeting each other as friends. They joined in prayers said by the curate, heard the passages from the bible about Christ's birth and sang a few hymns, accompanied by three of the men playing violin, bass viol and flute. The curate's sermon, spoken to the congregation without any notes, was based on the Magi travelling from the East, and finding a baby in a stable.

Sarah, sitting near the back of the church, thought only of visitors from the East who had come to their village, not finding a baby but losing one. The Christmas Story was one of joy but the Burrator visitors must have been full of sorrow. Sam had found the baby though, and this little life had brought happiness and joy to their family.

As Sarah sang the hymns, feelings stirred within her, surging through her body and tightening her throat.

> *Eastern sages at his cradle*
> *Make oblations rich and rare;*
> *See them give in deep devotion*
> *Gold and frankincense and myrrh.*

Singing in the candlelight, she glanced at the babe in her arms, at Sam and their own baby Will sitting between them. Sarah clasped Annie tightly to her and smiled down on Will. She was rewarded with a beaming smile in return. 'Eastern sages at his cradle'… they should be rejoicing around Annie's cradle but instead she had kept her in their humble dwelling. No riches would come to Annie at Outhome.

Snow on snow on snow on snow, the words filled her brain. Pure, unsullied, attractive and innocent as snow – that's how the villagers imagined Sarah. She had been born amongst them, grown up and played with them and given a new lease of life to poor lonely Sam on the moor. Underneath this pretence was the guilt and the torment. Would the truth ever be known? Would the hidden culpability come to the surface?

As the folk left the church, the little Shepherd family were the centre of attention.

'I didn't know you'd had another baby, Sarah.'

'You kept that one quiet, Sam!'

'Not left much time after the first one, Sarah.'

'Must 'ave been difficult up at Outhome in the blizzard, missus.'

'You'm a dark horse, Sam.'

Sarah kept the baby covered up against the chill weather and smiled back at them all.

'Yes, it's a girl. Her name is Annie, Annie Shepherd. She'll be a companion for Will,' Sarah held her head high.

The breath of the talk and laughter rose in the frosty air as they made their farewells. Each of the farming families returning to another week of labour and hardship in their humble dwellings, had a new topic to discuss.

'That's the biggest obstacle over,' her mother said, walking with them to the east gate. 'You'll be able to face them all again now.'

Sam had been quiet. Everyone was used to that.

'Take no notice of insults, Sarah. Cruel remarks are soon forgotten when there's something else to talk about. You needn't concern yourself.'

This was quite a speech for Sam. A solitary man of few words, he nevertheless had a sensitive nature.

Returning to their homes, the circumstances of the Shepherd family at Outhome was the topic of conversation. Fancy old Sam, and he a bachelor who hadn't so much as looked at a girl before Sarah. Perhaps the rumour was true. Some were saying that one of them foreign visitors over to Burrator had taken advantage of Sarah. What a fine fellow old Sam was to take on another man's child. The village buzzed with gossip and tittle-tattle.

Will and Annie were baptised together on a Sunday afternoon in the spring. Many came to church to witness the event or to take a look at Annie. No one passed a displeasing remark to Sarah but the women regarded Sam with pitying eyes. Will was a year old and Sam carried him in his arms. Sarah held Annie wrapped tightly in a shawl.

Annie was diminutive, her dark hair and eyes in stark contrast to the fairness of Will with his eyes of blue. Sarah told folk that Annie had been born prematurely during the blizzard in December, less than nine months after the birth of Will. The villagers recalled that Sarah had worked at Burrator in the year, when there had been people from Borneo staying with the Rajah. In the church's baptismal register in church, the curate wrote in the margin next to the name of Annie Sarah Shepherd, 'The particulars of this baby are unusual'. Nevertheless, the two little ones grew up at Outhome, happy in each other's company. In sunshine or in snow, indoors or out, they were inseparable. Will was a sturdy boy, tall for his age. Annie was petite and dark, and looked much younger. When they were old enough to walk to the village, Sarah left them with her mother who delighted in their company. The villagers accepted this strange duo and marvelled how happy and content the family were. Sarah once again worked at Burrator on mornings when she was needed, planning inwardly to keep Annie at Outhome if any visitors from Borneo were expected. Grace Thorn was always pleased to welcome Sarah.

'How's them little ones of yours, Sarah?' she asked. 'Bring 'em over to see me some time.'

'Yes, I will, Mrs Thorn. Are any more visitors expected while the master's away?' Sarah asked.

'None that I know of, Sarah. But then, who knows what's going on in this house. I suppose they could come any time. Sir James is very generous and a kind host.'

Sir James had laid the foundation stone of the school, Miss Coutts had given a generous donation and now the building was in use. The schoolmistress lived there with her daughter and a young boarder. Sarah took Will and Annie when they were four years old on mornings when she worked at Burrator. The oldest pupil was twelve years of age and some of the children left school when they were only eight. Boys went to work on the farms or to Ware's Warren where they lived in and were taught all about the catching and trading of rabbits. The girls went into service, at Burrator, Longstone Manor or the Vicarage.

Mrs Creber was convinced that Annie would be noticed by the Rajah one day when he went, as he did sometimes, into the school to talk to the children about his eastern country. The children were in awe of the Rajah, as was the schoolmistress, all believing the tales of his adventures were fairy stories which he had read in a book. Yes, he was sure to spot Annie, so obviously different from her friends and so like those of his adopted country, and ask about her parentage.

Sheepstor village and tor from Portland Lane 1981. (EH)

Sheepstor village and tor May 9th, 1891. (RB)

HM Prison, Dartmoor, 1913. (T)

Burrator House 2000 (PH-L)

Yennadon House in Dousland, 2000.

Eylesburrow Mine north-east of Sheepstor. (T)

Harry Terrell

Deancombe Farm, on the right bank of Deancombe Brook. (T)

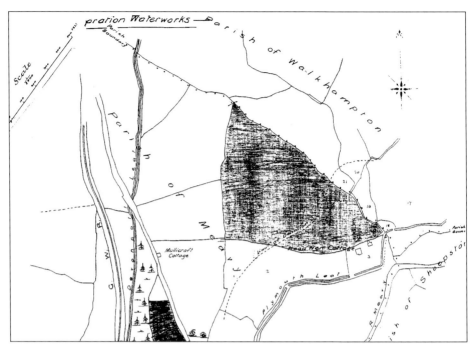

Three parishes meet in this area as shown on this nineteenth century plan. (SWW)

Out over the moor, below Eylesburrow. (EH)

The well for drinking water, at the south-west of Burrator House.

Sir James Brooke (1803-1868) at Sheepstor in 1864.

Prince Muda Hassim who enlisted the help of James Brooke to quell the rebellion in Sarawak. Hassim gave the country to Brooke who became the first white Rajah.

Burrator with Down Tor in the background. (T)

Royal Oak Inn in Meavy. (RB)

Sheep graze on the moor on the walk from Outhome to Sheeps tor village.

Angela Burdett-Coutts 1814-1906).

Tavistock in the nineteenth century. (T)

Old Sheepstor School as it was in 2000.

Venerable Revd W Y Daykin, curate of Sheepstor who lived in Brook Cottage near the church.

Sea Dyaks in Sarawak, dressed for war.

CL 621586

CERTIFIED COPY of an   ENTRY OF BIRTH
Pursuant to the Births and   Deaths Registration Act 1953

Registration District			West Devon						
1866.	Birth in the Sub-district of		Buckland Monachorum		in the	County of Devon			
Columns: - 1	2	3	4	5	6	7	8	9	10
No.	When and where born	Name, if any	Sex	Name and surname of father	Name, surname and maiden surname of mother	Occupation of father	Signature, description and residence of informant	When registered	Signature of registrar	Name entered after registration
225	First March 1866 Burrator Sheepstor	James William	Boy	John Souls	Mary Souls formerly Branning	Coachman to Sir James Knt Brook	John Souls father Burrator Sheepstor	Seventh April 1866	Richard Toop Registrar.	

Copy of the birth certificate of the Sauls' baby, born in the Coach house at Burrator.

Tomb of the Rajah of Sarawak in Sheepstor, 1870.

HH The Rajah of Sarawak. Charles Johnson Brooke, second white Rajah of Sarawak succeeded his uncle in 1868.

One of the Malay ladies who befriended Ranee Margaret.

The sixteenth century St Leonard's Well was restored in 1910 with part of the east window from the church.

The waterfront in Kuching with the Matang hills in the background. Centre is Fort Margherita built in the 1870s in honour of the Ranee.

Up to sixty families may live under one roof in an Iban longhouse in Sarawak.

Mrs Ware with calf at Ditsworthy.   *Ditsworthy in its heyday as a warren.*

Sheepstor taken from Sheepstor Brook showing the position of Brook Cottage near the lane, sold to be the Vicarage by Revd W Y Daykin, later renamed Greystones. (EH)

SOUTH DEVON,

BETWEEN TAVISTOCK AND PLYMOUTH,

Four miles from Horrabridge and six from Bickleigh, both Stations on the direct Line of the South Western Railway, but equally accessible by the Great Western System viâ Plymouth.

PARTICULARS, PLAN AND CONDITIONS OF SALE

OF A HIGHLY PICTURESQUE AND MOST INVITING

Freehold Residential Property

KNOWN AS

"BURRATOR,"

In the PARISH OF SHEEPSTOR, in the COUNTY OF DEVON, for some years the Residence of the late Rajah Sir James Brooke, K.C.B, situate near the Village and Church of Sheepstor, the eminence known as

SHEEPSTOR,

Famous in the Legendary History of Devonshire, being a conspicuous feature in the Landscape.

The RESIDENCE comprises Four Sitting-Rooms and Eight Bed and Dressing Rooms, Stabling and Appurtenances, is placed amidst Grounds which owe but little to art, but possess a wild romantic beauty of their own, to which it is difficult to do adequate justice. A sequestered path leads to

BURRATOR WOOD, THIRTY ACRES IN EXTENT;

Herein (at the junction of Burrator Brook with the River Mew) are the

FAR-FAMED FALLS OF BURRATOR,

Renowned throughout the District, and visited by every Tourist, irresistibly reminding the spectator of some of the

CHOICEST "BITS" OF SAXON SWITZERLAND

ON A SMALL SCALE.

Indeed, the whole Property presents so many scenes, possessing a BEAUTY AND ENCHANTMENT THAT ARE POSITIVELY BEWILDERING, that Mr. Robins very confidently recommends the Property to any one desiring a most Charming and Healthful Retreat for the Summer months, while to those of Artistic or Poetic Tastes it cannot fail to prove the source of fresh inspiration.

Excellent Trout Fishing may be had, and there is Good Shooting. The greater part of the Land is let off on Yearly Tenancies at a remunerative Rental. The Total Area of the Estate is nearly

SEVENTY-TWO ACRES.

IMMEDIATE POSSESSION may be had on Completion of the Purchase, of the House, Lands and Woods in hands.

WHICH WILL BE SOLD BY AUCTION, BY

M.R. ROBINS,

At the Mart, Tokenhouse Yard, Lothbury, by the Bank of England,

On **WEDNESDAY**, the 9th day of **MAY**, 1877,

AT ONE FOR TWO O'CLOCK PRECISELY—IN ONE LOT,

By Direction of His Highness The RAJAH OF SARAWAK.

These Falls are celebrated throughout this part of Devon, and are visited by every Tourist. A projecting Rock affords an admirable "coign of vantage" from which the imposing spectacle of this NATURAL WATERFALL can be safely and agreeably viewed.

Sale particulars of Burrator in 1877, (P&WDRO,874/65). In comparison the sale particulars of 2001 epitomised the same attractions with additions that Burrator House, 220m above sea level within Dartmoor National Park, was once owned by Harry Terrell, Sir James Brooke the White Rajah of Sarawak, Charles E Brittan and Lord Carnock.

Eylesburrow Mine buildings, taken 19 January 1889. (RB)

Cuckoo Rock (pronounced Goo-goo Rock on the moor). Looking down the valley to the reservoir. (AD)

Old Deancombe with granite trough. (EH)

Adit near Deancombe amongst the trees. (EH)

The lychgate, western entrance to Sheepstor churchyard. The initials W E, for Walter Elford, are carved on the coffin stone. (T)

Albert Philpott Prowse of Yennadon, 1817-1893.

Prowse's Crossing in Iron Mine Lane, Dousland. (T)

Site of Burrator reservoir in 1884. (T)

The train snowed up on Peak Hill.

Haymaking in the fields near the reservoir. Henry Creber is seated and Gilly stands with his pitchfork. (AD)

Longstone Manor, c.1890, then a farm. (T)

Middleworth Farm. (PH-L)

The Windstrew at Longstone. (T)

Park Cottage Inn, Sheepstor. (T)

Narrator Farm. (PH-L)

Henry Creber 1858-1941, who lived with his wife and children at Mullicroft. (AD)

George Shillibeer, son of Amos. (T)

Lowery Cottage. (T)

Sheepstor Bridge, now under water.

On Sheepstor Bridge before the flooding. (RB)

View of the reservoir from Yennadon in 1898.

14

A s the Rajah sailed up river into his eastern country in his steamship the *Rainbow*, a present to him from Miss Coutts, hundreds of little boats welcomed him. The people, waving flags and shouting to him, were glad to see him and his heart was full of pride as he saw this native community. Sir James wrote to Miss Coutts of the great rejoicing at his return and pleaded with her to encourage the British Government to protect Sarawak and British interests there.

His letters to her were full of grateful thanks for her support and funds:

'I was broken in heart, health and fortune. You gave me life and hope. My love to dear Mrs Brown. Kindness and sympathy attract me so strongly that I could almost leave undone what I came to do and return.'

Above the town of Kuching the mountain of Santubong rose to 3,000 feet, covered to its summit with luxuriant forests. Brown huts, made of dried palm leaves and built on poles, scattered the beach and little brown children played about in canoes. The scenery was exotically beautiful. Mists hung in ethereal drapes over the watery forests, riverbanks and on the high mountains of the interior. Members of the Rajah's government were also there to welcome him. The influence of the old Rajah over the Malays had always been great.

On 29 April, the Rajah's 58th birthday, he sailed in the *Rainbow* to see the Sultan of Borneo, receiving a cordial welcome wherever he went. He sent little flowers from Sarawak to Mrs Brown and in return received snowdrops and crocuses. Outbreaks of head-hunting and piracy could still break out at at any time amongst the Dyaks – the common name for the indigenous people of Borneo though there were land Dyaks, sea Dyaks and many other different tribes.

The Rajah had to deal with their chiefs, communicating by means of boat on the numerous long rivers that flowed from deep in the interior, the roadways to trade in the country. These aboriginal people respected the Rajah; he dealt justly with them and respected the ways of an oriental country, whilst taking the precaution of having servants guard him with loaded muskets! But despite such uncivilised undercurrents, harmony and artistic sensitivity was evident in many other ways, like the exquisite satin sarongs with elaborate embroideries produced by the Malay women. While he was living in Sarawak, Brooke was truly enchanted by it and became a mixture between a Dyak and a Malay.

After eight months he sailed home once again, a much happier man than when he arrived. He had secured peace with Borneo, had sorted out the natives' skirmishes without bloodshed and had given fresh hope to his people. It had been thought by those faithful to him in Borneo that his absence during his two years at Burrator had in fact been due to his death. His visit, a long tortuous journey by a man not in good health, had satisfied the Sarawakian people. Trade was improving and the country was thriving. He sailed home to England in only thirty seven days, thanks to the *Rainbow*, appropriately named by Miss Coutts.

Back home at Burrator and Sheepstor village, a different but just as genuine welcome awaited; no waving flags, cheering or being met by canoes, but snow, a merry peal of bells from the church tower and the barking of his dogs. His household, too, were more than pleased to have him back; John Sauls, the 31-year-old groom who also oversaw the seventy-two acre farm, Grace Thorn, the 61-year-old housekeeper, her 23-year-old daughter, Ann, and a young man, his secretary Mr Prout, who also lived in the house. Servants came in daily from Sheepstor village. The Rajah wrote to Miss Coutts about his welcome:

'Dick, one of the dogs, barked at the gig coming up the drive, accompanying it barking to the door. The house was warm and snug though very shabby. I was glad to be at home with a mind at ease, which was not so before. I had a woodcock for dinner and ate him up. I have not seen my neighbours yet, nor the ponies, nor the cows, nor the pigs, ducks and chickens.'

He wrote about his canaries and bullfinches twittering in the south window, of the snow outside tempting him to walk amid the granite masses of Sheeps Tor. A week later he wrote of killing a pig for meat and of his other country pursuits. He was a happy man at Burrator.

Miss Coutts and Sir James were both prolific letter writers and daily newspapers arrived at Burrator. In his absence he was sad to learn of the death of the Queen's Consort, Prince Albert, at the age of forty-three, shortly before Christmas. He felt sorry for Her Majesty who had lost her mother earlier that same year. Sir James knew Victoria would be devastated by her husband's death and thanked God for his own health, such as it was at that time.

He enjoyed walking along the banks of the Plymouth Leat near his estate, casting spring flowers into the flowing water and wondering if Sir Francis Drake who engineered the leat had ever done the same thing in Queen Bessy's time. The wide headweir and sluice gate were just below Lower Lowery farm on the right bank of the River Mew. Mr Shillibeer told him the leat was almost seven miles long. Walking on the path by the side of the fast flowing water gave him immense pleasure. He sent violets which he picked in the hedgerows to Miss Coutts and she sent him forget-me-nots in return. He travelled widely, going to Paris in the spring with his two lady friends to see the great International Exhibition. He felt sprightly and alive.

A new young curate had come to live in Sheepstor village, in a cottage near to the church, opposite the old vicarage. It was called Brook Cottage, named so because the Sheepstor Brook rushed between its banks through the garden. The brook then passed across Portland Lane where there was once a ford, on through the school garden, into Burrator grounds and plunged over a rocky precipitous bed with a forceful noise into the River Mew. Sir James often walked with the curate, William Daykin, showing him the village and countryside and soon they became firm friends.

Reverend Daykin was married to Mary but they had no children. Old Mary Daykin, his elderly mother, lived with the young couple, as did two young boys who attended the school and two servant girls. As well as his herd of cattle Sir

James kept two Guernsey cows which supplied milk to the household of Burrator and to the Daykins at Brook Cottage. Every week, 13¹/₂ pounds of butter were sent to the market at Tavistock made from surplus milk.

Sir James had a flock of sheep out on the moor, wild and tame ducks on his lake and foals which were frequently born in his stables. Mrs Brown sent him a ram and a ewe, Adam and Eve Sheep as she called them, as a trial to rear a fresh breed. Far from the worries and negotiations of far-off Sarawak, his island paradise on the other side of the world, he delighted in all this management and was thrilled to hear the first cuckoo in April.

His friendship with the two ladies was most unusual. A deep love held the three close, but not a physical love. They wrote constantly to each other from all parts of the world and rejoiced in the other's company. The curate or Mrs Daykin were also often to be found at Burrator, ready to do anything the Rajah requested. They read to him, drove him about in his little Norway cart or sat with him in his favourite seat by the waterfall in the grounds. A rustic bench and table were placed in the most picturesque spot, halfway down the fall and some boughs on the trees cut to let in the distant view. Here he would sit for hours, alone or with company, among the trees.

Writing from Burrator to his sister Emma on paper headed with his crest, a badger and the family motto, *Dum Spiro Spero, While I breathe, I hope,* he included the wishes of Miss Coutts with his own... *'Miss Coutts and I both think you should come and stay,'* he wrote.

Since his stroke, Sir James enjoyed riding in his carriage. He purchased two ponies, each thirteen hands high, to suit his new vehicle. Friends and relations were alerted to look out for items he needed to keep him comfortable and a white chaise duly arrived which perfectly suited his old horse. In this he transported his guests to and from Horrabridge station. Burrator was four miles from the railway station at Horrabridge and six miles from Bickleigh in the other direction. Both stations were on the direct line of the South Western Railway, but equally accessible by the Great Western system via Plymouth.

With John Sauls he bought a pair of ponies at a local sale for his phaeton, which he used in the summer. Sauls was kept busy with the number of horses and conveyances in the Rajah's possession.

Descriptions of the weather were a constant subject in his letters. Gales, cold, wet, sunshine, stormy, snow – all conditions he found pleasant, except for the east wind. The following is a typical letter, wrtten daily from his retreat:
'March 20, 1862
My dearest sister,
I have nothing to tell you in my solitude beyond the delightful saunter I had yesterday. A day to be enjoyed and the disappointment to find the east wind blowing this morning. It is not the ill that wind and weather do us, but the deprivation of enjoyment when they are bad...'

Much of Brooke's energy was still devoted to the concerns of Sarawak. Writing from Burrator in April the Rajah sent a report to Lord Russell, stating that the support of the British Government was needed for Sarawak, a question of refuge or ruin:

'Sarawak and the North-Western coast of Borneo hold a position important for steam navigation and electric communication, situated as it is on the Southern shore of the China Sea.

Possessing navigable rivers, gold, antimony, iron and silver in abundance, the soil calculated for the growth of cotton, sugar, coffee and other tropical productions and the forests yielding timber of fine qualities; the populations are alive to the benefits of good government and increasing trade.'

He wrote that the Malay, a proud and sensitive people, would become the government; the Dyak, a body of warriors, would defend the country; and the Europeans and Chinese would be the workforce. He was in constant communication with all those who might assist in the development of Sarawak. The Rajah was regarded by the Dyaks as almost superhuman, sent for their salvation while the Malays looked up to him as a great chief.

Miss Coutts and Mrs Brown came to stay again at Burrator that summer. He insisted they have the whole house and went to stay at a nearby inn. He took them to the local beauty spot at the Dewerstone, to the waterfall at the foot of his garden, to the tor and the church. The spectacular waterfall is where the brook plunges down the granite-strewn hillside to mother-stream, the Mew. There is never silence in Burrator Woods. Just as Maggie and Sarah had done a few years earlier, Sir James and the two ladies sat near the water, admiring the beauty and solitude.

The two ladies much admired this lovely part of Devonshire and were amazed to see the improvement of health and spirit in their friend. The three laughed together among the rocks and trees.

'What do you think about out here, Sir James?' Mrs Brown asked one afternoon.

'I love the solitude,' he disclosed. 'I love to come here and loll by the side of the stream, under the shade of these melancholy boughs, eat sandwiches and drink ginger pop! That's happiness – a fig for all the rest!'

But another cloud was on the horizon at the end of this year when James fell out with his nephew John Brooke Brooke whom he had left managing his affairs in Sarawak. His sister's sons had both changed their names from Johnson to Brooke. Sir James ordered Brooke to return to England and never return to Sarawak, causing much family agitation. In his place he sent his other nephew Charles Brooke to become the Rajah Muda, the heir to the Brooke throne. Sir James visited Sarawak for the last time in 1863 and received a letter from Lord Russell at the Foreign Office saying that he was ready to propose recognition of Sarawak to the Cabinet. It was accomplished. Sarawak came under British protection. He left his precious country in September and returned to Sheepstor.

15

WILL and Annie made other friends at the village school but they much preferred to be at home together. Will liked it best when he was allowed to be out with Sam and Annie would follow them around the farm. When Sarah and the children were due to arrive home at the end of a morning from the village, Sam rode his pony to meet them. Sam and Sarah walked home side by side, Sam leading the pony which carried Annie with Will behind holding her tightly.

At the beginning of the year Sir James wrote to Mrs Brown in London:

'May I petition for the overflow of the London schools for poor Sheepstor, as we had one year before, in the form of books and dolls etc. We have had a Christmas tree at Mr Lowther's and a few prizes for our scholars. I am pleased with the progress of the children and the attention Mr and Mrs Lowther pay them.'

Mrs Rebecca Williams had left the school, her spelling was not too good. Sir James had noticed little Annie Shepherd in the schoolroom one morning and as Mrs Creber anticipated, had asked Mrs Lowther her name.

'That's little Annie Shepherd, sir, and the boy sitting next to her is her brother Will. I believe their mother works for you some mornings. That's when she brings them here.'

'Thank you, Mrs Lowther, of course,' Sir James said smiling towards the children. He thought of Sarah Shepherd at his house recalling the pretty young woman who helped Mrs Thorn and how on one of his first visits to Sheepstor, Harry Terrell had shown him the lonely valley where Sarah lived. He guessed it had been one of his visitors that had fathered the child.

He thought to himself, 'I'll take more notice of her when I return to the house. Who am I to censure? I have a 31 year-old son, and not many here know that.'

Over the following months Sir James held shooting parties at Burrator which he joined in the afternoons; guests dined on woodcock, pheasant and hare among other game. Replying to his prolific letters Miss Coutts hoped he enjoyed the shoots, telling him the winter weather was mild in London and a great disappointment to the skaters. On Dartmoor, however, John Sauls made sure there were good fires in all the rooms.

Then the unusual friendship, with all its genuine mutual loyalty and kindness, was put to an unprecedented test over the affairs of Sarawak. Miss Coutts spoke her mind. It was her money supporting the country and she wanted a say in all matters. She was forthright in condemning the actions the Rajah was taking.

Writing from Burrator he sent warm friendship to her, explaining that even closest friends cannot be always in agreement. The lady had wounded his feelings and he asked her to spare him any more pain. One of her complaints was that she did not approve of Charles Johnson, his nephew who became Charles Brooke, being nominated by him as the heir to Sarawak, although she knew that

Sir James had left to her the revenues of Sarawak in his will. Letters from her ceased for a while but in the end they agreed to differ.

His letters to the two ladies never ceased, however. He told them of the improvements he was making to his property costing £1,500 for rebuilding the back and repairing the front of Burrator. The house pleased him:

'It looks very well outside. The drawing room is an excellent room and the new bedrooms are very comfortable, with a sunny aspect. By the time it is finished, it will be a gentleman's house.'

He had a new kitchen range and boiler fitted and took a keen interest in the embellishments being added to his house, both inside and out. A verandah was chosen by him for the front of the house which pleased him as he could take fresh air and exercise there in bad weather. In Bath, where he was taking the waters again, he chose wallpaper for his new drawing room and bedrooms – *'very cheerful and cheap'*. Carpets and furniture were sent for the new part of the house.

In the spring he bought a dogcart in which two of his ponies could take him around the country lanes. He had suffered another mild stroke but enjoyed the year's familiar routine on his estate. Undaunted by his illness he resumed his travels to friends all over England and even contemplated another visit to Sarawak.

At the end of the year he met with another stroke at Burrator and now the two ladies travelled to be near him. The doctor would not permit them to see the Rajah. Friends and his two sisters arrived in Tavistock by rail but they could not see him either. John Sauls cared for him with the Rajah's old friend Spenser St John. This time he lost the use of his limbs and his speech became slurred.

Despite his own misfortunes, he was moved to read in the local newspaper how a 13-year-old boy, Samuel Bray, had saved a younger child from drowning at Devonport. Sir James sent the boy a half-sovereign and stayed in touch. Sir James was always generous and kind. In return others were pleased to assist him. The parishioners of Sheepstor thought of him as a great man.

Mrs Brown sent the books and rag dolls for Sheepstor school and it was the girls who delighted in them, especially Annie. Will was not interested in reading, writing or arithmetic but Annie, only five years old, would sit for a long time turning the pages of a picture book, hugging one of the London dolls. Will and Annie were accepted as Sam and Sarah's children. It is surprising how quickly a thing that at first looks odd becomes the accustomed sight after a short space of time.

Grace Thorn and her daughter retired from Burrator and went to live on the east of the moor. John Sauls had by now married Mary Browning who was expecting their first baby in January. She was also to be the new housekeeper at Burrator.

Charles Brooke now governed Sarawak in the Rajah's name with his headquarters at Simanggang where he built a fort. Miss Coutts gave up her right to inherit Sarawak and accepted that Charles Brooke was the Rajah's chosen heir.

Charles wrote his autobiography, *Ten years in Sarawak*, with a preface, at the publishers' request penned by Sir James. This he wrote at Burrator, praising his nephew for keeping the peace and making the country safe for trading:

'*He has inspired its people with confidence and Sarawak has now been recognised as an Independent State by America, by England and by Italy.*'

The Rajah amazingly continued to gain strength at Burrator. He loved having company, especially his young friends, and would walk with them in the morning and ride in the afternoon, returning for afternoon tea. Between tea and dinner he valued time to read and every now and then he would put down his book or newspaper and talk of any question that was then interesting him. After a while he would resume his reading when the silence was companionable. When he had sufficient company he enjoyed the game of whist.

It was at this time that George Shillibeer, the water bailiff of the Plymouth Leat, died at his home in Sheepstor village. Revd Daykin took the burial service, his first since coming to Sheepstor, and the little church was filled by the humble and the affluent from the area. The Shillibeers were a well-respected family, a Sheepstor family who worked for the Plymouth town council controlling the flow and cleanliness of drinking water for the town from the River Mew at Sheepstor. George's son, William, who had learnt all he knew from his father, was to carry on the work of his father as water bailiff. William's son, Amos, would follow in the family tradition.

The school was closed for the day so that Mr and Mrs Lowther could attend the funeral. Listed in the school register were sixteen children but there was never a day when all the children were at school. Some days only two attended, the others being kept at home to work or to care for their younger siblings. Little children, like Will and Annie Shepherd, only came when their mothers were able to bring them.

Children listed on the school roll from the parish in 1867 were Charlie and Fred Ware (Ditsworthy), Mary, Jessie, Ellen and Richard Legassick (Collytown), Henry Stanbury (Yellowmead), Jane Butland (Yeo), Emmeline and John Creber (Longstone), Sarah Jackman (Narrator), Annie Andrew (Hellingtown), Bessie and Polly Crocker (Essworthy) and Will and Annie Shepherd (Outhome). All who attended had to pay at least one penny a week.

In the schoolroom was an American organ, desks, shelves of books and a cupboard; decorating the wall, a clock and some picture maps. The premises lived in by the teacher consisted of a sitting room, back kitchen and bedroom with a stove in the kitchen and fireplace with fender-surround in the sitting room. The whole building was just nineteen feet long, fourteen feet wide and thirteen feet high, its ambience cosy and homely.

Annie loved to write on her slate while Will copied her. Though he was good at sums he did not enjoy writing things down. They were both pleased when Sarah finished work at Burrator and came to collect them at the end of the morning. The children skipped along with their mother, holding her hands, and Sarah was overjoyed to have them with her again. They called in on

Sarah's parents in the cottage before their long walk home across the moor. Granny Creber always had something ready to eat for them and she, too, took much pleasure in these brief visits.

'Mary Sauls had her baby this morning, Mam,' Sarah burst out as the three of them entered her parents' cottage. 'It's a boy and they're calling him James after the Rajah. James William.'

'There's not been a baby born in Burrator for a good few years,' Mrs Creber exclaimed. 'How are mother and baby?'

'Fine. The Rajah's pleased. The first of March is a nice day to be born, isn't it? Funny that someone leaves the world and a baby comes along to fill the space.' They both thought of George Shillibeer.

As the young mother and two children walked home along the lane between the high hedges, Annie said, 'The Rajah came into school this morning, Mum, and told us about Queen Victoria. She's been our queen for nearly thirty years.'

'Do you know, Annie, I was born on the day she became Queen? That's why I was named Sarah Victoria.'

'Are you that old, Mum?' Annie asked.

'Not as old as the queen, Annie.'

'And the Rajah's her friend, Mum,' Will added. 'He told us all about her. She's very old, about fifty... I'm hungry. Race you to the next gate, Annie.'

Sarah picked up her skirts and ran after them. The family joyfully returned home where Sam usually met them, absorbed in their family life in the little Deancombe valley.

16

IN THE year of 1867, another son was born to John and Mary Sauls in the two rooms over the coach house at Burrator, where they lived. They named him Alfred John. Sir James enjoyed the company of his coachman John Sauls which was just as well, as these days he had to accept being driven everywhere as his riding days were over.

Unknown to the Rajah, or indeed to any member of the Brooke family, Charles Brooke also became a father that year in Sarawak. His son was born on 27 August at Simanggang, the mother Dayang Mastiah being of Malay aristocracy. The boy's name was Esca. The birth of Alfie Sauls was recorded in Tavistock, Devon and Esca's in Sarawak in arabic script.

Charles Brooke was relieved that year to receive a copy of his uncle's new will handing down the sovereignty of Sarawak to him and his heirs. The Rajah, at home in Burrator and unaware of his nephew's Malay attachment, wrote to Charles suggesting he looked for a rich wife. He was warning his successor of the great debts and financial obligations that he must meet in Sarawak. Sir James drew Charles's attention to a distant cousin, Lily de Windt, a wealthy widow who was living in Wiltshire in England.

At the end of the year Miss Coutts and Mrs Brown welcomed Sir James to their home in Torquay to spend Christmas with them.

'I feel wretchedly unwell. I don't know what the matter is with my frame. I hope I shall get better soon,' he said to the ladies one evening shortly after Christmas. 'I shall leave you in the morning and take lodgings nearby.'

'It was our pleasure to welcome you here for the season, please don't leave,' Miss Coutts pleaded. 'I do not understand your action.'

'I beg your pardon, I do not wish to hurt your feelings, Madam.'

'You must do what you feel is right, Sir James,' Miss Coutts declared. 'Life is too short and uncertain for me to dwell on circumstances which have upset you.'

'You are all that is kind. I hope you will forgive me.'

Her statement was truer than she knew. James Brooke had not many more months to live. Mrs Brown believed that James was unwell and did not wish to embarrass his host with his infirmities. How sadly life had changed.

Returning to Burrator in the New Year he still managed to write letters to the ladies blaming his state of depression on the unsettled weather. His last letter to them was a month before he died.

Three weeks after she received the letter Miss Coutts was telegraphed in London by Dr Willis from Devon: *The Rajah is gradually sinking there is no hope of his recovery.*

On the morning of Wednesday 11 June, as the Sheepstor folk were milking cows and busy with other daily tasks, just before seven o'clock, the Rajah died. Mrs Johnson, her son Stuart, Mr Crookshank and Mr Daykin were with him.

Arriving at the house after taking Will and Annie to school, Sarah noticed the blinds at the windows and knew immediately what it meant as she was met in the drive by the coachman.

''Tis as we expected, Sarah. The Rajah passed away this morning in his sleep. The doctors said he was very peaceful.'

'I'm glad of that, Mr Sauls,' Sarah said solemnly. 'Do they want me today?'

'Go on in and see Mary. I think she'll need you more than ever. I'm going up to tell Mrs Daykin the news, Mr Daykin is still in the house.'

Mary Sauls was weeping as Sarah entered the kitchen.

'James and Alfie know there's something up. I'm so pleased to see you, Sarah. The Rajah's family will be staying here I expect and we'll have all the beds to make up. Can you help the other maids?'

'Of course, Mary. Mr Sauls said life must go on.'

'I knew he was passing away and I thought I was prepared for it. But when death actually occurs it hits you inside.'

Mary Sauls and Sarah crept in sorrowfully and reverently to take their last look at the Rajah. He looked in death as Sarawak had known him in the full vigour of his manhood.

Six days later, the first White Rajah of Sarawak was buried in his chosen spot in Sheepstor churchyard, east of the church under a great beech tree. Mrs Daykin placed roses from her garden on his body. The brass plate on the oak coffin sparkled in the sunlight, *Sir James Brooke K.C.B. Rajah of Sarawak*.

'Make sure I am buried there, John,' he had said to his friend and coachman one day. 'It will be so jolly to lie there.'

Sarah's father, Tom Creber, was one of the bearers who carried the coffin to the resting place at the lychgate and then into the church.

The bells pealed, instead of tolling, before the service conducted by the Reverend Daykin. The little church was packed with family and friends. He had been the Rajah of the Eastern country for 27 years yet Mr Daykin made no mention of his status in the burial register, simply writing *'James Brook* (spelling his name incorrectly), *June 17. Officiating minister W. Y. Daykin'*.

An account of the Rajah's funeral appeared in the *Western Daily Mercury* on Thursday 18 June 1868:

'The mortal remains of Sir James Brooke, Rajah of Sarawak, were interred yesterday morning in the parish church of Sheepstor, near Horrabridge. The burial service was performed by Archdeacon Sinclair and the Rev Mr Dakin. The following were amongst those who were present: General Jacob, Rev Mr Walker, Dr Willis, Stewart Johnson Esq., Ed. Evelyn Esq., – Cruikshank Esq., – Fairburn Esq., G. Grant Esq., W. Collier Esq., J.H. Gill Esq. J.P., and Messrs Hodge, G. Brooke, Bailey senr, Bailey junr, Knox and Butt. Sir James is deeply regretted, especially by the poor of many parishes in the districts around Burrator, to whom he was always a friend, and his death will be a great loss to them. The funeral arrangements were undertaken by Messrs. Popham and Radford of Plymouth.'

John Sauls continued reading the report to his wife: *'"He was a bold, upright and somewhat over stern adventurer, with a talent not only for conquering, but for conciliating Eastern races."'*

Mary interrupted him. 'It doesn't mention us or any of the villagers.'

'No, it wouldn't print names of the likes of us, nor does it mention any of the ladies present. It isn't recorded that the sun shone and that every pew in the church was filled.'

'He got his wish. He'll lie forever in the soil he called home,' Mary spoke tenderly. 'Sheepstor will always remember him.'

'Listen to this last bit, Mary. *"Worse men and feebler have ere this been laid in Westminster Abbey, but we suppose no claim will be made for the last Englishman who has waged and won a private war."* Sir James wouldn't have wanted to be buried in London. This was his home.'

'Mr Daykin will sorely miss him and the church has lost a good churchwarden. Yes, he'll be missed all right.'

'It was good to have Ruby here with us.'

'You must call him George, my dear,' Mary said quickly. 'He dropped his name of Reuben when the Rajah recognised him as his son. He wishes to be known as George Brooke not Reuben Walker.'

'I know, my dear, but he's more like one of us and he understands I'm only baiting him.'

'He was in a hurry to return to Nottingham, to his wife Eliza and their four little sons. One of them is a wee baby.'

On 3 August 1868, a simple but moving ceremony took place in Kuching when Charles Brooke was installed as the second Rajah of Sarawak. A large number of the population witnessed the occasion when the responsibility of governing James Brooke's beloved country was entrusted to his nephew. He clearly shared his uncle's devotion to the country. It was the beginning of a new era for Sarawak.

In his will the Rajah left his estates in England and Borneo to Charles Brooke. To his son George, his wife Eliza and their children he left £5,000. To John Sauls and his family he left £25 a year and a request that the Sauls family should stay at Burrator as caretakers. To other young men he left sums of money which Charles had an obligation to transfer.

Miss Burdett-Coutts planned to erect a memorial to the Rajah in Westminster Abbey but this was never accomplished. She placed a large tombstone of pink granite over his grave, brought from Scotland, a distance of over six hundred miles. His grave was dug on his chosen spot, under the canopy of a great beech tree which gave both shade and beauty beneath the clitter of Sheeps Tor.

The memorial reads:

Sacred to the Memory of
Sir James Brooke, K.C.B., D.C.L.
Rajah of Sarawak
Born at Bandel in Bengal

April 29th 1803.
Died at his residence, Burrator,
in this Parish
June 11th, 1868.

A much longer and flamboyant eulogy was proposed and written by the family but was never perpetrated. If Miss Burdett-Coutts had known Dartmoor she would have realised that pink granite was obtainable less than five miles away on the Trowlesworthy tors in the neighbouring Plym valley.

At the end of the year, a more humble burial took place, that of Thomas Creber, Sarah's father. Mr Creber had not enjoyed good health for some years but Sarah's mother had devoted her time to caring for him. The village folk and members of the large Creber family filled the church on a snowy December morning. Will and Annie were at school. Sam and Sarah sat in the front pew, one on each side of the widow, Lily Creber. Thanks to the late Sir James Brooke the church was in good repair and Mrs Creber kept the church clean. Mr Daykin read the service and spoke over the grave as the coffin was lowered into the ground. The mourners hurried home afterwards, cold and wet in the wintry weather.

There would be no money for a memorial stone for this humble villager. He was buried next to the grave of John Andrew of Redstone, who was blind when he died aged ninety-six in 1754.

> *I twenty years in darkness lived*
> *None heard me to complain*
> *Having full hope in Christ that I*
> *Shall live in light again.*

17

LIFE at Outhome, in its quietude and remoteness, was blissful for Sam and Sarah. The two children brought family blessings and a happiness to Sam he had never known. Times did not change at Outhome. The rent was paid on the due date and there was enough money to feed and clothe the family. Sam and Sarah had all they needed.

Plymouth was as remote to them as was London or Sarawak. Built of stone, the upper window of the cottage peeped from under the thatch, giving forth a mellow warm appearance. The outside world seemed far away. Their garden was the moorland turf of Dartmoor and their world was never silent with its constant music of the babbling brook and birdsong in the woodland trees. When they were not helping their parents, Will and Annie played in the brook and the trees close to the house. Will showed Annie how to climb trees and look for birds' nests. They played hide-and-seek among the old ruins left from the tinners and created little boats from sticks, sailing them down the brook. Never far from the cottage, they ran indoors when Sarah called them.

In other parts of the country, people were moving away from the countryside into the towns. Wheat was grown in plenty on farms off the moor but on the craggy hillsides Sam cultivated grass and grazed his sheep. Hedges and stone walls were kept in good repair, trees felled for fuel and the wild creatures on the hillsides, such as rabbits and game birds, were killed to feed the household. The dairy cow in the field, pig in the shed and poultry in the yard supplied daily luxuries. It could be said that the tenants at Outhome did not keep abreast of the times but they were self-sufficient and independent.

During August Sarah and the children picked whortleberries which grew profusely on the banks of the old tin mine. On such fruit gathering expeditions, the three Shepherds returned home covered in the purple stains of the whorts and in a jolly mood. Sarah made the fruit into tasty pies and puddings, much liked by Sam. In September there were wild mushrooms and blackberries to be gathered in with the harvest.

As a tenant Sam Shepherd was not a problem for Massey Lopes and the landowner did not compel him to modernise. When the Shepherds would eventually move out of Outhome he planned to merge the land with that of Deancombe and to let the house fall into disrepair.

Sheepstor was a little place where the only activity was agriculture. The rabbit warrens out on the wild moor were going concerns and the farmers in small farms around the village were able to eke a living. The last tin mine in the parish up on Eylesburrow had closed down nearly twenty years before and families had moved out of the cottages on the hill.

As a boy Sam had worked at the tin mine which was on the south slope of Eylesburrow when Mr Deacon was captain of the mine. Mr Deacon lived in the captain's house, known locally as 'The Mansion'. There were cottages built nearby for the miners but Sam walked up the hill daily. It was not far to walk from Outhome and Sam was pleased to take his wages home to his mother. Returning home in the evening he enjoyed looking downstream on the Deancombe Brook, in the knowledge that his mother would have a meal ready for him in their secluded home.

When his father died in 1851, mine operations at Eylesburrow were closing down and Sam devoted his time between caring for the farm and his mother though he missed the company of the other lads at the mine. As well as Sheepstor men, others from Walkhampton and Meavy worked there. It had been a busy place for a few years, the noise of the mine workings carrying across the moor for miles.

Sam recollected that Mr Deacon had lost his baby in snow once when the family were taking it from Eylesburrow to be baptised at Sheepstor church. Luckily for them there was no blizzard or falling snow as there was on the day when Sam had found Annie. The Deacon baby was strapped to the family donkey, ridden by Mrs Deacon, whilst Mr Deacon rode his pony ahead of her. Realising the baby was missing as they passed Nattor Farm they were able to retrace their tracks, still clearly visible. Mr Deacon found the tiny bundle in deep snow at the foot of the mine road near the ford. There had been anxiety but no grief, only joy on the baby's discovery. The bank of snow had cushioned its fall.

The men of the parish frequently met at Park Cottage for a mug of ale and to pass the time of day with a neighbour. Gossip and wisdom were passed on and taken home to the wife from the ale house. Tom Reed was a jolly host and there was little he did not know about the goings-on in the parish. Sheep rustling was a common topic of conversation.

'Creber lost several sheep last week and Pengelly only t'other day,' Reed said to the farmers sitting around his table.

''Tis thought men come down from Nuns Cross and drive the sheep back up to Princetown,' Farmer Northmore stated.

'Us can't be out on the moor watchin' for 'em all the time,' Legassick said. 'But someat will 'ave to be done.'

'It may 'elp if the sheep were marked,' said another.

'Ow could that 'elp we, now?' Legassick asked. 'Us won't know where to find 'em.'

'No,' the warrener joined in. 'But they bain't going to be able to sell 'em at market, be they?'

The men's talk was usually about their flocks in this tightly knit community.

Appearance at church on Sunday was a necessity. The parson or curate, riding his horse out to the distant farms, called during the week to enquire the reason for any absence, causing the toughest farmer to recall days when he was a naughty boy at school. Quoting scriptures from the Bible had the effect of making the family feel they were condemned to hell. Mr Daykin, being a farmer as well as the curate, understood their way of life and no excuse was accepted.

Her Majesty's prison on Dartmoor lay on the other side of the headwaters of the River Mew near Prince's Town. This high moorland was often enshrouded by low cloud and cloaked in a damp dense mist.

Sheepstor was only a few miles down the valley of the Mew from the prison where the worst convicts were sent from all over England. It had a fearsome reputation as a tough location for both prisoners and staff with rigid discipline, hard labour and dismal weather conditions.

The prison building had been a French prisoner-of-war camp but about twenty years earlier the inmates had been forced to convert it into a convict prison under the guard of army soldiers. The prisoners had to clear the surrounding moor of rocks for ploughing using hand tools. Stones were taken from nearby quarries for wall building, the convicts marching to the quarries chained together at the ankles. Thus, a prison farm was created on this desolate part of the moor where some of the inmates helped to rear stock.

An escaped convict, on occasion, followed the course of the river downstream to the first inhabited village, Sheepstor. Even the worst offender must have been given new hope to discover the pure flowing stream and find himself walking down its gentle valley. Lost on the high moor, many a convict found he had walked around in circles for hours and was soon recaptured.

One farmer in the Deancombe valley left a pile of old sacks in his outhouse so that a desperate man would not attempt to break into his cottage to be rid of his unmistakable attire covered in arrows. Sam knew of this but told no one for fear of reprisal such as a public whipping for the tenant.

Sam warned Will and Annie to tell him if they ever saw a stranger near their home. Always there was the hope in the valley that an escaped convict could be apprehended and the reward of £5 claimed for his capture. A recaptured prisoner was punished by being placed in heavy chains and put on a diet of bread and water for many days.

Occasionally Sarah felt like a prisoner in her own home, enveloped in the beautiful countryside. Perhaps Sam's mother had felt the same. Sarah's late mother-in-law had not lived long after her husband had passed away; it was a lonely place for a woman to live. Sam did not speak much about his parents. Sarah was only just able to remember them, an elderly frail couple coming to church with Sam. She was a girl at the time, working for the Terrells at Burrator. It was never truly silent at Outhome with the music of the brook, the wind in the trees and the birds overhead but there was peace. Sarah found rest in reading her Bible and saying her prayers to a God who was her invisible friend. She put her trust in her creator.

But she carried the fear within her, of withholding the truth about Annie. Indeed she and Sam had saved the life of this child but she had kept the truth from all but her mother. In her mind Mr Daykin's sermons exposed her, as though he knew her secret. His text, Sunday by Sunday was, 'Jesus said, I am the way, the truth and the life'.

Sarah was both a help and companion to Mary Sauls at Burrator. The Sauls' sons, James and Alfie, who had been a delight and distraction to the Rajah, were hardly more than babies when Mary gave birth to their third child, Mary Ellen in the January following the Rajah's death. All three children were baptised by Mr Daykin in Sheepstor church.

Young Annie loved to mother younger children and the Sauls' brood had taken to her. When Sarah allowed it, Annie delighted in caring for these three babies born at Burrator; not least because when she had put them to bed, she was allowed to read the Rajah's books if there were no guests in the house. Annie was already able to read and write and Sarah realised she was far cleverer than the family that had reared her. Annie's accomplishments, in fact, were not shared by most of the folk in the village.

Annie helped the teacher at the school with the little ones and decided that she would stay on at school as a pupil teacher. Will could think of nothing worse and was longing to be given permission to stay at Outhome all day and help his father in the running of the farm.

The respect and affection held for the late Rajah in the countryside round about was remarkable, given that he had lived in Sheepstor for only nine years. Two of these were passed in Sarawak and in the remaining years he was away much of the time. But he had loved children, given them a school and they in turn delighted in his visits. He took them little gifts and at Christmas time all who worked for him had presents for the whole family.

Sarah said to Sam one evening, 'A presence has left the village with the passing of the Rajah. When he entered a room I was in, it was like being with a great person. Yet in his manner he was like us and ever so kind.'

'You preferred the Terrells, though?' Sam posed.

'Maggie was my friend and Mr and Mrs T were always so kind to me. But in his last years Sir James went out of his way to be nice to me. He always enquired about the children.'

18

JOHN and Mary Sauls waited for the newly-weds the day following the quiet wedding in Wiltshire. The new Rajah, Charles Brooke, and his bride the former Marguerita de Windt, spent their first night in Exeter. The hapless bride soon found out what sort of man she had married when he tucked into a hearty meal in the evening at the hotel, insisting that his wife make do with bread and butter. From here a one-horse cab conveyed the couple to Burrator where they were to spend their honeymoon. The luggage was taken to Sheepstor by a horse-drawn bus, in the company of their two servants. Charles had brought a Malay boy from Sarawak and Marguerita brought her French maid Adrienne, who had been with her for six years. Mary Sauls prepared an early dinner for them and placed the wedding cake she had made and decorated in the centre of the table.

'Oh, what a pretty cake,' the twenty-year-old bride exclaimed as they entered the dining room.

'Quite an unnecessary expense,' the Rajah said disapprovingly.

'Oh Rajah, Sir,' cried Mary Sauls, 'I made it for you myself, for you and your young bride with my own money.'

Mrs Sauls left the room in tears to be consoled by the maids in the kitchen. The incident illustrated only too well Charles's unpleasant, autocratic character, and what John and Mary Sauls would have to cope with over the next few months. For Marguerita, soon to be robbed of even her name, it was to be a much longer ordeal. Rajah Charles seemed almost inhuman after spending years controlling the natives of Sarawak. His wife was overawed by him, utterly dominated and manipulated by her husband. To him she was just one of his possessions.

'I can't stand your fanciful name,' he told her one day. 'You will be known as Margaret.'

'That's a hard, cold name. Can't I be known as Ghita, I have been so called all my life?'

'No, too sentimental and flowery for a woman in your position.'

He disliked the name Marguerita and although she had always been known as Ghita, she now had to accept being called Margaret. A name she loathed. Despite this formality, he did not mind her referring to him as Charlie. Now she was the wife of a Rajah and in Sarawak she was to be known as the Ranee.

All Margaret's fortune, he told her, including £400 a year from her mother, belonged to the Sarawak treasury. He showed her no display of affection and was not aware of her fear of him as a husband. Margaret disliked it intensely at Burrator, finding it lonely and dull. Sir Massey and Lady Lopes invited them to dances and parties but Charles declined politely all invitations sent to Burrator.

'I'll never allow another man to place an arm around your waist,' he declared whenever Margaret implored him on such occasions.

He was forty years old and set in his ways. Burrator had been left to Charles by the late Rajah who had hoped that the house would remain in posterity as a retreat for the Brooke family members. But Margaret hated it there and the new Rajah planned to return to Sarawak with his new wife in due course. He had not told her of the child he had fathered who was living with his Malay mother in Simanggang.

'You'll never guess what the master did today,' John Sauls said to his wife in bed one evening. 'You know how last week he harnessed two wild Dartmoor ponies to the small carriage and went for a drive on his own. Well, today he took Madam with him and made her drive the carriage.'

'Oh my goodness,' Mary exclaimed, 'where did they go?'

'Around the lanes and through the village. When they got to the brook the ponies tried to jump the wall and the carriage turned over on its side.'

'That's why Madam's face was scratched. Adrienne was bathing it for ages.'

'Yes, she walked back here. The trouble is the Rajah enjoys adventure and is out to tame those animals. He came back here to fetch me and the lads. He was laughing heartily and was full of excitement. We had to go and rescue the carriage.'

'Madam is too young and innocent for him. When are they leaving here for Borneo?'

'After the New Year. They will be sailing from Devonport.'

'We've got Christmas to get through first. Our three little ones take up much of my time. I don't know what I would do without Annie to help me.'

'I should approach Madam about the preparations for the festival. You may get a more favourable response from her about turkeys and plum puddings than from him.'

'Yes, I will. Goodnight, John.'

Sarah worked at Burrator when she was able. The children were nine years old and Will was a strong lad, a real help to Sam. Annie went to school and helped the other children with their work when Sarah was employed at Burrator.

'Mrs Johnson the Rajah's mother and her daughter are coming to stay tomorrow, Sarah. We need to prepare the rooms.'

'Right you are, Mrs Sauls. How's your little ones today?'

'Much better, thank you for asking, Sarah. James and Alfie are a handful and I'm still nursing baby Ellen.'

'Would you like Annie to come and help you again? She's lovely with little ones and she adores your three babies.'

'It would be a Godsend, Sarah. I'll keep her out of sight of the Rajah and the mistress like you asked me to last time she came. I realise you don't want her to be seen by them.'

Sarah coloured and looked embarrassed.

'It's not that I'm ashamed of her, far from it, but I don't want her to be bothered by all the questions that would arise if they saw her. The master coming from Sarawak, that is.'

'Yes, I see,' Mary Sauls smiled. Although she didn't see and had never understood how Sarah and Sam Shepherd had two children so completely different from each other.

'How does Mr Sauls get on with Rajah Charles?' Sarah asked, changing the subject.

'He knows his position with him, Sarah. He treats John like his Malay servant. To the dear old Rajah, John was a friend. Yes, Sir James was a true friend to my John.'

Sir James had been delighted that the first child born to the young man he brought to Burrator as his coachman, had been named after him. Alfie John, the second son was born near to the Rajah's sixty-fourth birthday but he had not lived to see Mary Ellen, now ten months old.

'Did you know Sir James left us money in his will, Sarah?' Mrs Sauls stated. 'We'll have £25 a year for our lifetime.'

'You cared for Sir James better than anyone. I thought it was a pity the Rajah never married.'

'That wasn't meant to be, Sarah. He was always on the high seas in his yacht or fighting in Sarawak.'

'I thought he might have married Miss Burdett-Coutts,' Sarah said simply.

'The lady certainly cared for him, as did her companion. I don't think we shall see them in this house again.'

'You know that George is his son, I suppose,' Mary Sauls added. 'I was pleased to see him at his father's funeral.'

'Yes, he's a handsome man. The villagers all know he is the Rajah's son, Sir James told of it eventually.'

'He was proud of him. Mr George spends much of his time at sea, just like the old man did.'

As they chatted companionably, Mary and Sarah had been preparing the bedrooms for the next visitors. In her heart, Sarah hoped Burrator would be sold to a Devon family so that she would not have to worry about Annie being seen by visitors from the East.

Sarah thought this new Rajah was far too old for the elegant young lady who was his wife. Speculating about their age difference she became aware that it was probably the same as between her and Sam. This realisation made Sarah think that how others regard a situation from the outside was a matter of little consequence to those involved. As her mother often said to her, 'As you make your bed, so you must lie in it.'

19

RAJAH Charles and his wife left Burrator for their long journey to Sarawak in January. Charles Brooke had placed the estate in the hands of his London solicitors and indeed it was mortgaged until the new Rajah decided whether to sell or retain the estate. For poor Margaret, their passage to Singapore and on to Kuching was a nightmare. The Rajah hardly spoke to her, showing little sympathy on the voyage when she and her maid Adrienne were constantly seasick. Cockroaches infested the cabin and rats scuttled across the floor, scratching at her bed clothes. The tropical heat was suffocating and her European clothes clung to her body. She longed to reach their destination.

She was not disappointed, at first anyway. As they approached Kuching she went on deck and gasped at the beauty she beheld. The mountain of Santubong rose up from the water, its summit emerging through the mist which hung in the mangroves along the river.

The longhouses of the natives were built on stilts above the water and on a hill she saw the white bungalows of the small English community. She followed her husband who had been met by many dignitaries, to her new home, the Astana or palace. This had been built for the couple in the Rajah's absence from the country and for his return with his new wife, the first white Ranee. It was a few months, however, before they lived in the palace as they waited for their furniture which was being shipped from England to arrive.

Many young Malay men rowed a decorated boat across the water, carrying the Rajah and Ranee to a waiting reception of uniformed servants. The beauty of the gardens took her breath away, flowers and trees she had never seen, radiant and graceful scenting the air.

But in the weeks that followed she was lonely once again. Charles ignored her and the English women made it clear to her they thought her far too young for the status of a Ranee. Conditions were very primitive, especially after the life she had been used to. Despite his unfeeling treatment of her, Margaret marvelled at the respect and honour her husband received from all he met and was truly proud of him when she saw how he was greeted as a friend and leader.

The wives of the English officials in the Rajah's government and the wife of the bishop kept themselves apart from the Malay women. So they did not approve of the Ranee's behaviour when she chose to make friends with the natives rather than with them. She soon adopted the Malay women's style of dress and invited them into her home, one action that *was* admired by Charles who felt at home with the Malay families.

Margaret Brooke loved the heat and compared her life in the East with her first months of married life at Burrator. She could not forget how cold she had been.

'Please don't make me live in that isolated house and village again, Charlie,' she pleaded. 'Can we not purchase a house in Wiltshire and live nearer to London when we make return visits to England?'

Rajah Charles considered Sarawak to be his home anyway. They had now lived there together in his country for more than two years. Margaret had given him a baby daughter and was now heavily pregnant again. During the birth of her daughter, whom she named Ghita, an old Malay woman attended her. Less than two years later Margaret gave birth to twin boys, a fascinating event to the Malay women to whom it was highly unusual. The boys were named James Clayton and Charles Harry. But Charles did not seem at all interested and was up-river at the time. Two wet nurses had to be found and an English nurse was sent from England. The Malay people sent a goat to supplement the milk.

The Ranee became depressed and sick, the birth of three babies in two years being not the only cause of her physical and mental exhaustion. Malay gossip had reached her ears which disturbed and distressed her. She confronted her husband one evening.

'Charlie, they are saying you have another son. A son born to a Malay girl in Simanggang. If it is true, please do not deny it.'

'Yes, it is so. He was born before I met you. The boy lives up-river with his mother.'

'Why did you not tell me? Why have I to be the subject of gossip? Everyone in the palace knows about the boy.'

'I never hid the fact from my people, Margaret. It was expected of me that I took a Malay girl when I lived here alone. She is Dayang Mastiah and I cared for her.'

'How old is this bastard child?'

'He is five years old. I went through a sort of marriage ceremony with Tia, but not one that would be adopted in England. I accept the child as my son but not as my heir. You know I married you to provide an heir for this country.'

Margaret had known he had not married her for love. She knew for a fact that he had arrived at her home intent on asking her own mother to marry him for the sake of her money. Seeing her mother, Lily de Windt, was past child-bearing age he had asked Ghita instead and, for what reason she never knew, she had accepted him. Lily was amazed and astonished by her daughter's decision, if not a little hurt.

Jealousy over this half-Malay child and his mother now festered within the young woman. Margaret became seriously ill and a year after the sons were born gave birth to a still-born child. The doctors advised the Rajah to take his wife to England if she was to recover.

'Would it please you, Margaret, if we were to travel to England, taking our three children with us? We will also take the child you never wish to see, away from this country of ours.'

The Rajah continued. 'Before you protest, I will find a home for us in Wiltshire as you desire and take the boy to Sheepstor. A member of his mother's family will travel with him and you need never set eyes on him.'

Margaret listened in silence. It was dawning on her that her husband was showing some care and actually trying to please her. She looked at him in some astonishment.

'Daykin, the curate of Sheepstor, and his wife are childless so they could take him. Dohl and I will take him there.'

Margaret thought about his proposal. She did so dearly want to go home and to take her children with her. The other child would be removed from Sarawak and to a place where she never wanted to visit again anyway.

'I shall agree to this, Charlie. I shall never, however, visit Burrator again. I do not wish to set eyes on the brat during our voyage.'

'That's settled then. We shall sail next week so you must choose who is to sail with us. I shall take a Malay boy for myself.'

This news delighted her. Amazingly, Margaret recovered from her afflictions quickly which the doctors put this down solely to the thought of her going to England. In Margaret's mind she was getting rid of her husband's first child but was disturbed that perhaps her husband slept with other Malay women at Simanggang.

The Brooke family and their entourage set sail for England on the P&O steamship *Indus* departing from Singapore on 20 September 1873. A week later they arrived in Ceylon and departed from Galle on the P&O steamer *Hydaspes*, operating between Calcutta and England. Margaret had spent a little over three years in Sarawak, giving birth to four children. With the family on the voyage was Harry de Windt, Margaret's brother. All were in good spirits and she found this sailing much more bearable than the voyage to Sarawak after her honeymoon. It was after leaving the port of Aden on 12 October, where an epidemic of cholera was raging that tragedy struck. All three Brooke infants became ill and within hours of each other all died. They were buried in the Red Sea.

Sailors and other passengers were deeply moved by this tragedy, the young mother devastated. Her outpouring of love was on her children so cruelly taken from her. The *Hydaspes* called at Suez and Port Said before reaching Alexandria on 23 October where Charles, Margaret and Harry left the ship to visit Egypt. The two men were kind to Margaret in her grief and hoped, if rather vainly, that sight-seeing would help her overcome her heartbreak.

The servants with the Malay child journeyed on to England in the *Hydaspes*, calling at Malta and Gibralta, arriving at Southampton on 10 November. The six year-old boy had survived the plague which could have only made matters worse for the Ranee. It tormented her. The boy's name was Isaka, but he was known as Esca, and with much care and attention he recovered from the fever. After two months at sea Esca stepped ashore on English soil.

Shortly before Esca's arrival Sarah received a letter from her friend Maggie Terrell. The two women were not in regular correspondence but Maggie had written to Sarah when she moved to London, giving her the new address. With help from Mary Sauls, a letter was sent from Burrator telling Maggie of the death of Sir James Brooke. Sarah wrote about her two children and included news of villagers.

Maggie now wrote to Sarah telling her of her father's death. Harry Terrell had become ill in Devonshire so both her parents moved to London to live with Maggie. Annie read the letter to Sarah telling how broken down Maggie's father had been to leave Dartmoor:

'He never recovered from leaving Burrator, he should not have sold the estate. I also lost my truest friend, dear Sarah. I am glad to know you and Sam are happy with the children. John and I expect our first baby in a few months. Father did not like the city and always searched for grass and trees.'

Harry Terrell was buried in a cemetery in London, aged 63 years.

20

CHARLES and Margaret stayed in London when they eventually reached England and he reluctantly allowed her to purchase some new winter clothes. Not clothes made for her by a dressmaker which she had been accustomed to but, to her dismay, clothes off-the-peg. He insisted at being present at the purchase of the garments, grumbling all the time at the expense. They were presented to Queen Victoria as Mr and Mrs Brooke; their positions as Rajah and Ranee of Sarawak, to Margaret's fury, were not recognised.

A house was purchased in Wiltshire as planned and Charles was able to hunt and drive a carriage with untamed horses. Margaret made friendships and moved in high society circles. She was pregnant again and realised she must endure this for a fourth time to produce the heir to Sarawak.

In London, on 21 September 1874, their son Charles Vyner Brooke was born. She adored Vyner but six months late dutifully set sail again for Sarawak with her husband. Breaking her heart, she left the baby with Bishop and Mrs McDougall, friends of the first Rajah, whom she hardly knew. Not wishing to risk the health of her baby and heir to the Sarawak Raj on the long sea voyage, she agreed to the arrangement.

Meanwhile, Esca and the servants had travelled to Sheepstor. Charles had written a letter to the Reverend William Daykin, ahead of the visit, briefly explaining the situation. He requested that the couple should care for the boy and, if they so wished, adopt him and bring him up as their son. Mary Daykin could not hide her delight. She adored children and waited in anticipation for the visitors to arrive. It was a great sadness to the Daykins that they had not been blessed with a child of their own.

The adults were to reside nearby whilst Esca and his attendant Dohl were to stay with the Daykins at Brook Cottage. Charles had forewarned them that Esca's mother was a native of Sarawak, a lady of high breeding. The childless couple made preparations and set the wheels in motion to adopt the boy.

When Esca arrived in Sheepstor he was greeted warmly. Mary Daykin was concerned at his frail appearance, wearing Malay clothes and speaking very little English. For poor Esca it was a bigger shock. At the age of six he had been taken from his mother and his Malay family, forced to endure a distressing voyage where he almost died of fever in the intense heat and arrived at the isolated moorland village of Sheepstor in the winter. The temperature on Dartmoor was a considerable contrast to the tropical heat of Sarawak.

Dohl told the Daykins of the Brookes' tragedy of losing their three infants at sea and emphasised the fact that Esca had survived. It was a sign, he said, of the importance of this child. Esca had suffered from heat exhaustion on the sea crossing but his strength had pulled him through. All at Brook Cottage believed that Rajah Charles would come to visit some time, but he never did. Tenants now resided in Burrator, Mary Costine and her parents with young servants. The boy never saw his real mother or father again.

The Reverend Daykin wrote an article for the Sarawak *Gazette* after Esca's arrival, and sent it to Kuching by Dohl. He wrote of his sadness at the deaths of the three Brooke children, and of the disappointment of the villagers that the Rajah of Sarawak did not visit Sheepstor. To the people of Sarawak he made it manifestly clear that there would always be a welcome for them in the tiny Dartmoor village where the body of their Rajah, and Sheepstor's friend, lies buried. He did not mention Esca. It was presumed in Sarawak that the child had also died.

William and Mary Daykin gave much attention to the little boy, and although he found it cold and lonely he liked to please these new parents. He was not able to ask them why he was with them or if he was to return home again. Esca became the centre of attention in this new home and, despite the language barrier, began to get his own way. In Sarawak he was one of hundreds in the longhouse and did not receive this much notice from adults. Mary was devoted to him and the curate set about educating him.

The first-born son of the second white Rajah was not to be recognised as the Brooke heir. Charles was persuaded by his wife that the British Government would not look kindly upon him with a half-Malay son. His obligations were to their family. The Daykins were sent £100 a year from the Sarawak Government for the boy's care.

From this time he was known as Esca Brooke Daykin, but to the Sheepstor folk he was Esca Daykin. With the letter of introduction, Charles had sent Esca's baptismal certificate. That Esca had been christened into the Church of England in Sarawak by the Reverend Crossland at the age of four was all the proof Daykin needed that he was the son of Charles. His mother Mastiah, known as Tia, was the daughter of a native chief and was present at her son's baptism at Port Alice. The certificate, signed by Reverend Crossland, read:

'This is to certify that I, William Crossland priest of St Luke's Mission, Sarawak, Borneo did, on the twenty eighth day of January 1872 baptise Esca Brooke, son of Charles Brooke and Tia at Port Alice, Simanggang.'

Esca looked like a Malay child but possessed Brooke features, the high fore-head and shape of the nose, though as far as the Brookes were concerned, and indeed most of Sarawak society, Esca Brooke died at sea.

Sir James had made allowances for the Sauls family to remain at Burrator for as long as they wished after his death. John Sauls, however, wanted to find meaningful employment and missed the Rajah at Sheepstor. So he secured another position as coachman and left Devon with his family before Esca arrived at Brook Cottage. The new Rajah, however, was obliged to pay the Sauls family money from Sarawak funds for as long as they lived. Annie Shepherd was more concerned over how much she missed the three little Sauls children.

'Where could they have gone, Mum? I should like to write to them. I want to know how the little ones are getting along.'

'No one knows, Annie. The new people at the house haven't heard from them and they didn't have any relatives who visited them,' Sarah told her. 'John Sauls promised he'd write to me when they were settled. That's four years ago now.'

'Mary Sauls told me the old Rajah left money to them in his will so perhaps the Brookes know where they are. I haven't liked to tell you but there's talk in the village that the Sauls family have all perished.'

'Oh don't, Mum. I can't bear to think of that.'

It was a sad fact that the Sauls family were never heard of again though Annie questioned any visitor to Sheepstor of their whereabouts.

The first Rajah's son, George, was a happily married family man with several children but once again, tragedy was to strike. He was drowned at sea in a shipwreck in the same year that Esca arrived in Devon. His widow Eliza had the following inscription written on the gravestone of her little son in a Nottingham churchyard, in memory of his father.

In
Memoriam
Reuben George Brooke
only son of
Sir James Brooke, K.C.B.
Rajah of Sarawak
who was lost on his passage
to Australia in the
wreck of the ship British Admiral
May 23rd 1874. Aged 40 years.
Also
Stewart
his son
who died Oct. 12th 1870.
Aged 2 years and 4 mos.

At varying times both illegitimate first-born sons of the two white Rajahs found their way to Sheepstor, played on the moor, visited Burrator and attended services in the church. Both had lived in Sarawak but neither was to play any part in the governing of that country and they never met. The first Rajah announced his son to the world when George was twenty-four-years old. The second Rajah denounced the existence of his son Esca when he was six years old. Such actions confirm the difference in principles of the two Rajahs, of uncle and nephew.

21

SIR JAMES Brooke was remembered with great affection for many years after his death in the parish of Sheepstor. Another family was now living in Burrator but Mary Daykin took Esca to see the house where his great-uncle had lived. She visited the farms and cottages in the parish with him and all were pleased to see how happy the curate's wife was to have a child of her own to care for, this adopted child from Sarawak. Esca was full of energy and skipped along beside her.

One Monday morning she set off to visit Ditsworthy Warren, telling her husband not to expect them home until the afternoon. They followed the Sheepstor Brook upstream through the village, passing Collytown and Nattor farms. Everyone liked Mrs Daykin and called out to her and the boy. Turning off the track to the right, they crossed the moor beneath Gutter Tor and saw the smoke rising from the chimney of the ancient warren.

Boys and men were scattered over the moor setting to their daily tasks. It was early spring and the sun shone on the young woman and six-year-old boy. Mr Daykin was much respected in the community as he was one of the men, farming land and raising stock. Only on Sunday was he different, dressed in his long black clothes and preaching to them on the virtues of a Christian life. The adoptive father was proud of the boy from Sarawak. He was learning his letters, enjoying scripture stories and was already talking the English language. Perhaps his birth mother had taught him the few words he already knew from Charles Brooke.

As Esca and Mrs Daykin approached the warren she explained to him the life of a warrener. Locally the warren was known as Ware's Warren as the Ware family had lived here for a long time. Rabbits bred naturally on the moor and the warrener encouraged this, creating a thriving rabbit farm. Mounds were built around the warren out of stones, soil and turf in which the rabbits lived and multiplied. In the early hours of the morning the animals left these burrows and searched the moor for food, enjoying even the gorse and heather. It was then at about four o'clock in the morning when the young boys who worked and lived at the warren, went to all the burrows, covering them with nets that they and the warrener's wife had made with string.

An hour or two later the warrener went to the outside dog kennel, a walled-in courtyard with sleeping quarters for the dogs built into the walls, and drove out the seventeen or so dogs. These animals were not pets and used only on the moor for chasing rabbits. The dogs were wild in nature and fed on dead ponies or cattle thrown to them in their courtyard after their morning's work, where they were enclosed again until the next morning.

The rabbits, chased by the dogs, would scamper for the burrows only to get caught in the nets and become ensnared, unable to escape. The men and boys then killed them by knocking them on their heads or twisting their necks.

Loading the dead animals on to carts, they then hung them in the large shed near the warren house. During the day the rabbits were skinned in 'big shed'. Rabbit meat was much sought after and butchers sold it up and down the land. The warrener took the rabbits to Plymouth and Tavistock by horse and cart, even sending some to London by train, and the skins were sold to be made into fur clothing.

Esca was excited at the story and surprised to see so many boys working here not much older than himself.

'Come in, Mrs Daykin, do, and you've brought the young man with you,' Mrs Ware smiled as she led them to the settle by the large fire. 'Sit yourselves down.'

'We won't disturb you, Mrs Ware, but I thought you may like to get to know our boy. This is Esca, say how do you do to Mrs Ware, Esca,' Mary Daykin said proudly addressing her son.

The young boy held out his hand which was taken by Mrs Ware. She shook his hand and smiled at him.

'Welcome to Sheepstor, lad. You'll have a lovely home with Mr and Mrs Daykin, I'll be bound.'

'How do you do,' Esca said slowly. 'It is good to greet you.'

All three smiled at each other and Mrs Ware chatted about the old Rajah to Esca.

'It is a pity you never met he. The last time he came here he was on horseback as he heard my son was ill. Mind you, he didn't look very well himself. He brought me a partridge to cook for the lad and offered me an armchair or a bed if it would be of comfort to him. He was kindness himself. If it hadn't been for him, we'd have no school to send our little ones to.'

Mrs Ware went on to Mrs Daykin. 'The poor man's fingers were limp and his speech was slurred and me and the husband had great pity for him. Not that he'd have liked to know that. Yes, he was a loss to Sheepstor.'

Mr Ware came into the house and Mrs Ware told Esca that her husband had become the churchwarden after the death of Sir James.

'Yes, he's a great loss. A kind, sweet gentleman that ever was,' Mr Ware declared. 'He told me himself he wanted to be buried under the great beech tree in the churchyard, and he was. Us wouldn't have been happy if he'd been taken to London.'

After some refreshments at the Ware's, Mrs Daykin and Esca left for their long walk home. Mr Ware walked a short way with them still talking of the gentle, patient Rajah. Esca asked his new mother to tell him about this Rajah and the walk home seemed to take no time at all as Mary Daykin tried to explain about Sir James, the first white Rajah of Sarawak. She wanted the boy to look upon Mr Daykin as his father and to forget Rajah Charles but she saw no harm in telling him about the life of the first white Rajah.

'You were only a baby when he died, Esca, and living in a far-off country. All the parish came to Sheepstor church for his burial.'

'Can we go and see his tomb on the way home, mother. I should like to see it again after our visit to the family on the moor.'

'Why, of course, my love. We'll go in the church gate by St Leonard's Well. It is a beautiful spot and especially so now with the new spring leaves coming out on the great tree.'

Mary Daykin chatted easily to the little boy.

'The Rajah always found it effortless to forgive a person and urged others to do the same. He did not quarrel or bear resentment against anyone.'

Esca touched the large tomb of pink stone which was placed near the church-yard wall under the tor. He looked up at the huge tree and took his mother's hand.

'Shall we go home?' Esca enquired.

His mother nodded and smiled. Passing through the lychgate they saw Mrs Andrew at her cottage gate.

'You been looking at the old Rajah's tomb, I expect. He was a good man, for sure. He knew everybody's kitchen in the village,' she said laughing to herself. 'My husband was his gamekeeper when he first came to live here, and some-times Sir James went shooting with him. He was a good sport.'

They left Mrs Andrew and crossed the lane to the gate of their cottage.

'My goodness, Esca. You have certainly learned today what a kind man the old Rajah was and how much he was respected in the village. It is good to see how the kind acts we do for others live on after we die. Let's go and see what we shall eat for dinner.'

'Did the old Rajah build the church, mother?' Esca asked as she prepared the evening meal.

'No, the church is very old, hundreds of years old, but he collected a lot of money from his friends before we came to live here and had it repaired. People say it was in a bad state before he came. Some say it had no roof and at one time a service was held here only once a year. Your father had the window in the east put in, in his memory. It is so colourful and is the story of the exaltation of Joseph in Egypt. You remember the story, do you not?'

Mrs Daykin went on to tell him. 'After removing his coat of many colours, Joseph's brothers sold him to merchants, who took him to Egypt. Joseph did well for himself and was rewarded by the Pharaoh, who made him ruler of the country. Your father thought it was an appropriate memorial to Sir James. Last year our little church was full of soldiers at Matins each week. There were hun-dreds of them holding manoeuvres nearby on the moor which was spread over with bell-tents. Your father and I certainly did not know what an eventful life we were to have when we came to this village, far from anywhere. Our great-est joy is to have you, Esca. You are now our son, and I am so very happy.'

Esca smiled at this gentle woman. He could not remember much about his old life, except that the climate had been hot, and here he always felt cold. That there had always been many people around him and so many children to play with; here there were few. He felt close to this new mother.

'What about the other window in the church with the picture of the two ladies?' Esca asked.

'That is in memory of a well-loved teacher of our school, Mrs Ware. She married old Mrs Ware's son in the year the old Rajah died. I remember her as Miss Sendey, a governess. Your father married the couple then had to bury her three years later, it was most sad. She died in the year before you came here to live,' Mary Daykin explained. 'The two ladies, as you call them, are St Cecilia and St Catherine. We saw the teacher's gravestone under the beech tree near to the Rajah's tomb.'

Mary Daykin called to mind the great sadness when William Ware junior was left a widower. Celia had written her own epitaph:

> Dear Husband, Weep not for me, my life is past
> My love for you was to the last
> Then do not weep but comfort take
> From Christ, your Saviour, for my sake.

'Will you and father have a picture window in the church, mother?' Esca was asking looking at her.

'Oh, that's a long way off. It is a way to be remembered in this village, though, and I have happy memories.'

Some days when his father was too busy to tutor him Esca was allowed to attend the village school with the other children. He enjoyed these mornings especially when Annie Shepherd was there. She came in to help the teacher and he liked to look at her. In fact, Annie enjoyed helping the little Daykin boy and they smiled a lot together. He believed that Annie was somehow a link with his past but he was not able to solve the riddle.

22

EVEREND William Yate Daykin missed his friend the Rajah. Then, his
mother, who lived with them at Brook Cottage, died leaving him a sub-
stantial legacy. He was a well-educated man and seeing no prospects of pro-
motion if he remained in Sheepstor, applied for the post of Archdeacon of
Durban. He was successful and in 1875, with Mary and Esca, set sail for Africa.
Bishop Colenso of Natal had known James Brooke personally. The Rajah and
Daykin had talked of helping the bishop in his cause, in forming his own church
in South Africa. After only two years in the country, and perhaps because of the
Zulu war, the Daykins returned to England and to Brook Cottage.

It was a sad return for the Archdeacon. Sheepstor parish had recently separated from Bickleigh and he hoped to become the vicar of the parish he loved
so well. Sir Massey Lopes, however, patron of the living, had given this position to the Reverend Warneford Gompertz and was looking for a property in
the village to purchase for use as the Vicarage.

Daykin visited Sir Massey Lopes.

'There is nothing for me any more in Sheepstor,' he told him. 'I'm going to
sell Brook Cottage and find another living. I wonder if you would like to consider it for the vicarage?'

Realising that it would make an ideal vicarage with its close proximity to the
church, Sir Massey agreed on the purchase. Brook Cottage now became the
Vicarage and the Daykins left the village for the second time. Daykin found
work assisting in various parishes throughout the Church of England, never
becoming an incumbent of a parish. But his last act for Sheepstor was to give a
stained glass window in the north wall in memory of his parents, Bewes and
Mary Daykin.

After a few years the Sheepstor villagers heard that Archdeacon Daykin had
become a missionary in Canada. He was appointed rector of St John's Church
of England at Madoc in Ontario. Another voyage, another steamship, another
country for Esca.

On Wednesday, 9 May 1877, by direction of His Highness Charles Brooke the
Rajah of Sarawak, Burrator was sold by auction at the Mart in London next to
the Bank of England. The particulars, plan and conditions of sale were produced in a large eight-page document. Burrator was described as:

*'Highly picturesque and most inviting, situated near the village, church and eminence
known as Sheepstor. Comprising of four sitting rooms, eight bedrooms and dressing
rooms, stabling and appurtenances the residence is recorded as being highly desirable.*

*The grounds are portrayed as possessing a wild romantic beauty of their own to
which it is difficult to do adequate justice. The property is recommended to anyone
desiring a charming and healthful retreat for the summer months or a source of inspiration to those of artistic or poetic tastes.*

The natural waterfall in the grounds, above the confluence of the Sheepstor Brook and the River Mew, is described as the far-famed falls of Burrator, renowned throughout the district. It likens the area to the choicest bits of Saxon Switzerland on a small scale.'

Sir Massey sent his London agent to the sale by auction of the property, who successfully purchased it for the Sheepstor landowner. Charles Brooke sent the proceeds of the sale to Baroness Angela Burdett-Coutts, thus repaying her for the kindness she had shown his uncle when she presented him with the funds for the purchase of the estate eighteen years earlier.

Sir James had become strongly attached to the place and ever perceived himself truly at home here. The pure and bracing Dartmoor air relit the lamp of his life which had been almost snuffed out when the Sarawak affairs were in a bad state.

The villagers of Sheepstor knew nothing of the sale until Sir Massey let it be known that he was the owner of the Burrator estate. These final years of the decade were ones of movement in both Sheepstor and Sarawak. The Ranee Margaret left Borneo before the birth of their third surviving son and returned to England. She was becoming more independent and able to stand up to the strange requests of her husband. She bought clothes on her own and attended parties and dances without the Rajah. Leaving her three children, Vyner, Bertram and Harry in England, she returned to Sarawak yet again but on her terms, and from this time lived mostly apart from her husband, bearing no more children. She was aware that wherever in the world the Daykin family lived, they received from the Sarawak Government, through her husband, money for the upkeep of a boy she wished to forget.

And what of Miss Coutts? She had been in love with James Brooke but with his death lost interest in both Sheepstor and Sarawak. The people who knew her in Sheepstor were interested in her acts of kindness although she never visited the village again. Her name was reported almost daily in the newspapers and even Mr Daykin had sought her assistance. Miss Coutts had founded the bishopric of British Columbia, providing thousands of pounds for the maintenance of the clergy. She also had contacts with Bishop Colenso of Natal although the South African church became independent of the Anglican church.

All over the British Isles, and indeed the world, she gave money and help to various causes, especially to poor and neglected children. Her love of animals was also intense and she became a founder member of the National Society for the Prevention of Cruelty to Children as well as the leader of the Royal Society for the Prevention of Cruelty to Animals. With fantastic energy she funded the building of model housing estates, schools, churches, fountains and monuments, and provided scholarships at universities.

In 1871 Queen Victoria conferred on her a peerage under the title Baroness Burdett-Coutts of Highgate and Brookfield, Middlesex, the first woman to receive such an honour. The City of London granted her the Freedom of the City the following year and Edinburgh the same tribute a year later. She recalled all those years ago when James Brooke told her she was worthy of such distinctions.

At the age of sixty-six, thirteen years after the death of Sir James Brooke at Burrator, Baroness Burdett-Coutts married Mr William Ashmead-Bartlett who was then twenty-nine years of age and assumed her surname. The humble folk of Sheepstor were amazed that this lady, who had repaired their church, placed the tombstone on the grave of James Brooke in the churchyard, improved the estate of Burrator and walked among them, was such a public figure. They remembered the tall, stately and slender lady, graceful in manner when she spoke to them, in the company of Sir James with her companion. The three attended church together, walked the lanes, and had often been spotted chatting and laughing along by Drake's leat.

It was announced in the church at Sheepstor that her companion, Mrs Brown, who so many of them had known ten years earlier, had passed away. A new vicar for Sheepstor was appointed in 1879, the Reverend Cornelius Hargreave Crooke. Mr Crooke moved into the Vicarage where he enjoyed the peace and tranquility and was amazed at the stories the villagers told him of the famous personages that used to live amongst them.

Will had his twentieth birthday in the spring and now in the month of July the school was closed for the summer holidays. He and Annie slipped away from Outhome, as they often did, and walked up over the moor. It was growing increasingly difficult at home to be alone together.

'I can't remember when it exactly happened, Annie, but I have ceased to look upon you as my sister. I know you feel the same way about me, I can tell when our eyes meet.'

'This is true, Will. I am afraid to look at you at meal times when mum and dad are there. You must have noticed I am never hungry. I am sick inside with love for you.'

'Oh, Annie, what shall we do?' Will implored her.

23

WILL held Annie tightly in his arms, tenderly stroking her shining black hair. They lay in the afternoon sunshine on the Dartmoor turf in a hollow created not many years before by the tinners on Eylesburrow. Tears of joy, or of sorrow, Annie didn't know which, trickled down her cheeks.

'Annie, I love you. I suppose I've always loved you. You have been always part of my life.'

'You know I love you, Will. At night in bed I make up poems of my love for you. You are as much a part of me as my heart or any limb. But it is wrong – you are my brother.'

'Look at us, Annie,' Will said indignantly. 'Do you think we look like brother and sister? Do you?'

Will sat up and rested on his elbows.

'Brothers and sisters don't always look alike,' Annie declared.

'Annie, for goodness sake. We are as different as east and west. You look like all them visitors as come to Burrator way back. In fact, Esca could have been your brother. I'm like the other lads in Sheepstor.'

'Don't get angry, Will. What are you saying? That I don't belong?'

Will wiped the tears from Annie's cheek.

'Of course you belong. This is where you have lived all your life, but I can't believe you're my sister. There's talk, too, in the village.'

Annie sat up now, and was the one to be incensed.

'What do you mean? What is being said? What kind of talk?'

Will began to feel uneasy. He kicked at the turf and pulled at some heather stalks.

'Oh things. I've asked Dad but he just moves off and Mum – well – she gets embarrassed when you and me are close, she makes funny remarks.'

'I've noticed that. She refers to you as 'your brother' when she addresses me, as if to emphasise the fact. Yes, her tone is of violent disapproval.'

'I love you, Annie, and I want the world to know. When we sit down to supper tonight I'm going to speak my mind. I'm going to ask right out if you're my sister. They can't deny us the truth. You can go out of the room if you want to.'

'No, I'll be with you. We'll tell them we want to stay together.'

'Not as brother and sister, Annie. I'm going to tell them I want to marry you.'

Annie flung her arms around Will's neck and they clung to each other. Will twisted a blade of grass into a circle and put the ring on Annie's finger. They were inseparable.

'Annie Shepherd, will you marry me?'

Walking hand in hand across the moor to the cottage, laughing and full of joy, the young couple jumped down over the banks into the yard. They released hands and their smiles disappeared when they saw three horses they didn't recognise tethered to the gate post.

A man in black came out of the cottage door to greet them. It was the Reverend Cornelius Crooke, vicar of Sheepstor. Will greeted this unusual visitor.

'Good afternoon, Mr Crooke. Have you been visiting my mother? Who else is with you?'

'Is something wrong at the school, Mr Crooke?' Annie enquired.

'You'd better come inside, both of you,' he replied grimly. 'There are people waiting to see you, Annie.'

'Me?' Annie said in great surprise.

They entered the room and stared in shock at Sarah who was clearly distraught. Two visitors were seated at the table.

'You must be Annie,' the man said standing up.

The woman was staring at Annie. She smiled. Annie returned her gaze and her heart missed a beat. It was like regarding herself in a looking glass.

The man came forward.

'My wife, she has not very good English but she understands much of what we say. Mr Crooke brought us here because we met him in the village and we told him that nearly twenty years ago we were here. The old Rajah Brooke was our friend and we stayed at his house. Your mother is upset by our visit, but she need not be. We are truly grateful to her.'

'Mother, who are these people? What are they saying?' Will burst out.

'It is all right, Will,' Reverend Crooke interrupted. 'Your mother has had a bit of a shock. It is my doing, I brought these people to your cottage. Perhaps you could go and find your father, Will.'

'Where is Dad, Mum?'

'He went to cut the grass in Homer Meadow, Will.'

Sarah whispered her reply, not looking at her son.

'Come on, Annie. Let's go and fetch Dad.'

'You go alone, Will,' Mr Crooke intervened quickly. 'Leave Annie with your mother.'

Will frowned but went out into the sunlight in search of his father, in a humour much altered to the one he was in a short while before. All the time Annie was regarding the strangers. Her heart was pounding within her and her inside churning. She went to Sarah.

'Please tell me why they are here, Mum. Did you know them twenty years ago?'

Sarah shook her head. She looked with guilt at Annie who at once had compassion for her and put her arms around her. Tears were streaming down their cheeks when the vicar asked Sarah if she should like him to tell Annie what the strangers had told him. Sarah nodded in agreement.

Annie looked from the minister in his black coat and leggings to the middle-aged couple in their light clothes.

Reverend Crooke explained that he had seen the Sarawak couple, Mr and Mrs Lim, looking at the tomb of the late Rajah at about noon. They told him that they had travelled to England in memory of their daughter who had become lost on the moor twenty years ago. Standing under the shade of the great beech tree they told their story. They had been friends of the first Rajah and stayed at Burrator during the winter.

The vicar cleared his throat.

'As Mr and Mrs Lim told me the events of their fateful visit to our village, I began to think of Annie. Their baby daughter would have been nearly twenty years old had she not slipped from the horse and become buried in snow. She was presumed lost and believed to have perished in the blizzard.'

'I have only known your family for one year, Mrs Shepherd, but it is obvious that Annie is not the true daughter of you and Mr Shepherd. She resembles Mrs Lim,' the vicar observed.

Annie blushed. She looked at Sarah. How had she been so blind? Why did she not want to see that she could not be the flesh and blood of the people she called her parents? 'There's none so blind as them that won't see,' she mumbled to herself.

Mr Crooke was still talking. 'As the lady and gentleman talked I perceived it to be my duty to tell them of Annie's existence. The same age and obviously of the same origin. The baby had been lost. Could it be that the baby had been found?'

'Anyway, we hired two horses for them in the village and I brought them here.'

If he was looking to be congratulated by Sarah, his hope was in vain.

Meanwhile, Will had found Sam in the meadow and shouted to him even before he was near him that two people from Borneo were in their kitchen.

'Mum's in a state, Dad. What's going on?' Will demanded.

'I don't know, son, but I tell you this. Your mum and I have dreaded this moment should ever come, if it is what I think.'

Sam put down his scythe against the hedge, called his dog and began walking back to the cottage.

'Tell me, Dad. You've got to tell me,' Will shouted.

''Twas nearly twenty years ago, in the winter. There was heavy snow and a blizzard was raging and I found a baby down by the river,' Sam stammered. 'No tracks, nothing. No baby was reported missing. Nothing was said, so your mum and I kept her.'

'And that was Annie?'

'Yes.'

'I've told her all along I wasn't her true brother but she didn't want to believe me. Where was I?'

'You were but a babe yourself. I took the bundle home to your mother and she called it Annie. We were going to take her down to Burrator the next day but the snow was so deep, we ended up being snowed up for about a month. By that time, Annie belonged to us.'

'Did no one claim her? No one speak of her loss?'

'No. As the weeks and months passed by, we realised whoever had lost the baby supposed she was dead. I had saved her and we couldn't let her go.'

Will had never heard his father make such a long speech in all his life. He tried to think of them caring for Annie along with himself. He wanted to shout at his father, he couldn't forgive them for withholding the truth. On the other hand, he and Annie were free to marry.

'By heck, Dad, can't you see Annie and I have fallen in love? I was going to ask you at mealtime tonight if I could marry her.'

Sam was silent. They had reached the cottage.

He walked in front of Will and opened the door. Sam stared at the five occupants.

Mr Crooke broke the uneasy silence.

'Annie is going to walk to the village, Sam. You come too, Will. You go in and look after Sarah, Sam.'

Mr Crooke hastily left the dwelling. The enormity of what he had done was beginning to sink in. If he hadn't told the strangers of Annie's existence, surely someone else would have done. Wouldn't they? Should he have left well alone?

He was stumbling over his words saying something about Sam saving their daughter's life as they went out into the sunlight. Sam touched his hat and hurried in to be with Sarah.

Will rode the horse the lady had ridden to the cottage and the three men rode up on to the moor towards the lower end of Eylesburrow mine road. The two women followed on foot. The moorland turf was dry but the lady trod carefully as they walked behind the riders.

Annie had guessed the lady to be her rightful mother from the moment she saw her in the cottage. As they walked on the springy moorland turf there was, at first, an awkwardness as Annie struggled inwardly to come to terms with the situation. Part of her was saddened that dear Sarah and Sam were not her parents and another part – a big part – was filled with sheer delight that she was not Will's sister.

Annie gazed at the woman from Borneo. 'Are you and your husband my true parents? Are you my mother and father?' Annie was bewildered.

The lady haltingly told Annie the story of losing her baby. She spoke of the terrible weather conditions and blinding snowstorm when they left Burrator, with their baby tied in a bundle at the rear of her horse while she clung to the mane with her eyes closed. Annie was told of the anguish and devastation there had been in this woman's life. Of boarding the train and steamship, thinking of their daughter buried alive in freezing cold conditions. Never for a moment did they believe that anyone would be on the moor in such atrocious weather, find the baby and rescue her.

'By birth you may be my mother, Mrs Lim, but I shall always honour the woman who cared for me as my mother.' Annie spoke quietly. 'I know she loves me and I love her in return, as a daughter. It was a cruel fate.'

24

THE LITTLE party reached the village and Annie started to realised that her humble upbringing was of material contrast to the one she might have had, had she not been lost.

The Lims bore no resentment or malice towards Sarah and Sam. Only appreciation for the care of their daughter for twenty years. It was clear to see that Annie was well and happy.

'If Mr and Mrs Shepherd allow it, would you like to come with us to London, Annie? We should like to buy you fine clothes and get to know you. Perhaps you will come to Sarawak with us, to meet other members of your family.'

'Annie's fine,' Will stated firmly. 'When we've saved up a bit we are to be married and rent a farm of our own.'

'You come, too, Will, for a holiday,' Mr Lim suggested.

'Mum won't let Annie go,' Will declared.

'Don't be too hasty, Will,' Mr Crooke said to the young man. 'Annie may live to regret this chance of a lifetime. Your mother would not stop her from being with her true parents, I am sure.'

Will desperately did not like the situation. He could see Annie was tempted by the prospect of fine clothes and the opportunity to travel and see the world. He wanted to shout at the vicar, to tell him to keep out of this dilemma and to mind his own business. Annie would have been startled if she knew Will's thoughts, but the young man restrained himself.

He looked at the two women. They were regarding each other, holding both hands and smiling warmly. Mother and daughter. Will could see the bond. What of Annie's loyalty to Will?

Mr and Mrs Lim planned to return to Sheepstor church in a week's time. Annie promised to meet them there with a decision – to say farewell or to meet them prepared for the journey.

As Will and Annie walked slowly back to Outhome, Annie was silent.

Trying to make light of the dilemma Will said, 'One problem is solved, at least, Annie. We shan't have to confront Mum and Dad tonight.'

Annie did not smile.

Will attempted a new tactic.

'You're only a woman, Annie. You believe all things you hear and talk so freely with these strangers. You must stay here.'

Annie burst into tears in her distress.

Will tried to reason with her. 'What I'm trying to say is you need me to protect you, Annie.'

'I cannot obey you in this matter, Will. When we are married I shall always do what you tell me. We have not yet made our solemn contract, but I have given myself to you. There are so many unanswered questions. They have put no pressure on me, it is up to Mum and Dad.'

'Does your past matter, Annie? We are your family. You are going to be my wife, can you not forget about it?'

'Forget it, Will? Forget it? You don't understand, do you? I have just met my real mother and father and you tell me to forget it. We have the chance to travel, to have new clothes and to learn about my other family. Please come with me, Will.'

'No, Annie. I shall not go. I shall never leave Sheepstor. My home is here, I want no other. If you leave you will change.'

'I shall go if Mum and Dad let me. I shall return to become truly Annie Shepherd, when I am your wife.'

Was it only that afternoon that they had lain together, so close, on Eylesburrow? As they made their way back into the cottage, the two young people sensed the troubled atmosphere within. The visitation had brought unhappiness to the four occupants in different ways.

Sam involved himself in his work out on the moor. Sarah was bewildered that the strangers were so grateful to her for the care she had shown to Annie; she ached with guilt. Will was desperately worried that he was going to lose Annie. At length, Sarah and Sam made it clear to Annie that it was her decision whether to travel with her real parents or to stay in Sheepstor. They had kept her all those years ago, now she must decide, and she alone. Annie was torn between the family she knew and loved and the temptation of riches and wealth. She trusted she could have both.

Annie must decide the future for them all. Each in their own way dreaded the week ahead. Sam was his usual quiet self, out on the moor and the hills, or around the farm, saying little at mealtimes. Sarah was unusually harsh, finding fault with Annie and taking to her bed with headaches.

Will and Annie talked. They loved, they cried and held each other. Will knew in his heart that Annie had made her decision to travel.

'Will, I shall come back to you very soon and I shall bring money for us to rent our own farm. When I used to listen to the old Rajah talk about his other country when we were children it stirred feelings within me. It made a lasting impression. I should like to get to know my true parents. You know I love you, Will. I shall always love you.'

Annie and Will were sitting beneath Cuckoo Rock, a huge rock not far from Deancombe. The moorland landscape subtly changed colour as clouds scurried across the sky.

'I wish I could paint like John White Abbott at Meavy Parsonage, Annie. He's the same age as us and I saw him only yesterday down on the Mew painting a picture of the tor. It was beautiful, just as I saw the scene in front of me. His grandfather was a famous artist and his parents gave him the same name. The rector, Mr Abbott, doesn't paint at all. I'd like to paint a picture for you to take with you.'

'I need no painting to remind me of you and the moor, Will. Dartmoor is in my blood.'

'I love you, Annie. I'm ready to give my life for you. They have tried to keep us apart but I love you with a fierce intensity. I tell you, no one has ever loved like this before.'

But all Will's pleading with Annie did not alter her mind. On the day set to meet her relatives in Sheepstor church, Annie packed a small bag and walked to the village on her own. Sam had hugged her with tears in his eyes, Sarah cried and held her tightly and Will was inconsolable. When she left the cottage he was nowhere to be seen. Will was walking the moor with manic energy.

'I shall be back. You all think I won't return but I shall, I belong here. You are my family. Do not be sad, rejoice. Prepare for the wedding.'

Blinded by her tears, Annie stumbled up over the hillside, crossed the moor and walked down the lane to the church, alone. Annie pushed open the heavy oak door, the noise of the latch causing the three people inside to be startled in the hushed surroundings. It was cool and dark inside where she found the couple and Mr Crooke waiting for her. Seeing Annie on her own, carrying a small bag, the lady rushed forward and took her hands. 'You are coming with us!'

No more was said. Mr Crooke watched as the carriage conveyed the three occupants to the railway station. Annie looked sad, the couple elated.

'I must go out to Outhome soon,' the vicar muttered to himself as he walked across the lane to the Vicarage. 'There will be much sadness in that little cottage.' If he had only known the despondency out there he might have remembered his resolve.

25

THE next few days and weeks were agony for Will. He tormented himself that Annie would never return. His friends in the village tried to convince him that she would be back, telling him to prepare for the wedding. It did no good.

The wretchedness and pain he endured overwhelmed him to the point of unbalancing his mind, the edge of madness. Sam and Sarah were at a loss to know what to do. He was pining for Annie with his body, mind and soul. Friends called at the house to help in any way they could but Will was never at home, always up on Eylesburrow, walking and walking amongst the old tin workings. Sam and Sarah's hearts were breaking over Will, overshadowing their own grief at Annie's departure. Sarah prayed in deep devotion.

One morning in late August, Sam made the grim discovery.

Will was hanging from a branch of an oak tree not far from the cottage. Sam rushed to cut him down and hugged the already stiffening body.

'Son, son, don't leave us,' he wailed, knowing it was in vain.

Sam took off his own coat and lay it over Will's body. The ordeal he now faced, to tell Sarah, was almost too much for him. With his dog at his heels, bent and breathing quickly, he slowly approached the open door, where Sarah stood.

'He's gone. I knew he wasn't in his right mind,' Sam mumbled. Tears trickled down his face.

Sarah was still. There were no tears left for her to shed.

'I had to suffer, Sam. I have dreaded and dreaded that the truth might be unearthed. From the moment we hushed things up I deserved to be punished. I shall weep with the psalmist, *Unto thee will I cry, O Lord my rock; be not silent to me.* Oh Lord help me!'

'Don't fret yourself, maid. Those people told you it was us as saved the girl's life.'

'And what for? To forfeit the life of our only child?'

'Come and see the boy.'

Together they knelt at Will's side, where they were found about an hour later, hunched in the same position, by the farmer from Combeshead. He rode down to the village and told the vicar what he had seen, suggesting he called on the widow, Mrs Creber, before going out to Outhome.

Deep within, Sarah had always lived with misgivings about her failure to own up to the truth about Annie. If she had told of Sam finding the baby in a blizzard nineteen years ago she might have been praised for her actions, in rescuing and caring for a stranger. Not now. She considered she was being accused of abduction, deceit and lies. At night, Sarah wept uncontrollably.

A memorial service for Will took place three days later in the church with his friends and family in subdued mood. Almost everyone there tortured themselves with guilt. Should they not have foreseen this might happen? His body was laid in a grave dug beyond the churchyard wall in unconsecrated ground beneath the tor. The weather was hot and thundery. No informal words were spoken, only those uttered by the vicar. The weather mirrored the gloom over the village. In the margin of the burial register Mr Crooke wrote, *Committed suicide, buried without the office of the church.*

Sam and Sarah walked home. The villagers did not know how to console them. Annie had been gone for nearly two months and it was thought that she had gone to the East with her newly found family. The village itself was bereft of all joy and hope. Will's untimely death troubled not only every household in the parish but also those in the outlying farms in the valleys around the village.

Summer evenings were drawing in and the days were cooler. Sarah couldn't face picking whortleberries on the moor on her own. She took to helping Sam on the farm like she used to before she had had the babies. Early in September her mother became ill and died within a week. The hearts of Sheepstor folk went out to Sarah yet again.

On the afternoon of the burial of Mrs Creber, a carriage stopped outside the Vicarage and a young lady alighted. She walked to the lychgate. She wore a brown dress and matching coat and bonnet.

'Why Annie, I hardly recognised you,' Emma Crooke the vicar's wife said as she passed through the church gate, admiring the beautiful young lady before her. 'We all thought you had travelled to the East.'

'Good-day, Mrs Crooke. No, I have only been staying in London. I wrote to Will that I hoped to arrive today. Whose funeral is it?'

'Oh, Annie. It's your grandmother, Lily Creber. She became ill and died all in a week. Annie, are you all right?'

'I must go to my mother, please forgive me.'

'But Annie...'

Annie hurried to the lychgate with its high granite coffin stone. She pulled open the old wooden gate which creaked noisily, closing with a slam behind her. She walked up the church path. There at the side of the grave she could see her mum and dad – but where was Will?

Annie waited for Sam and Sarah to leave the graveside. The man and wife, who Annie looked upon as her parents, with bowed heads left the churchyard by the east gate to begin their walk home. The villagers watched horrorstruck as this young lady hurried after them, calling, 'Mum, Dad, wait for me!'.

Hugs were followed by tears, then silence. Up the lane, through the moor gate, across the flank of Sheeps Tor. Annie had been feeling full of joy but the sudden news of her grandmother's death had shaken her. The sight of this grieving couple, appearing so much older than when she left them, was most distressing. Strangely, to Annie, they seemed disturbed to see her and made no mention of her new outfit. She bided her time and waited for them to speak, longing to ask if Will was back at Outhome.

Slowly and little by little Annie learned about the passing of Mrs Creber, the woman Annie regarded as her grandmother; then about Will, her lifelong love whom she worshipped. Annie's screams could be heard from the hills in the village below.

Sam and Sarah had to almost carry Annie back to Outhome. It was then that Sarah realised that Annie was plumper than when she had left them.

Seated in the cottage, Annie told Sam and Sarah she was expecting Will's baby in five months time. Mrs Lim had taken Annie to a doctor in London as she was so sick and he had confirmed her pregnancy. Annie's surprise and innocence when she was told she was expecting a baby in February caused her to faint.

'All I wanted to do was to come home to see Will. Did he not get my letters? I wrote to tell him I had exciting news for him and that I should be home soon.'

'Why did he not wait for me? Mum, help me!'

Sarah held Annie's hands. She felt numb.

'It was the balance of his mind, Annie. Whatever anyone said, he sincerely believed you had gone away forever, he became unhinged. He wasn't thinking straight.'

Sam thought of the unopened letters he had found in Will's pocket. Sam wasn't able to read. They had gone to his son's grave with him.

Walking over the lonely moorland, in the months that succeeded her return, helped Annie to heal her inner torment. Outwardly it appeared to endow her with the strength to carry Will's child that moved within her. She found on Dartmoor tension-relieving solitude and wondrous silence where she was able to commune with the spirits and talk to her beloved Will. Annie loved the moor, she had hated London.

Every day she visited the mound of earth and stones that covered Will's body. She was in sombre mood but with Sarah's encouragement ate as much as she was able for the sake of the baby. Sarah did not want Annie to be seen in the village and Annie wanted to talk to no one. When Sam and Sarah attended church, Annie sat by Will's grave and listened to the ringing of the bells and the singing of hymns.

Christmas meant nothing to the Shepherds that year. Sarah and Annie sat in the gloom at Outhome in the long Dartmoor twilight evenings, sewing baby gowns made from old sheets. After the New Year Annie never left the cottage. In February she gave birth to a son, William Thomas Shepherd, named after his father and great-grandfather, in the same room, same bed where his father had entered the world.

It was a difficult birth. Annie was small and the robust baby had broad shoulders. She developed milk fever and left this world when her baby was five days old.

Sheepstor had witnessed the death of these two young people at Outhome and two contrasting burials. Annie was buried in the consecrated ground of the churchyard, near to the wall, close to Will's grave. Only a few villagers attended Annie's funeral service. It had been a harsh winter. The Plymouth Leat had frozen over and the road leading to the village was blocked with frozen snow. Annie's grave, dug by the sexton Richard Bowden, was shallow. In the bitterly cold conditions Mr Crooke spoke quietly over the modest coffin as it was lowered into the ground.

'We brought nothing into this world, and it is certain we can carry nothing out.'

Sarah had a headstone placed on Annie's grave, with the inscription:

The mortal life of Annie Shepherd

age 20 years

was terminated by a broken heart

1881

Sarah had a new baby to care for, her son's baby. Some women gave birth at the age of forty-three she told herself, but there would be no pretence this time.

'This little one can't replace Will,' Sarah told Sam. 'He'll give us something to work for, though. William will be told we are not his parents, Sam. We shall tell him the truth, no more secrets. We shall talk to him about Will and Annie, tell him they died when he was born. There is no need to tell him how his father died.'

'I am past sixty-three years of age, Sarah. I don't know if I can keep the farm going until he can take over,' Sam said doubtfully.

'We will have our hands full with bringing up the baby, Sam. Let's accept each day as it comes. *"Be ye therefore ready also; for the Son of Man cometh at an hour when ye think not,"* as the Good Book says.'

26

ONE day, later in the year, Sam came in from seeing to his sheep down on the banks of the River Mew.

'There's some noise going on across the valley, Sarah,' he told her. 'They're building a railway line up to Princetown.'

'Our peace will be shattered if the engine is like the one we saw at Horrabridge all those years ago.'

'No, I shouldn't think it'll be that big. We might be able to ride on it one day, though, and take the boy for his first train journey.'

Sarah forced a laugh. 'And our first one and all, Sam. We never did get to ride even as far as Tavistock.'

For sixty years there had been a horse-drawn tramway devised by Sir Thomas Tyrwhitt from Prince's Town down to Plymouth, carrying granite quarried from the tors on the moor, to be shipped to London. Prominent buildings and bridges in the capital city were constructed of Dartmoor granite including Nelson's Column. The GWR company had purchased this line and the track was being laid down for steam locomotion. Some deviations from the old track had to be made, especially across Yennadon where the curves on the horse-drawn track were too sharp for the steam engine. Sounds echoed across the valley to Sheepstor.

Prince's Town, the village built up by Tyrwhitt in the time of the Prince Regent and named in his honour, was growing in population. It was now known as Princetown and houses were being built near to the prison for the warders and their families. An increasing number of convicts were sent to the prison and the railway was becoming essential.

A memorial tablet was placed in Princetown church.

Sir Thomas Tyrwhitt, Knt.,
late of Tor Royal,
Lord Warden of the Stannaries,
And many years Usher of the Black Rod.
Died Feb 24th, 1833,
Age 71.
His Name and Memory
Are inseparable from all the Great Works on
Dartmoor,
And cannot cease to be honoured
in this District.

William Shepherd grew up at Outhome as his father Will had done, but without the companionship of a little sister. Sarah sometimes worked at Burrator for the new tenants and took William with her. When he was old enough he attended the village school where he enjoyed learning and absorbed all he was taught. William liked it out on the moor, too, with his grandpa but most of all loved to be with his grandma. His non-stop questions made Sarah smile and her fretting over Will and Annie ebbed considerably with the comfort William brought her.

In Sarawak the second white Rajah continued the rule of his uncle, bringing stability and peace to the country. Many more buildings were constructed during his reign. Among those he had built were the courthouse, the French chateau-inspired Sarawak museum and the Greek influenced Post Office.

Ranee Margaret was not so at ease but devised her own ways of coping. A keen musician, she had her piano sent out to Kuching so that she was able to entertain the many visitors. She learnt to paint under the guidance of a Miss North from England and set about copying the rare and colourful flowers of the jungle. These she pasted in a book and dedicated them to her husband. The vivid colours were to be enduring.

Sarawak, being on the equator, had twelve hours of darkness and twelve hours of glorious light. In the darkness Margaret Brooke entertained and played her piano, in the mornings she painted and wrote, resting in the afternoons. Always, including mealtimes, there were servants who fanned the English with large leaves. Charles and Margaret were Eastern royalty.

Much of her time was solitary. At Simanggang, when her husband was in the jungle, she watched egrets flying overhead at sunrise and sunset for the daily migration to the fishing grounds on the coast sixty miles away. She wrote of this wonderment in her notebook:

'The shafts of light breaking against their bodies in tints of orange and rose made symphonies of colour as they formed and re-formed with the movements of the birds. I fancied the beautiful things understood the pleasure they gave me as they flapped their great white wings over my head across the river, across miles of forest, finally disappearing like dots of glittering light in the morning and evening mists.'

William Thomas Shepherd was baptised at Sheepstor in the summer following his birth. Sarah chose her friend Mrs Lavers from Essworthy as his godmother. The two godfathers were Ben Andrews from Redstone and George Jackman from Narrator. Baby William did not favour the cold water poured over his head by Mr Crooke and yelled loudly. The villagers were happy the couple at Outhome had William to care for in their lonely existence.

The baby had come into the world as Annie was about to leave it, during one of the worst blizzards ever experienced on the moor. Annie's entrance and exit at Outhome were both at times when Dartmoor was blanketed in deep snow.

The talk in Sheepstor at this time was all about a battle which would decide the best place to construct a dam on the River Mew. It was either to be in the upper valley below the confluence of Harter Brook down from Princetown, or in Burrator Gorge near the headweir of the Plymouth Leat. Land had been bought up around the river on the moor by Plymouth Corporation in anticipation that a storage reservoir would soon be needed in the valley from which the town's water supply still flowed in an open channel. Meanwhile the Great Western Railway Company was buying land in the same valley on which they laid the track for the branch line.

The Princetown branch railway line opened from Yelverton, crossing Yennadon Down and following the contours of the hills upstream on the right bank of the River Mew. The Sheepstor folk out on the moor could tell the time by the usually prompt steam engine heard passing up and down the valley.

Albert Prowse had built Yennadon House on the side of the down in Dousland in the 1870s. When the Great Western Railway Company requisitioned his land on the moor to lay the track for the steam railway he was angry but despite spending a large sum of money in trying to save his land, lost his case.

Farmers who ran their stock on Yennadon were often seen driving their sheep away from the railway line when a train was due to pass. The animals had been startled at the coming of the noisy puffing engine that encroached on their territory.

Little William Shepherd looked forward to his mornings at school. Sarah walked with him as she had done with Will and Annie across the moor right to the school gate. She was protective of the little boy and would always wait at the gate to see him go in before walking the short distance to Burrator where she now helped the housekeeper of the new tenants, the Brittan family. Charles Brittan was an artist, usually to be found out on the moor standing at his easel in collar, tie, tweed jacket, plus fours and soft trilby hat, brush and palette in hands. His prolific moorland landscapes would make his name as one of the best known watercolour painters of Dartmoor.

'Good morning, William,' Miss Lang said, smiling down on the young dark haired boy. He was one of her brightest pupils. 'It's good to see you.'

William fetched a slate and a piece of chalk then sat on the floor with the other children. The children's ages ranged from four years to twelve years this morning, boys and girls, most of them wishing they were at home on their farms. Mary Lang was teaching her pupils addition and subtraction sums this morning using sheep to illustrate the examples.

'John, if your father had twenty sheep and bought three more, how many sheep would he have?'

John Pengelly was ten years old.

'He's got lots of sheep, Miss, so I don't know.'

The other children laughed. 'Who can help John? William Shepherd, how many sheep if you add twenty and three?'

'Twenty three, Miss,' William answered.

'Yes, now all write it on your slates.'

John Pengelly realised the children admired his amusing answers and it wasn't long before John was standing in the corner facing the wall. Mary Lang wished the morning was over when Mr Crooke the vicar entered the room. The school was the property of the church and Miss Lang's career depended entirely upon Mr Crooke's approval. Four schoolmistresses, prior to Miss Lang's appointment, had been dismissed in quick succession. Mr Crooke also had grave doubts about Miss Lang's discipline and her ability to spell but the school was also a home for Mary Lang and she was determined to stay. She was thirty-six years of age and was now all alone, her mother who had lived with her in the school having died the previous year.

'May I set your pupils a spelling test, Miss Lang, before they complete their morning's work?'

'Certainly, Mr Crooke. Clean your slates children and listen to Mr Crooke. John, come and sit down.'

'Why were you in the corner, John?'

'Don't know, Sir.'

Miss Lang spoke in her own defence. 'He caused a disturbance, Mr Crooke, and needed to be punished.'

'I'm sorry to hear that, John. Your father pays for you to attend school and wishes you to do well. What do you say for yourself?'

'Sorry, Sir.'

The children were silent. The vicar gave them ten easy enough words to spell but some of the pupils were not yet able to write their own name. There were four Williams at school this morning – Bowden, Mortimore, Shepherd and Shillibeer – all about the same age but only one, William Shepherd, did not feel threatened by the task. Bessie Worth, whose father was a road labourer, gained the highest score with seven correct answers, pleasing Miss Lang.

'This is not good enough, Miss Lang. I know they are young but cat, mat and sat should be taught to them all.'

'Yes, Sir. The children here today are very young.'

Mr Crooke told the children to put their slates away and read them the story of the Good Samaritan from the Bible. Standing up when he left the room they chanted, 'Good morning, Mr Crooke,' the boys bowing their heads as the girls curtsied. As Miss Lang showed him to the door, John was heard by the children to remark about the vicar being a crook and were giggling when Miss Lang dismissed them and sent them into the garden to play.

'William Shepherd, your grandmother will be waiting for you,' Miss Lang called. 'You did well today, William,' she said quietly to him. 'I wish you could come more often.'

William ran to the gate to the waiting Sarah. Some of the children brought a pasty for their lunch, others a slice of bread and a lump of cheese. A drink of water was obtained by pumping it from the well in the school garden. After much effort, Cecilia Ware and John Pengelly managed to pump up a small jug of discoloured water.

'We get our water from the brook next to our farm, Miss. It tastes good and it's always clean.'

'I know, John. This pump has been repaired many times.'

Mary Lang had been too agitated to complain about the pump yet again to

Mr Crooke this morning. Most evenings she took a bucket to Sheepstor Brook and filled it for her own use at school.

'Come indoors and get a drink from water I collected myself.'

In the afternoon, the few pupils left with her copied out the ten words from the morning's test. After this, in caps and bonnets, they sat under the tree sketching the tor as seen from the garden. After singing a few hymns it was time for the children to walk home, back to their farms. Mary Lang was not a well woman, she felt old and tired. Her salary was £18 a year; more money than this was spent on coal for the school fire over a year. There were no two days when the same pupils attended school and she was at a loss to know how best to educate these children who were healthy, good-looking and happy.

But she struggled through another four years before receiving a letter:

'The Managers request that you send in your resignation as teacher of Sheepstor school. We realise due to ill health that you are not equal to the task of efficiently conducting the school and we will pay you to leave at Michaelmas.'

She was buried in the churchyard less than a year later at the age of forty-one.

27

M{R and Mrs Lim returned to England to see their grandson in the summer after his sixth birthday. The journey to London by steamship and on to Plymouth by rail was arduous for them, but on arriving in Sheepstor to see the Shepherds, they looked refreshed and happy. Cornelius Crooke continued to live in the vicarage and gladly took them to the Deancombe valley.

'Thank you for writing to us at Mr Crooke's hand, Sarah,' Mr Lim said when the couple reached Outhome. 'It was a terrible tragedy that your son died. We were greatly saddened by Annie's death, of course, but you, who cared for her for twenty years, must have been devastated.'

'Why do you not hate me? I kept your baby,' Sarah pleaded piteously.

'Because you rescued her and gave her life. We had given her up for dead.'

William was told these people were his mother's parents and had offered to take him to London.

'Only if Grandma comes, too,' William declared.

Sarah and Sam thought of Annie leaving for London and over the next days Sarah prayed that she would be guided to do the right thing. Sarah and William took the Lims to see Annie's grave. The couple were too polite to ask the whereabouts of Will's grave; they would ask Mr Crooke.

The visit to London was talked over and over as offers of help poured in from neighbours and villagers to encourage Sarah to get away from Sheepstor for a while. Neighbours undertook to provide a daily meal for Sam and keep an eye on him.

'Go on, Sarah. This is a fine chance for you and the boy,' Sam told her. 'It will be great for him.'

Sarah and Soo Lim became well acquainted. Sarah told her about her old friend Maggie who had lived in Burrator before the Rajah, now married and living in London.

'A telegraph can be sent to say you will visit her on one of your days in London,' Soo Lim offered. 'Do you have her name and address? William will enjoy the rail journey.'

'She is Mrs John Peard and I have her address here behind the clock.'

It was decided. Sarah and William would spend a week in London at the Lims' expense. An unknown excitement of anticipation pervaded the cottage, in fact the whole of the Deancombe valley and in Sheepstor village. All told, Sheepstor parish comprised less than twenty inhabited properties.

Friends gathered at the church gate to wave goodbye to the four travellers. In grand style they left by carriage for the adventure ahead of them. Sarah gazed down on her young grandson who took after Annie more than Will. Looking at William she thought of Esca Daykin who was the same age when he embarked on his first long journey of his life. These people they were travelling with, were as much grandparents to William as were Sam and Sarah.

At Plymouth they boarded the train for Paddington Station. Sarah and William feasted their eyes on the panoramic views as they travelled to London. Sarah sat back and marvelled at the smooth ride along the railway lines. William asked questions about everything he saw from the windows.

The silhouettes of Dartmoor's tors from one side of the carriage windows and the stretches of red-cliffed sea coast on the other delighted them both. Mr and Mrs Lim pointed out landmarks to the enthralled boy and woman. Sarah delighted at the sight of Windsor Castle. This was the year of Queen Victoria's Golden Jubilee.

It was strange to Sarah that this couple from a far-off land knew more about her country than she did. They were also able to tell her news of the second Rajah and Ranee Margaret. She thanked them repeatedly for the kindness shown to her and William.

'It is our joy,' Mr Lim often said. 'We shall not come to England again, I think. Our family back in Sarawak are pleased that our grandson is to care for the land where our first Rajah lived. We feel honoured.'

Sarah imagined what the Lims had told their extended family in the long-houses on stilts. She was glad if it pleased them that William would one day farm on the land near Burrator – if there was to be any land left to farm.

In London the day duly arrived for Sarah's visit to Maggie. Nervously, she and the boy rang the bell at a tall terraced house. Maggie was overjoyed to see them. The two women held each other and Maggie wept a little.

'Come in, come in,' she cried delightedly. 'You haven't changed a bit, Sarah, I should know you anywhere.'

True enough, but Maggie saw a much older woman, drawn with greying hair. The sparkle that had once been in Sarah's eyes had long since died.

'It's nearly thirty years, Maggie, since we had that lovely picnic by the water-fall before we had to say goodbye. So much water has flowed under Sheepstor Bridge since that time.'

'I know, and here you are with a grandson,' replied Maggie.

Maggie had searched out the toys belonging to her own son years ago and William was spellbound at being allowed to fit together a miniature railway line. He pushed an engine along the track, fitting carriages and goods wagons. He was captivated for hours, leaving the reunited friends to talk without inter-ruption.

'Henry is at school today and John works in the City. I am sorry they won't be home until late this evening. I can hardly believe myself that Henry will be sixteen years old next week.'

Maggie served tea herself and the two friends imparted family news on both sides.

'Henry was born three months after Papa died. He knew, of course, that we were expecting a baby but my deep sadness has always been that he never saw him. That is why John and I named him Henry Terrell Peard.'

Sarah told Maggie briefly how she came to be in London. Even to Maggie, she could not bring herself to disclose the fact that Will had not married the Sarawak girl they had brought up as their own.

'Little William is obviously from the East, Sarah, but I can see a look of Sam in him.'

Sarah smiled.

'Now that Burrator is owned by the Lopes family, we don't get so many visitors from the East. Some come to see the old Rajah's retreat, as they call it, and visit his grave in the churchyard.'

Sarah found herself telling Maggie about Esca Daykin.

'A few years after you left the district, a young curate, with his wife and his mother were brought to the village by the Rajah. They purchased Brook Cottage with money given them by his mother. The church had been repaired so we then had weekly services. They had come from Stoke Fleming in South Devon where Mr Daykin had been the rector. He rented some land around Narrator and farmed those fields.'

'Anyhow, after Sir James died, the new Rajah sent this boy called Esca to live with the Daykins,' Sarah resumed, after sipping her tea from a bone-china cup. 'You could see he was from Sarawak but strangely he looked like the Rajah, too. Our William has the look of Esca. All to do with our Annie coming from the East, I suppose.'

'What happened to this Esca?' Maggie enquired, offering her two country guests another piece of cake.

'The Daykins sold up and went abroad as missionaries. Mr Daykin became an archdeacon in Africa and then they went to live in Canada. They adopted the boy as their son. Mr Daykin had two beautiful stained-glass windows put in the church. One in memory of the Rajah, the other in his parents' memory.'

Maggie found it hard to believe all the events and tragedies that had taken place in Sarah's life and in Sheepstor.

'Nothing much took place in the village when we lived there, Sarah. The day you got married to Sam was one of the most special days I remember.'

'There's lots going on at the moment. The steam train goes up and down to Princetown two or three times a day and now they want to flood the river valley.'

Sarah told Maggie all about the proposed reservoir.

'A few years back in '81, the Plymouth leat froze over and no water reached the town for days. It was decided that some means of storage of water was needed for Plymouth and Devonport. The Water Corporation has had a real battle on their hands to find the best site to build a dam. It's been in all the local papers.'

'I can hardly believe so much has happened in the tiny village, Sarah. I should notice so many changes.'

'Indeed you would, Maggie. The site of the reservoir was at first going to be under Hart Tor, near Princetown. Then we heard it was to be near the headweir and the Shillibeer's house. Apparently there was not enough water up at Hart Tor, which we all knew, and the rock was found to be too soft at headweir. We only need another freeze-up like that winter and the powers-that-be will realise a dam will *have* to be built soon.'

'But it will change the Mewy valley, Sarah. Do they mean to flood it forever?'

'So they say. As soon as someone comes up with a sensible proposal.'

'My goodness,' Maggie said. 'They'll have to put in new roads if the only road in or out of the village is under water. You must all be very worried.'

'Yes, we'll be glad when it's settled. It's hard to carry on farming the land when you don't know if next year it'll all be gone.'

'What about the farms?'

'There's speculation that some farmers will be told to leave their homes.'

'We still own the fields of Leaford between Burrator and Essworthy, you know, Sarah. Papa left the land in his will to Henry as his eldest grandson. Do you think it will be flooded? I receive the rent for the land from the Creber family until Henry comes of age, you see.'

The two middle-aged women chatted on for a long time whilst William had the time of his life with Henry's model railway. Maggie could see he was a solitary boy who enjoyed his own company. In the late afternoon Sarah and William made their farewells to Maggie and reluctantly prepared to leave.

As they parted Maggie expressed her hope that Sarah might visit her another time.

'No, I shan't ever leave Sheepstor again, Maggie, but it was a chance I'm glad I took, if only to see you. It might have given William the urge to see the world, though.'

They hugged and tears of fondness once again filled Maggie's eyes. She was sad to see the troubled lines and the sadness in Sarah's face.

'Enjoy the Jubilee procession tomorrow, and have a good journey home. Give Sam my best wishes,' she called as Sarah and William walked away from her along the street, back to their hosts.

'We have one more day to look forward to tomorrow, William,' Sarah smiled down on the little boy. 'It will be a grand day. What a lot we shall have to tell grandpa and everyone in Sheepstor.'

28

THE weather throughout the summer months of 1887 was glorious and became known as the Queen's weather. On the morning of Jubilee Day, 21 June, the Queen went in procession from Buckingham Palace to Westminster Abbey to attend a thanksgiving service. Along with her family, she was accompanied by many of the crowned heads of Europe and Indian potentates.

'Victoria was a young queen when I was born,' Sarah said at breakfast. 'I was born the day she came to the throne. She wasn't crowned, though, until the following year. Fancy being queen for fifty years.'

'Many happy returns, Sarah.' Everyone at the breakfast table wished her a happy birthday.

Mr and Mrs Lim took Sarah and William to watch the royal procession passing Hyde Park Corner. William, who had never seen such enormous horses or men in uniform, was speechless. Sarah waited in awe to see the open-top coach carrying Her Majesty the Queen surrounded by guards on horseback. Even the streets were lined with mounted guards to hold back the cheering crowds.

The next day Sarah could not find the words to thank the Lims. The Lims in their turn were sad at the departure of Sarah and their grandson. Grandmother and grandson. Dartmoor country woman fifty years of age with a six-year-old boy with Malay features. An odd couple but with an unmistakable love for each other.

Sarah and William were pleased to be on the train travelling to Plymouth. They would catch the train at Plymouth station for Horrabridge where a neighbour was bringing Sam to meet them in a cart. It was a joyful reunion at Horrabridge station after the only time Sam and Sarah had been apart at night since their wedding day, more than twenty-eight years before.

Sarah was glad to be back at Outhome. But she was delighted when the landowner suggested that the Shepherd family might like to take over the tenancy of Middleworth farm. She loved her home but there were too many unhappy memories of Will and Annie. Sam, as always, wanted to please Sarah so went along with the plan to move down the valley. They left Outhome when William was in his tenth year, old enough to be a good helper to Sam with the sheep out on the moor.

London now seemed far away though Sarah often wondered about the people she had met at Burrator many years earlier, all of them living across the seas. As she went about her daily chores, Sam often heard her mumbling, 'Wash me thoroughly from mine iniquity, and cleanse me from my sin.' He knew that she sat up in bed reading her Bible by candlelight when she thought him to be asleep and still blamed herself for the death of her son. William's looks also made her dwell on Esca Daykin and what had become of him, she would have liked some news of him.

Missionary activity was expanding rapidly in Canada and Bishop John Lewis had welcomed the Venerable Daykin, his wife and son to the diocese of Ontario. Esca found the winters even colder than those at Sheepstor, in the Canadian town of Madoc. It was not an easy mission for Venerable Daykin. He was in charge of six far-flung parishes.

As the son of a Church of England minister, Esca received a scholarship to attend Trinity College School near Lake Ontario, not far from Toronto. After four very happy and successful years at this school Esca returned to Madoc to help his father with mission work. The Daykins were sent to a more remote parish, many miles north on the Ottawa river. People liked Esca, the young unusual-looking missionary but the Archdeacon was not popular.

Esca soon realised missionary work was not for him so from funds given to him by his mother, bought a share in a foodstore. The venture failed and in a short space of time his mother died at the age of sixty-two after a long illness. William and Esca Daykin moved to Ottawa, a more comfortable parish for the Archdeacon, while Esca found a post with Ottawa's leading store.

After a few months Esca fell in love with Edith Webster who worked at the same store, and a year after his mother's death they were married in a ceremony conducted by his father. In the register of St Margaret's church it is recorded that Esca Daykin, son of Charles Brooke, Rajah of Sarawak, was born in Borneo.

Canada, far, far away from the moorland solitude of Sheepstor, was as distant to the village folk as Sarawak but they heard tales about these exotic places from those who read the newspapers. Life for the Ranee had changed considerably. She was now a society lady, living in London and Paris, surrounding herself with famous writers, artists and musicians. With her sons at school in England, she took a succession of suitors.

Rajah Charles was angered by his wife's lifestyle and the great debts she incurred. He was still further incensed that his eldest son, the Crown Prince of Sarawak, did not live with him in Borneo. Vyner, at the age of twenty-three, received an ultimatum from his father, which prompted the young man to sail for Sarawak. He was sent to Simanggang, his father's favourite place in the country.

On return visits to England Vyner found his mother's home full of wealthy young women. The Ranee had formed a female orchestra of well-bred aristocrats, all suitable partners for her three dashing sons. The young Brooke men made their choices, not for love but for money and connections from these young ladies in their mother's so-called orchestra. Vyner became attached to Sylvia Brett but theirs was to be a long courtship.

At one time in Sarawak Vyner had a close brush with death, indeed it was reported he had died, along with thousands of natives from an epidemic of cholera. The severity of the plague was due in no small part to the stupidity of the Rajah who, typically, believed himself to be above such afflictions. Even the

Rajah's people thought him foolhardy at this time of torment but he, equally typically, considered a tough life and contact with deadly illnesses to be character building for his son.

On Sarah's return to Sheepstor, Sam was to hear all about London many times over from his wife and young William. He was genuinely interested to hear news of Maggie; he had liked Harry Terrell. William told his friends all about the great city, the journey by rail and wonders he had never heard of that he had seen in London.

'I'd like to travel when I'm a man. There is so much in this world beyond our shores. When I learned about other countries at school I'm not sure that I really believed they existed,' he admitted to Thomas Creber.

The London experience faded from Sarah's memory but for William the urge to travel and to see the world never left him. Young Mr Vanstone at Meavy sailed to Australia that year to the deep sadness of his family. This event made William realise that he could never sail away from Sam and Sarah whilst they were still alive.

Plymouth Water Corporation was now forced into doing something about a dam and storage reservoir. As long ago as 1880 they had begun to review the purchase of land from the owners in the Mewy valley. In 1889 Sir Massey Lopes and his son Henry agreed to sell land to the Corporation, under a special Act, for thousands of pounds. The landowners were to instruct their tenants to allow any part of the valleys in the watershed to be tested for a storage reservoir.

A blizzard again left Sheepstor cut off from all communications with deep snow and freezing weather conditions. Early in 1891 the Plymouth Leat froze over again and soldiers were sent to Sheepstor to break the ice. As soon as water began to flow it froze again making all their efforts a waste of time.

Three trains were snowed up on their journeys across Dartmoor on the evening of Monday, 9 March. On the train which left Princetown in the early evening were eight passengers and staff. It got no further than Peak Hill before becoming completely buried in snow. The following morning, it took the guard two hours to walk the three miles to Dousland to alert the outside world before returning to the train with food and drink. It was considered too dangerous to allow anyone else to leave the train but there was no warmth or heating aboard. It was not until Wednesday morning that the passengers were able to walk to the nearest farm where they were given a hearty breakfast by Mrs Hillson.

With the water supply cut off from the town for several weeks, Plymouth Water Corporation set about finding an engineer who would find the best site for the long-awaited dam.

Two of the Brown family members outside the Smithy in Meavy. The advertisement reads: 'PURITAN SOAP used in Britain's happiest homes.'

Revd Sabine Baring-Gould, 1834-1924.

Meavy Parsonage, next to the Royal Oak Inn.

Sheepstor from Portland Lane. Lether and North Hessary tors on the skyline to the left, the massif of Sheeps Tor on the right and Maiden Tor on the slope behind St Leonard's church. (EH)

Two horses were needed to pull the cart back down to the Warren. (AD)

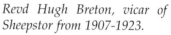

Revd Hugh Breton, vicar of Sheepstor from 1907-1923.

Charles E Brittan, one of the best known water-colour painters of the moor, 1870-1849.

Rood screen in Sheepstor Church at Eastertide 2000.

This could be Sarah Shepherd, matriarch of the fictional family, and William's dog Shep. (Elizabeth Creber, nee Bowden, 1844-1915).

Mrs Evans and her daughter with the pupils of Sheepstor School c1906 when Will Legassick and Fred Glanville were 4 years old.

The tombs of the first two white Rajahs of Sarawak.

Stenlake Farm. (T)

Kingsett Farm.

Dickie Pengelly shortly before his death at Combeshead. (AD)

Dickie Pengelly in the doorway of Combeshead Farm in the 1920s. His two daughters, Millie and Bertha, lived with him until he died. (AD)

*Horrabridge station opened 21 June 1859 and closed 31 December 1962.
In the 1860s it handled large quantities of copper ore from local mines. (T)*

The steamship **Metagama** *which left
Plymouth for Vancouver in 1924.*

Workmen raising the dam, pose for the photographer in 1923. (SWW)

The suspension bridge placed across the dam in 1925. (T)

Dickie Pengelly outside the home he refused to leave in the 1920s.

Dickie working at Combeshead with Sheeps Tor visible in the far distance.

Combeshead Farm two years after its last tenant was carried in his coffin off the moor. (T)

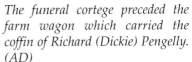

The funeral cortege preceded the farm wagon which carried the coffin of Richard (Dickie) Pengelly. (AD)

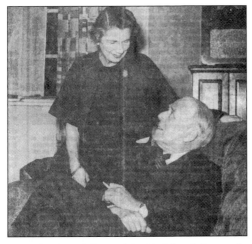

The third and last white Rajah of Sarawak, Sir Vyner Brooke, and Ranee Sylvia in 1946.

The stained-glass window in Sheepstor church was placed to commemorate all those who lost their lives in Sarawak during the war 1941-1945. Above the heads of the saints are two coats of arms of the Diocese of Borneo on the left and of Sarawak.

Menhirs and stone rows at Thrushelcombe beyond Ditsworthy Warren.

The Rajahs of Sarawak remembered in Sheepstor church with memorial tablets and a bust of Sir James.

Down Tor from the lane between Nosworthy and Kingsett. (EH)

The four concentric stone circles on Yellowmead Down. (EH)

The rails were removed from the track as the last train came down the Princetown railway.

Removing the rails.

Nelson Palmer and his children outside Sheepstor stores in the centre of Sheepstor village, 1968. (NP)

Amos Shillibeer on the village cross.

Outhome and the Deancombe Brook in the year 2000.

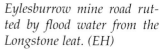

Eylesburrow mine road rutted by flood water from the Longstone leat. (EH)

The summit of Sheepstor which overlooks the lake. The wind always blows here and the views are spectacular.

The author emerging from Pixies Cave. (EH)

North-east of Sheepstor churchyard where members of the Brooke family are laid to rest.

Slotted gatepost at Deancombe. (EH)

The ruins of Combeshead Farm looking towards Yennadon. (EH)

Down Tor and Cuckoo Rock on the horizon, from Combeshead Brook.

One of Emma's photographs of Burrator House which she was taking to Canada for her grandfather Tom.

Ernest Prowse, grandson of Albert, who emigrated to Canada, named the district Yennadon and was Mayor of Vernon, near Vancouver, six times.

Rosa, Katherine and Laura Prowse at Yennadon in the 1870s. Katherine married Revd James Catton, rector of Meavy.

Couples meeting on Meavy village cross by the famous ancient oak tree, early twentieth century.

Burrator and Sheepstor Halt in the year 2000. The GWR 'kissing' gate leads down to the reservoir.

An early photograph of Marchants Cross.

Old Meavy school by the side of the village green.

School children exploring the wildlife in Drake's leat as it leaves Burrator in the woods below the dam.

This Moorland Solitude. Emma's photograph from Portland Lane with the church and village nestling under Sheeps Tor.

The Lychgate at Sheepstor today.

Gorse is always in flower on Dartmoor. Emma's last photograph as they travelled away from Sheepstor, from the tranquility she now called home.

29

SARAH walked along the rough track from Middleworth farm towards the village with William. He was going to help George Creber at Longstone with the hay harvest. Men and boys from the village and surrounding farms enjoyed the warm summer days, helping each other to collect the dried grass to be used as fodder for the animals in the winter. Sarah was going on to Burrator House where she still did cleaning jobs a few mornings a week.

William was twelve years old. The grass had been cut by the men the previous day with scythes and bill-hooks and lay in neat rows in the sunshine. William and the other boys, using hay forks, turned the hay over, shaking it in the air as they did so. It was hot, thirsty work and the midday meal brought out to the fields by George's wife and sisters would be heartily welcomed. The occupiers of the two neighbouring farms of Redstone and Essworthy, Ben Andrews and Bill Lavers, brought their horses and carts to help George Creber. He would do the same for them at their harvest. The day was long, from sunrise in the early morning until the dew began to settle in the evening. Tomorrow the hay would be gathered in, using the horse and cart where possible.

The old granite manor of Longstone was on the left bank of the River Mew above the steep gorge. For a hundred years now it had been a farmhouse but the granite arches in the gardens, granite doorways and windows still had the manorial appearance of former days. The road from the village passed the arched gateway leading to the cobbled courtyard. Water flowed through the farmyard as it had for centuries by a leat taken from the River Plym out on the high moor; its headweir above Plym Steps many miles away. The leat provided running water for many inhabitants of Sheepstor village as well as for Park Cottage and Redstone farm on its journey to Longstone before flowing into the River Mew in the valley below.

The ancient manor had been the home of the Elford family, a family of some repute in the neighbourhood and seated in Sheepstor early in the thirteenth century. Sheepstor Church contains several memorials to members of the family, the Elford monument of 1584 bearing many coats of arms. The family had added to its possessions, in customary fashion by marriage, and had been wealthy landowners for centuries.

The Elfords owned another house and farm about three miles further down the valley which they called Elfordtown. This exposed moorland area was becoming increasingly popular with the coming of the railway and since the opening of the station there, six years before, the name had been corrupted to Yelverton. Wealthy business men from Plymouth were building large family houses near the station and Yelverton was becoming a holiday resort for people attracted by the bracing Dartmoor air. Shops were opening and some houses even had a telephone.

William loved these summer days. He liked helping Sam to cut and save their hay but he and his grandfather could manage the few fields of Middleworth on their own. Sam was old but continued to work from dawn to dusk. At the age of seventy-six he was much slower and bent in his body but 'as strong as an ox,' as the neighbours said.

'Where's your dog today, Will?' Charlie Lavers called.

'He's home with Grandpa, and you know you're not to call me Will. Grandma gets real mad. My name be William.'

'Sorry, I forgot. It's cos of your dad, isn't it?'

'Yes, he was called Will, and he died before I was born. It upsets Grandma to hear his name.'

His friend Thomas Creber came to William's defence.

'I'm always called Thomas by the family, it's the same thing.'

'Just as well,' Tom Northmore joined in. 'We'd get addled if we were called by the same name.'

The four boys, all of the same age, walked up and down the fields turning the hay. It was hard, sticky work but they each enjoyed the company of their friends. Charlie lived at Essworthy, Tom at Yellowmead and Thomas lived here at Longstone. They had all left school to work for their fathers.

'We'll be saving this hay tomorrow,' Thomas called to the other boys. 'Shall we meet up at Pixies Cave tonight?'

'I'd like that,' William called back. 'I have to be home by nine o'clock though.'

'Me, too,' Tom said. 'Let's meet there at seven.'

Near Longstone was the headweir of the Plymouth Leat. On a higher contour was the Devonport Leat, constructed a hundred years ago to take fresh water to the ships in dock. The source of this flowing water was from the West Dart river in the middle of Dartmoor. A cottage had been built for the foreman of the leats by the Water Corporation twenty years before, near to the headweir of the Plymouth Leat. Known as Headweir Cottage, it was now lived in by Amos Shillibeer and his wife Emma. Amos, son of William, and Emma had lived above the stables of Burrator when they were first married when Amos had been gardener for the Rajah.

There were many Creber families living in Sheepstor. About a mile up the road from Headweir Cottage, near where the railway crosses over the road by the bridge, is Mullicroft Cottage where one of the Creber families with young children lived. The families in Sheepstor were neighbourly and cared about each other's well-being, knitted together by their common bond, agriculture.

In one of the fields not far from Longstone, high above the valley, is a wind-strew, the threshing floor in the days of the manor. On this, in olden days, corn was thrashed by men, the chaff blowing away in the wind leaving the grains to be harvested. Carved on one of the stone steps leading up to the platform is JE 1640, supposed to be the initials of John Elford. His father, Walter Elford, carved his initials on the large stone at the church gate, where coffins are rested before being carried into church for burial.

It was at John Elford's cavern, or Pixies Cave, that the boys were to meet that evening. It was the tradition in the parish that during the Civil War, John Elford hid in this cave amidst the clitter under Sheeps Tor. The story is told that Elford frequently concealed himself there from the pursuit of Cromwell's soldiers, hiding with him the church silver and surviving on food taken by the villagers. Sam had told William that when he was a boy there were still paintings on the wall of the cave which are said to have been painted by Elford to pass away the time. Born in 1606, John Elford was married four times and had fathered eighteen children. It was never quite clear whether he was a Royalist or a Puritan.

At about seven o'clock the boys found each other as they scrambled over the granite boulders beneath the tor. Each generation passed down the knowledge for finding Pixies Cave. Amidst the most confused masses of rocks, that look as if they had been tossed about in battle, is the cave with an overhanging stone at the entrance. This, the hiding place of John Elford, was big enough for the four boys to sit in comfortably and walk about.

The boys went the way of generations of boys from the village. Under the tor, not far from the gate to Yellowmead farm where Tom lived, they looked for the huge rock, paler in colour than all the grey rocks surrounding it. The cube-shaped rock is of a finer grain granite and once the boys spied it they clambered at speed over the fallen clitter.

As they approached they made for the left of the rock and dropped down through the entrance. Visitors to the cave, believing it to be the home of pixies, left silver coins or pins. Although adults down the ages had told their children not to remove these in case of bad luck, all children did. This was the attraction of the cave this evening.

The four boys sat in the cave with the little collection of offerings. Sounds of dripping water further back the cavern added to the mysterious feeling as they groped about in the darkness.

'I'd better be getting back home,' William said after a while.

The boys scrambled out into the light of the setting sun. Tom made his way home to Yellowmead as the others went down the lane to the village.

'Do you think there are such things as pixies?' Charlie asked in a careless manner.

'Maybe,' Thomas said. 'My gran told me they are too small for me to see, and they can make themselves invisible.'

'Grandma has shown me fairy rings which she says the pixies make when they dance on the hillside,' William added.

'When our cow fell down dead,' Charlie said, 'Dad said it was the work of the pixies.'

'Well, I won't believe in pixies 'til I see one,' William declared.

The boys parted and made for their own homes.

The next day dawned warm and sunny. Men and boys were back in the fields early, raking in the dry hay. Sam came with William this morning. It was well-known in the area that Sam was the best maker of hay-ricks. Other men's ricks lent over by the time winter came but Sam's ricks remained as straight and upright as the day he made them. Hay was loaded on to the carts and taken by horse to Sam putting up the rick in the field above Narrator. Using only his pitch-fork, and stamping on the hay with his boots, he built up the rick until it was higher than a cottage. The other men helped Sam down after he had put a sloping hay roof on the rick.

'Thanks to you all,' George Creber called at the end of the day. 'Any man who wants can have a pint of ale at Park Cottage tonight.'

Young women had come out to help in the afternoon. Boys much older than William appreciated this and not so much work had been done by them in the afternoon. But they would all be cutting hay in another field tomorrow. The maidens and boys returned home, the men walked to the ale house. This had been the pattern unchanged for centuries, seeming as natural and permanent as the tors themselves. But as events were soon to prove, such apparent permanence was no more than illusion.

30

ONLY two months after these halcyon days, work on Burrator Dam began. A meticulous survey was undertaken by Plymouth's newly appointed water engineer, Edward Sandeman, then aged twenty-nine. Burrator Gorge was finally agreed on as the best site, the very place suggested as long as fifty years before. Work started on 9 August 1893 when the site for the foundations of the dam was cleared of bushes and trees.

Essworthy farm was to be completely submerged when the project was finished and the Redstone farmer was also told to leave his farm and his land. They had saved the hay in the fields, building the hay-ricks up on land away from any danger of being flooded, sold their animals and moved their families.

'I'm that sorry for 'ee, Mrs Brown,' Bessie Turpin, the farmer's wife from Narrator, said to Jane Brown from Redstone after church on Sunday. 'It's a bad time for us all but you've got to get out with your five little ones. We're all right sorry for 'ee.'

'Thank you, Mrs Turpin,' Jane Brown replied. ''Tis a bad time for us all, to be sure. Everyone's being kind but the chillern will miss their friends.'

No one in Sheepstor would remain untouched by this huge undertaking. Sheepstor Bridge, Headweir Cottage and the headweir of the leat would be under water. All the villagers could talk about was the flooding of the valley. The estimated time for the work to be completed was seven years.

In December, Albert Prowse died at Yennadon House. He had lost all his money fighting the railway company in trying to protect his land on the moor. The steam locomotive was a common sight now passing by Sheepstor on the other side of the steep river valley which was soon to be lost forever.

The deep gorge had been cut naturally by the River Mew over millions of years. For the next two years a deep trench was cut through granite bedrock for the foundations of the dam across the bed of the river. Crevices were cleaned out and filled with concrete. Some of the local men found employment here, walking to the site from nearby villages. The River Mew was diverted into a large wooden chute to enable work to progress. A few yards upstream a quarry was opened up in the side of the gorge, the granite from which was cut into blocks for facing the two dams. Mr Sandeman was always on site overseeing the vast undertaking.

In the year following the commencement of the dam known as Burrator, work was begun on a dam nearer the village. This Sheepstor dam was necessary to prevent flood waters reaching the village. Dozens of men with picks and shovels dug out the rotting granite, which resembled coarse sand. The deeper the men dug, the softer the granite became. Edward Sandeman soon realised this was to be a major venture in itself.

Machines were brought into the village to dig a trench to find solid rock. Some of the villagers could still remember a time when no cart or wagon had ever come into the village. Goods were then brought into, and taken out of, the village by pack-horse. Even now, no wheeled vehicles had ever been taken up the Deancombe valley.

At Sheepstor dam, not far from the gates of Burrator, water gushed in relentlessly from springs. Pumping equipment and pipes removing the water covered the area. Eventually bedrock was reached and the trench, one hundred feet deep, had to be filled with concrete. Sheepstor dam caused many problems but in the end all were overcome. The slope of the dam was faced with granite blocks cut at the quarry. This was built across the old and only road entering the village.

Across the road from Burrator House were the three fields named Leaford which still belonged to the the Terrell family, bequeathed by Harry Terrell to his grandson, the baby he had never seen, twenty-three years before. The young man was approached by letter in London, by Plymouth Water Corporation specifying that he should sell them the eight acres, land needed for the reservoir. Since his coming of age at twenty-one Henry Peard had received rent for the land from John Creber. Contracts were drawn up by solicitors and Henry never saw the fields bought by his grandfather in 1852. He agreed to sell the fields and received £450. Maggie included a letter with the agreement, perhaps in loyalty to her father, informing the Corporation that she knew the land well. She also enclosed her son's birth certificate as proof of his identity and age:

Henry Terrell Peard born 29 June 1871, son of Margaret Elizabeth and John Peard.

Grey old London was transformed into a temporary fairyland to celebrate the sixty years of the reign of Queen Victoria. Streets were decorated all over the city. Cunningly concealed in hanging baskets of flowers were electric lamps to make the streets even more brilliant at night than they were in the daytime. Cloth mills in the north of England were working at full capacity to provide flags and materials. Globes of red, white and blue glass sparkled in the sunlight. Planning for the day had taken months.

Bicycles were bedecked with streamers and every whip fluttered with national colours. Omnibuses ran under swaying decorations hung across the roads and even the horses seemed to sense the special atmosphere of the event. The crowds were immense; visitors surged on London for days to witness the celebrations for the longest reigning monarch.

Special church services of thanksgiving were held, the main one being in St Paul's Cathedral on Tuesday 22 June. This day was declared a public holiday by Her Majesty. On Monday the Queen travelled from Windsor to Buckingham Palace in the royal train. As usual, she was dressed in black except for white egret plumes in her bonnet. As she left the Palace for St Paul's on Tuesday morning the sun shone and the Queen's weather showed up for this momentous day in the great little lady's life. To all parts of the Empire her message to her people was transmitted by telegraph: *'From my heart I thank my beloved people. May God bless them.'*

On her progress through the city she was preceded by the colonial procession of troops on horseback from Canada, Australia, New Zealand, Africa, Trinidad and Cyprus. All men of the British Empire, including Sikhs, Chinese, Malays and Dyaks.

Then came the Royal Procession, led by a guardsman six feet eight inches tall on horseback. Carriages rolled by full of the Queen's family, children, grand-children and great-grandchildren, followed by the Queen's carriage drawn by eight cream-coloured horses. The tiny lady, dressed in black with a white parasol, was surrounded by a great army of men in brightly coloured uniforms, of scarlet, purple, emerald, white and always gold. Millions of her loyal sub-jects shouted in their exuberance of loyalty. Celebrations and parades around the country continued for weeks.

On Sarah's sixtieth birthday she reminded William of their London visit ten years earlier.

'There will be even greater celebrations in London for the grand old Queen I expect, William.'

'I'll never forget the sight of the horses and men in uniform, Grandma. I was only six years old but I remember everything clearly.'

'You were such a good boy, William. We had a grand week, didn't we? I think you enjoyed the journey as much as anything. I thought it might have given you the urge to travel, but here we are, still tending sheep in the Deancombe valley.'

'I'll be here 'til I'm thrown out, Grandma, don't you worry.'

'It's worrying times, sure enough. You don't think it'll come to that do you, William?'

'Well the water won't be far from our fields. The Crebers and Browns have got to go. It doesn't make us feel very safe, does it?'

'No,' Sarah sighed. 'I'm glad your grandpa doesn't realise the seriousness of the situation. I suppose we'd have been told by now if we had to go. It's all *most* disturbing.'

The tranquility in the valleys faded, there was too much agitation in the hearts and minds of those who lived there. Those farmers who had been served notices to quit drove their animals to market and made enquiries for farms, cot-tages or land to rent. Tenants like the Shepherds were sad to see neighbours forced to leave their homes and offered to help in any way possible. William realised that change and progress at the end of the century were inevitable.

31

THERE was little stomach for grand celebrations in this jubilee year in the Sheepstor valley. The men and women were used to hard work but not the helplessness that was overwhelming every home. Henry Creber was a stone-cutter's labourer and cut the blocks of granite from the new quarry which were to be used in facing the dam. He was thirty-eight, with a young and growing family to provide for. There was much talk at the quarry about the flooding of the valley so he believed his house to be safe, well above the expected water level.

Henry and Ann were the tenants of Mullicroft, an old farm above the right bank of the River Mew in the parish of Meavy. The old Sheepstor road went pass the front door and most people called in on the Crebers as they passed by. On the other side of the road the Devonport Leat flowed, a useful source of fresh clean water for the family.

Beyond the leat, the Great Western Railway went through Mullicroft land so the Crebers were never lonely. Up the hill from their cottage, known as Woodland Hill, the branch line crossed the road by a bridge and a little further along the track passed over the road. Here, at Lowery Crossing, in the crossing keeper's cottage lived Henry and Ann Heard with their son and daughter. They were good neighbours to the Crebers and Henrietta Heard, who was twenty-two, helped Ann Creber with her little ones.

It was two days after Christmas and the Crebers and Heards were having a fine and merry time at Mullicroft. The Crebers had five children. Alice, the oldest was twelve, then came the boys Harry, Fred and Lou and then little Annie. In the middle of a game of Blind Man's Buff a knock came to the door. Nobody knocked on the Mullicroft door, it was never locked and visitors just walked in, sure of a warm welcome.

Henry Creber went to open the door.

The assembled company inside the cottage went still as they heard him say, 'Come in, Dr Cornish. Would you care to take a glass of wine?'

'No, thank you, Creber. I'm sorry to interrupt your jollity but I've been asked to serve you this. There's no kinder way to say it, but it's a notice to quit. I'm afraid you have to be gone by Lady Day.'

'That's only three months away,' the listening group heard Henry say to his landlord. 'We were told we'd be all right here, up the hill away from the water's edge.'

'I'm sorry, Creber, I'm only passing on to you instructions I received from the Corporation. There it is,' Philip Cornish added, mounting his horse. 'Hope the news won't spoil your celebrations.' And with that he had gone, up 'Oolan Hill, as they called it.

Henry Creber closed the door. He was stunned.

'I suppose you all heard that. Three months we've got to get out of our home. Then they'll pull it down.'

His neighbours were as upset as he was. 'You are well above the water line, they may as well ask us to go and all.'

'Where are we to go, Harry? Can't we fight this?'

'No, Anne, the Water Corporation have got the powers to throw us out. I'll just have to look for another place.'

Nobody felt like putting on a blindfold and groping around in fun any more, the game was forgotten. The Heards put on their coats and walked up the hill to their cottage in sombre mood.

Mullicroft had been the Crebers' family home for twelve years and Henry and Ann saw no reason why they should be asked to leave.

'All five chillern are at Sheepstor school, is there no one to help us?'

'No. The likes of Cornish and other landlords will do all right out of it, you mark my words. They'll get compensation for losing a house and land. We're the poor devils who get nothing.'

Philip Cornish was the grandson of Richard Stranger who had made his money by selling his land between Sheepstor and Princetown for the development of the railway. As Creber so rightly guessed, he was to receive over £1,000 from the Plymouth Water Corporation. For the Crebers, Christmas celebrations had come to an abrupt end and there would be no merriment to welcome in the New Year. George Creber at Longstone, who rented some of the Mullicroft fields, was also served notice to quit.

Every farmer who lived within the watershed of the River Mew was now concerned about their tenure on their farms. Most of the men, and their sons who were old enough to do so, worked on the building of the two dams as well as caring for their land and flocks of sheep. It was a hard life and the worst weather of the winter was ahead of them.

The farmers who were served notices to quit by Lady Day 1897 were those at Essworthy, owned by the Creft family, once a large but now empty farm and the only farmhouse to be submerged by the reservoir; the family at Mullicroft, occupiers of the old Sheepstor manor Longstone above the valley on the left bank, and the family at Redstone. The owner of this old farm, Alexander Duncan, lived in Weymouth in Dorset and had already sold the house and land to the Water Corporation. The Plymouth Corporation Water Act of 1893 was served on the tenants of Redstone, William and Jane Brown and their five children, Ethel, Percy, Arthur, Lily and Mary. They were almost identical in age to the Creber children at Mullicroft and were all friends at school together.

'Fine Christmas present we had, eh Henry?' Bill Brown asked as they worked in the granite quarry in the new year. 'Don't expect we shall see any of the compensation they are paying out.'

The Shillibeers at Headweir Cottage had always expected to move but Burrator Lodge had been built for the family as Amos was the water foreman. The farmers in the farms further up the valleys all felt reasonably safe and secure – Narrator, Stenlake, Lower Lowery, Higher Lowery, Vinneylake, Lethertor, Kingsett, Nosworthy, Middleworth, Deancombe and Combeshead.

All these farms were on land within the catchment area of the River Mew but well above the dams now almost completed, ahead of schedule. Outhome was falling into disrepair and no one had lived there since the Shepherd family moved to Middleworth.

Sir Massey Lopes owned large tracts of the land from Sheepstor to Plymouth now being dug up for the large pipes that were being laid to carry the water. The Water Corporation purchased the rights for the purpose of making, maintaining, inspecting, cleansing and repairing a line of pipes or conduits under lands in the parish of Sheepstor and others down to the coast. Landowners received compensation for the damage caused by the diversion of the Plymouth Leat and for the coppices and timber removed from the land. Machinery and materials conveyed across land caused much disruption to the farmers and their animals.

The new roadway was staked out in Sheepstor. Permission was granted for two wooden huts to be erected near Park Cottage Inn. One to be used as the office for the reservoir, the other for the shelter of the men working on the dams. All the tenants in the farms in the valleys received notices that they 'should give the Corporation facilities for entering at once to lay the line of pipes'. The Corporation were given powers to compulsorily purchase any land required by them.

By Lady Day, 25 March 1898, both Creber families had left their homes, Mullicroft of fifty acres and Longstone of sixty-eight acres. The three main occupants of Longstone, Mary, James and George Creber, were in their late forties and all unmarried.

Charlie Mortimore was the beer retailer at Park Cottage. This dwelling and land in the valley had been owned by Septimus Oliver Jackson, together with the Trustees of the Poor of Sheepstor. Fields known as Little Park, Middle Park, Western Park, Cattle Marsh, Old Marsh, Old Bitt Craff and Little Gratton were soon to be under water.

Park Cottage Inn was doing a thriving trade due to the great numbers of men employed on the building of the dams. The house stood in a field known as Gratton and in this year it was purchased by the Tavistock Brewery Company. They sold the inn the next year for £1,600 to Reginald Watts. Charlie Mortimore, the innkeeper, received only scant compensation for his pasture field going under water.

Lowery farm, not far from the Heard's Crossing Cottage, was lived in by widow Anne Hamlyn and her three grown-up children. Though there were seven years to run on their lease, they did not want to live under the threat of being made to move out. Anne's son Bill Hamlyn took a lease on another farm in Walkhampton parish and offered the farmhouse to the family at Mullicroft, wonderful news for the Crebers who by the spring were in their new home. The five children attended Walkhampton school where, no doubt to their dismay, they found a headmaster with much stricter discipline than at Sheepstor.

Harry Legassick, a busy carpenter and mason, moved into Mullicroft when it was empty knowing he would be thrown out in a few months. The view from the little cottage on the hillside was striking – steep Lether Tor on the left side of the valley facing the mighty Sheeps Tor, with the other tors of Cramber, Combeshead, Down and Maiden backed by the rounded hill of Eylesburrow. Below these lofty heights, farmsteads nestled in the valleys, smoke rising from the chimneys, surrounded by a patchwork of fields. Seen directly below Mullicroft was Sheepstor Bridge over the Mew, covered in creepers, and granite footbridges across the parallel lines of sparkling waters of the Plymouth and Devonport leats.

The steep hill from Sheepstor Bridge twisting up to the village made all travellers gasp for breath. Horses and ponies heaved on, pulling carts and carriages to their destination. Clouds traversing overhead changing the light, the Mew tumbling over boulders below making natural music, the rushing of the two flowing leats, the sound of the steam engine pulling up the valley, all such things were part of the excellence of living at Mullicroft. Life here would soon be extinct when the waters advanced to flood everything below.

There was no peace in Sheepstor, at this time either in the landcape or in the hearts and minds of the inhabitants. Noise and clamour in the valley, stripping of the trees in the woods and the railway on the hillside all destroyed wildlife. Those who observed such things wondered if serenity in this once secluded location would ever be restored.

32

FROM the time of Sir Francis Drake, when he took water to Plymouth by leat, to the day when the headweir was submerged by the reservoir three hundred years later, the ancient custom of 'Ye Fyshinge Feaste' had been held annually. This custom is still upheld and will continue as long as the River Mew sends its water to the town. The town's mayor and other notables bring silver goblets to the river from which they, and invited guests, drink water from the leat, drink wine and eat trout caught in the river at luncheon. The guests and members of the Plymouth Corporation each take the goblets in turn and repeat the toasts in memory of Drake, 'To the pious memory of Sir Francis Drake', and 'May the descendants of him who brought us water never want wine'.

This year of 1898 was a special feast. The dam was completed and to be dedicated in the afternoon of 21 September. In the cool, crisp air of the bright morning guests arrived by train. Some walked from Yelverton station, others caught a second train on the Princetown branch line and walked from Dousland station. Yennadon Down rang with the sound of walkers' voices as they made their way to the new dam. Other guests were transported in carriages and wagonettes along the new road cut to the masonry dam from Meavy village.

Not only was Sheepstor school closed for the day but all the schools and shops in Plymouth besides to enable as many as wished to witness the opening of Burrator Dam. Special trains ran from Plymouth to Yelverton every half hour from eleven o'clock in the morning.

'Why don't they erect a temporary platform on the line above the dam?' William asked his friend Thomas. 'Then everyone would turn up close to the site.'

'Mr Shillibeer asked that of the railway company and was told that in the interest of public safety the Board of Trade opposed it,' Thomas said.

'It seems daft to me. People are coming to Sheepstor now in wagonettes and charabancs as well as on the train to Yelverton and blocking the new road.'

After the Fyshinge Feaste, which was attended only by invited guests at lunchtime, more crowds reached Burrator. The ladies in dark, graceful gowns brought parasols, not usually seen in Sheepstor, to protect their faces from the autumn sunshine.

'That reporter told me there are six thousand people here,' William informed Thomas.

'Yes, and I reckon many are disappointed. They expected to find the valley already flooded.'

'All they see in the valley is the quarry they opened up to build the dam and Essery farmhouse pulled down. But the valley will be under water soon enough,' William added sadly.

Small white flags, planted at short intervals on both sides of the valley, traced the top line to which the water should reach when the reservoir was full. It gave some idea of the magnitude of the immense sheet of water which was soon to fill that portion of the valley of the Mew.

Dartmoor looked its best in the brilliant sunshine. Sam and Sarah stood on the Burrator side and watched the crowds approaching the dam. A neighbour from Narrator had brought them in his cart to see the happening at a distance. Sam leaned on his stick and mumbled to Sarah. Even she found it hard to understand her husband's speech these days.

'I never thought I'd see the day when our valley was drowned, maid.'

'It's put Sheepstor on the map, Sam, and we've got new roads into the bargain.'

'We got on all right before. I'm glad I shan't live to see any more so-called improvement.'

Sam wore the same clothes all year round, come rain or sunshine. Thick under garments, shirt, breeches, woollen jumper, jacket and cap. Sarah knitted his woollen socks and he wore leather boots. He was never heard to complain of either being too warm or too cold. Life in summer time was certainly easier in the country, less of a struggle.

By three o'clock the slope of Yennadon was alive with spectators, as well as the crowds on the dam itself. Everyone applauded as the Mayor of Plymouth dedicated the memorial stone weighing two tons. The inscription reads:

*Borough of Plymouth Burrator Reservoir, commenced 1893, completed 1898. J T Bond Mayor and Chairman of the Water Committee 1891 – 1898. James Mansergh, Edward Sandeman, engineer*s. The stone was to be placed in the parapet of the bridge over the dam. Another stone was placed in the parapet nearer to the Sheepstor side, which reads:

Plymouth Corporation Water Works, Burrator Reservoir, 110 feet beneath lies the foundation stone of this embankment which was laid on the 24th day of July 1895. Names of the mayors and engineers are inscribed on the stone.

Sir Massey Lopes made a speech and presented the Mayor with a silver loving cup. The crowds cheered and applauded other speeches, although most of them could not hear a word of what was being uttered. The cheering of the crowds reached Sam and Sarah on the other side of the valley. A Baptist minister offered a long prayer, all joined in saying the Lord's Prayer and the ceremony ended. The crowds of visitors vanished back to Plymouth and the villagers and farmers of Sheepstor returned home.

In the evening a banquet was held in Plymouth Guildhall. For the first time on such an occasion ladies were invited. Their dresses brought a little more colour to the regulation black and white attire of the men. The toast list began with, '*The health of her Most Gracious Majesty the Queen and Royal family*'; no residents of Sheepstor were present.

One speech praised the army and navy forces in the region of the Nile under the generalship of Sir Herbert Kitchener.

'Looking at the dam at Burrator today,' the officer stated, 'I am reminded of the barrage which crosses the Nile below Cairo, and the best I can hope is that the town of Plymouth might increase in prosperity and riches in the same way as Egypt has prospered in consequence of that undertaking.'

There was much applause and praise for the engineering at Burrator after the dinner that evening.

At Sheepstor William and Thomas wandered across the bridge over the dam and looked up the valley, their valley. The river was snaking its way towards them, passing under the high ivy-covered arch of Sheepstor Bridge and proceeding below the new road by culvert beneath the dam.

William Shepherd and Thomas Creber were young men of seventeen, both doing a hard day's work on their tenanted farms. After work they went down to the river bank waiting for the valley to fill with water. The slopes and banks had been their childhood playground and the bridge over the river the spot where they had caught fish with string and pin. The boys used to have picnics on the banks and light fires to cook the brown trout they caught in the river.

'The water's creeping up the banks, Grandma,' William told her one evening. 'The water is flowing to town in pipes now so it will be clean when it gets there. It should never freeze up again.'

'What about the river bed below the dam, William?' Sarah asked.

'Not much water is flowing out at the moment but it picks up when Sheepstor Brook tumbles in from Burrator grounds. There's enough water flowing for Meavy mill leat to carry sufficient down to the mill. The Plymouth leat is nothing but a ditch now.'

William spent much of the day out on the moor. Sam worked near to home as he wasn't able to walk far from his farm. William was a good shepherd of his flock. His friend Thomas was not so fortunate. His family had to move out of Longstone and rent another farm out of the parish. Not much employment was to be had on nearby farms as each farmer had enough family of his own to manage his acres.

Sheepstor folk witnessed the flooding of their valley in the autumn and winter. For them the lake was not so much a thing of beauty as a covering up of their past. The natural filling of the valley brought problems, silt stirred up from the bed and animals wandered into the water, unable to get out. Gradually the machinery was removed and men ceased to work on the dam. Sheepstor would not be the same again but in the winter it retrieved some of its remoteness.

In February Sam caught a chill which developed into pneumonia. Sarah never left his side, day or night, but five days after William's eighteenth birthday Sam gasped his last breath.

'Your grandpa died the same day as your mother, William. It's hard to get a grave dug this time of the year.'

William asked no questions, it was not the time. This was the first occasion he remembered the date of his mother's death being mentioned. Sarah seldom spoke of his parents, and he never raised the matter.

'You are the man of the house now, William. We will manage as best we can.'

At Sam's burial Sarah remembered their wedding day forty years before. She reflected on their years together. Sarah's prayers were not for Sam that day but for William, that she might live until he found a good woman to care for him.

Sarah recalled the last words from the Book of Proverbs in the Old Testament: *'Who can find a virtuous woman? For her price is above rubies.'* Sarah regretted any hurt she may have caused Sam but she had been a good wife, knowing that Sam loved her dearly, even though he seldom expressed it. On her knees she prayed that William would stay with her to the end of her life.

Spring came again. Lambing occupied William's time. He did not labour for himself alone but for his grandmother and for the years ahead of him when he hoped to see the world. Meanwhile Middleworth was his home where he slept and ate and felt comfortable.

William had not had much fun in his life. Passing up the Deancombe valley he often visited his old home of Outhome where he had been born. He thought of his young parents and wished he knew what they looked like. For a long time, he had realised he looked different from other lads on the moor. But he was never able to ask his grandmother about them. All he knew of them he had picked up from village folk. He recalled the day when he was about nine years old. It was the beginning of a suspicion. William wanted to find out more about the boy who lived with the curate years ago. People in the village told him he looked like Esca Daykin so he confronted Sarah.

'Am I adopted, Grandma?' William had asked.

'Lord have mercy on you boy, what makes you say a thing like that?'

'People say I look like Esca Daykin and that he was adopted.'

'No, William, you are my own flesh and blood. You have always known Grandpa and me weren't your mum and dad, but we are your father's parents.'

'Why do I look different, then? Why do I look like this other boy?'

'Your mother was born in another country where old Rajah Brooke used to live and you are like her. Esca Daykin was born in that same country.'

Nothing more was said. There are such moments in life, touched on and passed by, but never forgotten.

33

WHEN she was alone, Sarah wept bitterly, for Sam, for Will and for Annie. Sam was eighty-two years old when he died, after a long hard life but he had always been there for her. William was not his son but he also grieved alone for his grandfather. Sam had been a father-figure and a companion whom William had looked up to. But the young man took over the running of the farm in his stride, stepping into Sam's shoes. Sarah gave up her cleaning job at Burrator and stayed at Middleworth farm to care for William.

William and Thomas met in Park Cottage Inn and made a new friend, Fred Brown from Meavy. His father was a journeying blacksmith, a branch of the Brown family who lived at the Smithy in Meavy. Occasionally a social was held at the inn when there was food and dancing. Young women from Meavy and Walkhampton, as well as from Sheepstor, came in groups to these events, walking and laughing along the lanes arm-in-arm. Among them was Fred Brown's sister, a pretty girl of seventeen with dark curly hair who came with her friends. William made sure to talk to Fred just to be near Ella.

On New Year's Day in 1900 the social was jollier than usual. William danced with Ella and told her about his work on the farm with his grandmother. Ella told him about the job she had at Meavy Parsonage, cleaning and scrubbing every day in the large old house. Reverend Tyacke was a kind employer, she told him. Ella was smitten by this good-looking young man whom she had never met before. He was unlike all the other lads, he was handsome and behaved like a gentleman. William walked to Meavy any evening he could following this first proper encounter so that he could meet Ella on Meavy Green with other young folk from the village.

It was not long before they were accepted as a couple though they never saw each other alone. Sarah was delighted that William had found a nice girl from a local family, a hard-working family. William needed a woman to care for him after she passed on.

Middleworth was an ancient farm and not far from the shores of the newly-formed lake. William kept his sheep on the high moor, much of his time spent repairing his hedges and stone walls to hold the sheep back from the water. Sarah, as she had done for Sam all her married life, dutifully cooked all his meals, washed his clothes, kept the house as clean and tidy and helped him outside when she was needed.

'Why don't you bring Fred and Ella to tea on Sunday?' Sarah asked. 'I'd like that.'

'Perhaps when I've got a bit more time,' William replied. 'I'm awfully busy this weekend.'

Though he loved to be with Ella, they had always been surrounded by friends and William was not yet sure of his feelings. His grandmother was the only woman he had really known. He had been shy with the girls at school who had teased him about the way he looked. If only he had a mother or a sister like other lads. Company enough for William during the day was his dog Shep who went with him everywhere. William had a good horse and he enjoyed putting it through its paces on the moor with Shep running at his side.

Fred and Ella asked William about his parents.

'I mentioned it to mother,' Fred told him. 'She said your father died young before you were born and your Ma died shortly after you were born in Outhome.'

'It's so sad,' Ella said. 'Fancy losing both your parents when you were a baby. Does it upset you, William?'

'Not really. It might have done if I'd got to know them, but I've always treated my grandparents like my mum and dad. My mother was only twenty and father not much older.'

William did not want to talk about them. He felt they were his secret.

'Grandma said my mother came from the country of the old Rajah, so I have Malay blood in me. Perhaps that what gives me the urge to travel.'

'You're not planning on going away, are you, William?' Ella enquired, alarmed.

'No, but I may one day. That's between the three of us, mind.'

When summer came, so did the visitors to see the lake. Surrounded by Dartmoor hills and tors the lake did indeed look very natural and those who had been to that country likened it to Switzerland. People walked from Dousland station across Yennadon for picnics near to the railway line, where they could look down on the still blue water reflecting the white clouds of the sky. Mrs Andrew in the cottage near the church served cups of tea to the visitors which rapidly became popular. Now that a road ran round the reservoir, visitors came for drives to admire the view. Undoubtedly, the roads had made life easier for Sheepstor folk. William bought a cart and another horse and was able to take Sarah into the village.

In the autumn and winter Sheepstor became remote once again. No more strangers on the roads in carriages, though groups of men would be seen walking out to the village and on Dartmoor. Not for mining, nor shooting, nor checking stock like the farmers but for pleasure.

'It beats me why any man should walk out over the hills to look at stones, William,' Thomas said one day after he had met three gentlemen who asked the way out to Yellowmead Circles.

'They were serious enough, I daresay. We take it all for granted. They probably know a lot more about the moor than we do who have lived here all our lives.'

Sabine Baring-Gould was one of those men, walking the moor for pleasure and restoring ancient monuments. Not only was he the vicar of Lew Trenchard in West Devon but a country gentleman and author of religious, travel and history books. Albert Prowse from Yennadon had driven him in his carriage to outlying villages, including Sheepstor, where Baring-Gould listened to folk-songs, collecting the words and music for posterity. Nursemaid to his two youngest children of fourteen, John and Grace, was Lily Salter, known to many in Sheepstor. She listened to him as he read her hymns he had written such as *Onward Christian Soldiers* and *Now The Day Is Over*. Sheepstor was a place of inspiration for this great man; in return, he not only produced books about the village but gave generously for the church's restoration. The story went that, meeting Lily with his own children in his home village one day, he enquired of her whose little ones they were, his mind obviously elsewhere! Sheepstor captivated the priest as it did many other men of note, with its antiquity and beauty. The tiny village was on the map to be explored.

In the year when the river valley at Sheepstor was filled with water, the Venerable W Y Daykin married for the second time. He was sixty-six and his parishioner and new wife, Hannah, was twenty-seven. Whether he ever knew of the flooding of the land he had rented near Narrator, no one knows. He had no contacts with Sheepstor from the time he left the village for the second time. Hannah Daykin gave him four sons in his old age and with this young family of his own he had little time for Esca and Edith Brooke Daykin who now, too, had a son and three daughters of their own.

In Sarawak, Vyner Brooke was being trained by his father to be the heir of the Sarawak throne. In the wet season in Borneo, from October to March, Rajah Charles left his country and spent the time in Cirencester, leaving his son in charge. But kicking his heels in England did not suit him, especially when Vyner took it upon himself to act as he thought best. Charles hurried back to Sarawak as soon as the weather in the tropics had improved. He enjoyed the power he had over his people too much to stay away, bitterly resenting what he saw as his son's interference.

The second white Rajah had not only taken many Dyak mistresses over the years but insisted on flaunting them, quite brazenly in front of his long-suffering wife. A good many children in the country were known to be of Brooke descent. Yet in later life he took on a distinctly bizarre and gruesome countenance following a riding accident in Wiltshire in which he lost the sight of an eye. With one empty eye socket he visited a taxidermist where he purchased a variety of fearsome looking glass eyes. His family found him totally unapproachable.

A poem written by Beatrice Chase on Dartmoor

The Music of Dawn

O the cuckoos mock my cuckoo clock

As the cuckoo clock strikes four,

And then there's a hush until the thrush

And his mate their songs outpour.

There comes the note from the brazen throat

Of the cock in the snug thatched farm

He is safe shut in, so his cheery din

Can do no sleeper harm.

But cuckoo is first to lead the burst

Of music from the moor and tree,

While it's still quite dark before the lark

Has left his nest on the lea.

Then blackbirds wake for the dawn's sweet sake,

And pipe and whistle and trill

While the curlew's cry down the sleep-flushed sky

Is echoed from hill to hill.

O I would not miss the daily bliss

Of the joyous songs without words,

Spontaneous praise in the gold May days,

From the glad wild Dartmoor birds.

34

THE month of May brings a carpet of bluebells in Burrator Woods. Walking home from Meavy, William admired the beauty of nature. The vivid haze of the flowers, the heady woodland scents and fresh green of the new leaves on the trees all filled him with a feeling of wellbeing.

Now a young man in his early twenties, he yearned for more adventure in his life. William worked hard in the daytime, went to church on Sundays and met up with friends two evenings each week. He was now a member of the bellringing team in Sheepstor and enjoyed the company of the other men. Many a time he would muse on the tales he had been told and never forgotten, of the adventures of Rajah James Brooke.

'If I had been born into a rich family maybe I would have sailed away,' he thought to himself. 'I wonder what happened to my mother's parents? They were kind to me in London all those years ago.'

Perhaps he did not seek such excitement as fighting head-hunters and pirates but there was a whole world to explore and maybe one day, just maybe, he would cross the seas. All this he kept to himself. Sarah always wanted to know where her grandson went and who he was to meet. He loved her dearly but also needed his own company. He would never do anything, however, to upset his grandmother.

The bells in the tower had not been pealed for years as the condition of the frame and fittings were in a dangerous state. With funds collected from the congregation and landowners, the five bells had been rehung and a new ringing team formed. Many of the old ringers willingly taught William and his friends the art of ringing. Room had been left in the belfry for a sixth bell when more funds could be raised.

A bishop had not been seen in Sheepstor church for more than thirty years. But on the occasion of the repair of the bells the Bishop of Exeter was to visit the village. The diocesan bishop, Dr Robertson, arrived at the Vicarage, now home to Reverend and Mrs Leigh Murray, on a January afternoon in 1904. At the service he dedicated the rehanging of the bells, accompanied by ten local clergymen from neighbouring parishes.

'In the beautiful moorland scenery and moorland air,' the bishop said in his sermon, 'the bells harmonise with the scene. The sound of the bells calls the parish to worship at church or to private prayer in their work out on the hills.'

At the social held in the parish hall after the service the villagers danced, sang songs and recited some witty poems.

'It's a good evening, Ella,' William said as he danced with her around the room. 'The fiddlers are certainly keeping us on our toes.'

'Yes, it is,' Ella answered breathlessly. 'Were you ringing the bells yesterday? They sounded lovely.'

'I was part of our team. Ringers came in from Bickleigh, Walkhampton and

Meavy as well. Peals were rung for most of the day.'

When they were seated William told her what the bishop had quoted in his sermon, from a poem by Alfred Lord Tennyson. *'Ring out the false, ring in the true'*, I reckon that's a good way to think of the church bells, isn't it, Ella?'

William and his friends sometimes walked up Portland Lane and turning left onto Ringmoor Down looked into the valley below. The cottages of Sheepstor clustered around the old granite church, with its tower surmounted by four pinnacles adorned with crockets and finials, all set against their backdrop of the massive Sheeps Tor and the shining blue of Burrator Lake, looked stunning.

The young people remarked on how natural the lake looked, twisting above the old bed of the River Mew. They looked down on the wooded valley below Burrator dam, all that was left now of the gorge, and saw the fields of so many farms spread beneath the high moorland hills of Dartmoor.

William knew who owned every field in the valley. Sheep, cattle and ponies were all marked with each farmer's individual markings, he knew them all. The insular society would never be as close as it was before the building of the dam but it was still an out-of-the-way community. Sarah liked Ella and could not help looking on her almost as a daughter. She was doing all she could to encourage William to marry her and settle in Middleworth farmhouse. It was an ancient granite building but Sir Massey Lopes had considerably improved the living conditions.

Almost three years were to pass before a treble bell was added in the tower. Every parishioner had contributed to its cost and they all crowded into the church for the dedication ceremony. Reverend Sabine Baring-Gould was there along with seven other vicars in the area. Mrs Murray, the vicar's wife, played the organ, the choir led the singing and during the hymn, *O Praise ye the Lord,* the clergy went in procession to the tower. The new bell was sounded, followed by a short burst of the whole peal. Baring-Gould preached his sermon on the theme that education without religion was like a peal of bells out of tune.

'You,' he said, 'the people of Sheepstor, saved enough money to add this bell in your tower however full of labour, toil, pleasure, pain, joy or sorrow in your life.'

His text was the ninety-second Psalm: *'It is a good thing to give thanks unto the Lord, upon instruments. He is my rock and there is no unrighteousness in him.'*

'How lovely to hear six bells ringing out,' Sarah said over a cup of tea in the vicarage, to which everyone had been invited.

A few days after Christmas, Sheepstor learned of the passing of Baroness Angela Burdett-Coutts in her ninety-second year. In her mind, Sarah always thought of her as ABC. It was reported that the lady had died in her London home, 1 Stratton Street, Piccadilly, of acute bronchitis. In the newspaper it was recorded that thirty thousand persons, rich and poor, paid their last respects to her while her body lay in state for two days. Her body was buried in Westminster Abbey, in the nave near the west door, in January 1907.

Her memorial stone in the floor bears the inscription, Baroness Burdett-

Coutts 1814–1906. This almost forgotten lady did much for the Church of England in the nineteenth century and entertained the great and famous in her homes. Street names bear her name in England and the Burdett-Coutts School thrives in London. In Canada, the two towns of Burdett and Coutts were named after her.

In that year a new vicar was appointed to Sheepstor. He was the Reverend Hugh Breton who was delighted to live amongst the hills of Dartmoor. One of his first duties, to Sarah's joy, was to perform the marriage ceremony of William Thomas Shepherd and Ella Mary Brown. Their courtship had been a long quiet one, the two young people becoming really good friends and soulmates. William was in his thirtieth year and a well-liked farmer in the Deancombe valley.

The wedding took place in Sheepstor church at four o'clock in the afternoon of Saturday, 7 May 1910. At this hour, in St James's Palace in London, the announcement was being made of the accession of King George V. His father, Edward VII, had died just before midnight at Buckingham Palace. There was no mourning at Sheepstor that afternoon as the news of the king's death had not reached the moorland village.

Ella had many family members at the happy occasion, enough to fill the little church, but William's only close relative was his grandmother, Sarah. The little old lady looked pleased and happy in her best coat and hat which she had decorated with flowers and ribbons. Many of the Creber family sat with her in church. Mr and Mrs Breton provided tea and cake after the ceremony and the vicar persuaded Sarah to stay and talk with them afterwards about their new parish.

'You and Ella get off home, William,' Hugh Breton said smiling to the happy pair. 'I'm sure you've got plenty to do. I'll bring Sarah home later.'

'Thank you, Sir,' William said gratefully, shaking the vicar's hand. 'Thank you for all you've done for us today.'

He liked this new vicar and could not see why some thought him unapproachable. At the old doorway of Middleworth farm, he scooped Ella up and carried her over the threshold. Laughing happily, they changed into their working clothes.

The beautiful flowers that decorated the church at the wedding were removed for the Sunday service, during which Mr Breton told the congregation that the world was in mourning for the late king. 'His body is to be taken by the Royal train to Windsor for burial in St George's Chapel,' he announced.

A tragedy closer to home touched hearts in Sheepstor more deeply than the royal death. This was the death of Isaac Moses, a farmer in Dousland of the same age as Sarah. Crossing the railway branch line on Yennadon Down with his flock of sheep, and being hard of hearing, he did not hear the engine of the delayed Princetown train speeding around a corner. Isaac was killed with many of his flock of sheep. Sarah, William and Ella Shepherd attended the funeral service for their old friend in St Peter's, Meavy.

Sarah was getting old and welcomed Ella wholeheartedly into the family. Just as Sarah had so many years before, Ella enjoyed helping her husband out on the farm, as well as being in the company of her grandmother-in-law indoors. The Brown family from Meavy often called at Middleworth to see Ella and this gave Sarah much pleasure. All she secretly longed for now was a great-grandchild before she left this world.

William was told that Ernest Prowse, whom he knew quite well, was emigrating to Canada and taking his father with him.

'What would you say if we went to Canada one day, Ella, and made a new life for ourselves?' William asked his wife.

'Well, I've always known your wish to travel, William, but your grandmother is too old to begin life in a new world. You wouldn't leave her, would you?'

'No, you know that but I thought that I should put the idea into your head.'

'The Prowse family have money, too. We would have to *work* our passage to Canada. I'm enjoying being your wife and love to care for you and Sarah.'

Nothing more was said of emigrating to Canada or anywhere else for many years.

Mr Breton enjoyed visiting Sarah Shepherd and in the year after William and Ella's wedding he brought the newspaper to read her the announcement of Vyner Brooke's marriage.

'That is thoughtful of you, Sir. You know I worked for the old Rajah and I met this young man's parents when they spent their honeymoon at Burrator,' Sarah said, remembering how she kept Annie hidden from the sight of the second Rajah.

'He's married Sylvia Brett, daughter of Lord Esher. Quite a society wedding, I expect.'

'I hope they'll be very happy, I'm sure,' Sarah replied.

Mr Breton found out much about the Deancombe valley and this corner of Dartmoor from the old lady. He made notes about Harry Terrell, the old Rajah and the past curates and vicars of his parish. This vicar took a keen interest in the school, replaced the old pump with a new one and placed a seat around the tree in the school yard.

35

T HE vicar of Sheepstor was determined to raise funds for the repair of the carved oak screen between the nave and chancel. The church had no dedication but because of St Leonard's Well, it was presumed to be dedicated to St Leonard, patron saint of prisoners. Hugh Breton made acquaintance with Sabine Baring-Gould, vicar of Lew Trenchard and both decided to write booklets about the moor to raise funds for the costly work.

Hugh Breton wrote short guide books on Dartmoor which were sold in bookshops in Plymouth, Torquay and Exeter and by the villagers, who dispensed tea and refreshments to visitors. These booklets were illustrated by Charles E. Brittan, who with his wife Ada and two young children, Ethel Betty and Charles, rented the old Rajah's house at Burrator. His father, Charles Edward senior, had also been a Dartmoor artist. Sheepstor folk were pleased the little books came from men in their midst.

They were amazed to see so many travelling to Dartmoor in motor cars and charabancs, crossing the upper moorland on the two roads from Moretonhampstead or Ashburton to Tavistock or Yelverton. With his clerical friend and two other lovers of Dartmoor, Robert Burnard and Hansford Worth, the vicar of Sheepstor explored the moor re-erecting fallen ancient monuments.

The vicar had long talks with Sarah when he visited her at Middleworth and in one of his little books described the walk she had undertaken for so many years when she walked from Outhome to Burrator:

One of the most charming walks from Sheepstor is over the southern shoulder of the tor into the Deancombe valley. Follow the track along the wall above Yellowmead. When the wall goes no further, keep straight on and strike the wall in front. Then follow this wall over a stream, and keep to it till the track passes through a gate into a grassy field with several large boulders in it. Then descend into the valley. The view down the valley is exceedingly fine.

Above, beneath, immensely spread,
Valleys and hoary rocks I view.'

Mr Breton read his notes to Sarah for her approval.

'Fancy anyone walking that way for pleasure,' Sarah declared. 'I walked that way to work in all weathers, sometimes with two little 'uns holding my skirts. How times have changed.'

'Do you want to speak of your two children you lost, Sarah. Or is it still painful?' The vicar had been told only gossip about Sarah Shepherd.

'It's thirty years ago now and best forgotten. I don't know what I should do without William and Ella.'

'William tells me there will soon be another Shepherd in the house. That must give you great joy.'

'Oh, it does. Ella is a girl after my own heart. I do so hope this country doesn't go to war, Sir.'

'I think it will, but we can only pray that it is not for long.'

The nurse from Clearbrook walked to Sheepstor on a lovely autumn day when she was told that Ella Shepherd had gone into labour. In her experience she would be there in plenty of time for this first baby in the family. Fred Brown had called on her to attend his sister. Sarah had pans of hot water ready on the stove and plenty of towels, recalling her labour with this baby's grandfather at Outhome and how overjoyed she and Sam had been when Will was born. William busied himself in the yard with Shep at his heels. Sarah and Ella's mother were having a cup of tea when they heard the baby's cry.

'Let William go to her, Alice. We'll know soon enough.'

Thomas Frederick Shepherd was a peaceful quiet baby. With a mass of dark hair and bright blue eyes he slept, drank and lay contentedly where he was put down. Middleworth Farm was constantly full of visitors and days were never lonely. William and Ella found much joy in their son and their family was established.

The screen was put in the church that year and in the month of May was dedicated to the memory of Sir Massey Lopes and Robert Bayly by the Bishop of Exeter. Mr Breton took the pamphlet containing the names of three hundred subscribers to show Sarah Shepherd.

'There you are, Sarah, the task that I visualised has come about. You see we raised £474.'

'It's wonderful, Mr Breton, and it looks very fine in the church. Would you kindly read me this little book?'

'I will read you the front page and some of the names that will interest you.'

Mr Breton read that Frederick Bligh Bond designed the screen and Herbert Read of Exeter constructed it: *'Funds remaining will be used for the reseating of the church with oak seats with finely carved bench ends,'* he read. *'This work will begin soon and the carving on the bench ends will illustrate the history of the English Church from its foundation to the present day.'*

'I shall be at the dedication, God willing,' Sarah proclaimed. 'You have done a good job.'

'Teas will be in St Leonard's Room after the service at sixpence each. Now let me read you some of the subscribers.'

The vicar read out names of the parishioners and of Sir Henry Lopes, the Bayly family and His Highness the Rajah of Sarawak.

'There are nearly one hundred parsons listed, Sarah, for each donating a half-crown. I asked them when I visited their churches,' he said with a smile. 'Here is a name you will recognise – Henry Terrell Peard.'

'Oh, I am glad he gave. It is good to think of Maggie's boy in part of the screen.'

'Miss Devitte at school gave seven pence to make up the children's pennies to a half-crown. The children's names put down are R Dark, M Pearse, G Matthews, T Matthews, M Moses, D Moses, W Manning, D Nelder, V Nelder, May Nelder, K Nelder and M Nelder.'

'May I keep this booklet, Mr Breton? It's a lovely drawing of the screen.'

'Yes, of course, Sarah. HMS *Indus* sent a contribution. Have you heard of that ship?'

'It was the ship on which Rajah Charles left Sarawak with his family and Esca to come to England, before his three little 'uns died. Fancy they sending you money.'

'Even the architect's mother is listed, as well as two Members of Parliament, Henry Hurrell the Mayor of Plymouth and Charles and Ada Brittan at Burrator.'

'All for our church, it is humbling.'

'And to the greater glory of God, Sarah,' the vicar added.

In the following year, when Britain was still at war, news reached the parish of the death of their one-time curate, the Venerable William Daykin, in Canada. His second wife, Hannah, and their three surviving sons were with him when he died. Mr Breton said prayers for his soul on Sunday. He had been told that his vicarage had once been the home of this curate who had sold it to the living for the purpose. This young curate, friend of Sir James Brooke who became an archdeacon and a missionary, had adopted the illegitimate first-born son of the present Rajah.

'I have seen a portrait of Archdeacon Daykin,' proclaimed Mr Breton to his parishioners. 'It hangs in the vestry of Stoke Fleming church where he was rector before holding the position of curate in this village.'

In 1917 the newspapers reported the death of Rajah Charles Brooke in Cirencester, England on 17 May. Now that his birth father and his adopted father had both died, Esca Brooke Daykin set about finding out about his birth in Sarawak, hoping for some recognition from the famous Brooke family. Although Esca received payment from the Sarawak government they considered it was perhaps circumspect if he kept his birth private. The body of Rajah Charles was embalmed. He wished to be buried in Sarawak but the events of the war made this impossible at that time.

Far away in Sheepstor, Sarah delighted in little Tommy's company as he sat on her lap to hear stories about his daddy. A few days after Tommy's third birthday, at the age of eighty, Sarah passed peacefully away in her sleep. In her last years, sufferings and sorrows turned to joy. The little child missed her and William wept.

Mr Breton took the funeral service and Sarah was buried in the same grave as Sam, next to Annie, near the church wall beyond which the body of Will was buried. Fallen leaves covered the ground and the air carried the sweet smell of damp earth. The church was full of folk from the parishes of Sheepstor, Meavy and Walkhampton. Sarah took to her grave truths which no living person could even guess. William and Ella could never bring themselves to ask her the many questions in their minds. Their son Tom looked like his father. He was a handsome little boy with slight Malayan features. Ella could see the serious look in his eyes that she found so appealing in William.

Plymouth Corporation Water Works had placed granite upright stones on land around the catchment area which they had purchased. The stones, marked PCWW 1917, were to show that all water that fell on the land within this boundary flowed into the reservoir and became drinking water for the townspeople of Plymouth, Stonehouse and Devonport, known as Three Towns. But it was becoming clear that demand was already outstripping supply.

Ella and William already talked openly about moving to Canada. When talk reached their ears that there was not enough water stored in the reservoir for the ever expanding populations of these towns, they knew life at Middleworth would soon be at an end.

'There's talk of raising the dam ten feet. They say that will double its capacity. We're almost at the lake's edge now so we'll surely have to go,' William said to his friends in Park Cottage.

What no one suspected was that the Water Corporation was planning to evict everyone who lived in dwellings within the whole catchment area. All agriculture activity was to be suspended on these thousands of acres. The justification for this action – hygiene and sanitary reasons it was claimed – made no sense to the inhabitants of the valleys.

'Why on earth do we all have to stop farming, William?' Ella asked her husband. 'It doesn't make sense to me.'

'Nor to anyone else, Ella.'

'The moorland will become overgrown and unmanageable in a short space of time, and where will we all go?'

'It will break the hearts of the older ones. I'm glad my grandparents aren't here to witness such stupidity.'

'Every family in the valleys has lived on this land for generations,' Ella stated sadly.

'The new landowners don't understand Dartmoor. Water flowing over granite purifies itself and anyhow it is filtered before it enters the pipes under the dam. It's madness.'

'And what of Tom's future, William? What will we have to pass on to him?'

'I reckon the time has come for us to think seriously of going to Canada, Ella. If you're in agreement I will look into the cost of passages for the three of us. I know you'll miss your family but there is nothing left for us in Sheepstor.'

'We have the animals to sell and our tools, there may be enough.'

'We'll at least get some compensation if we leave quietly. It may take a few years, so don't upset yourself yet. Talk to your family about our plans.'

'I will. Let's not mention it to Tom just yet. He will want to tell all his friends.'

'This war will have to be over first. What a world we live in, Ella.'

36

ONE day in 1918 the valleys of Sheepstor echoed with the piercing sound of the steam whistle. The engine driver of the train blew the whistle almost constantly on his journey from Dousland to Princetown. It was the signal that all had been waiting for, the war was over. Folk in their isolated farms rushed out in excitement at the long-awaited signal. There was not one household that did not know a young man fighting for his country.

That evening William and the other bellringers pealed the church bells in jubilation. It was more than a year, however, before the young men who had gone to war were back home again on the moor.

Sheepstor was once a thriving community when tin mines were working and the wool trade was flourishing. Though so out of the way, it provided a place of shelter and refreshment for the wool-traders en route between the abbeys of Buckfast, Buckland and Tavistock.

Centuries ago travellers found hospitality at the ale house next to the church with its tall tower, built with money from rich merchants and tinners, in thankfulness and to the Glory of God. Loaded pack-horses, joined together in long trains, needed to rest and graze, men required rest and sustenance. This was at a time when there were perhaps twenty sheep farms in the Mew valley. The tiny moorland village remained at the heart of the wool trade but could not survive the twin blows as its young men went off to fight and sheep farmers in the valleys were forced off land their families had farmed for generations. After the First World War its decline was sealed.

The old yeomen of the moor lie in Sheepstor churchyard, many without a memorial stone to show where they were laid to rest. Above the porch of the church is a stone skull and crossbones, representing wheat sprouting from eye-sockets and three Latin inscriptions. One translates, *Death is the gate of Life*. This was probably moved from a tomb within the church as it bears the initials of John Elford.

All around the parish lies evidence of man's labours; farmers, shepherds and stockmen caring for the thousands of animals out on the moor in all weathers; blacksmiths caring for the horses and mending tools and machinery; stone-masons cutting and shaping granite, building the numerous bridges over leats and streams; tin miners walking miles each day to the gruelling work and dangers before them.

Men worked from eight in the morning until five in the evening, six days a week, for about £2 10s. The weekly wage had to support large families and fathers were rarely seen by their children. The working man had to walk to where he could find work which was sometimes up to ten miles away.

'How do the Water Corporation expect animals not to enter the watershed, William? I cannot understand the necessity to clear the moor for the reservoir.' Ella and William were discussing the recent rumours in the village.

'Not after the area has already been the water catchment for twenty-five years, Ella. There are new people in charge, I suppose. They must be crazed.'

'Perhaps they think the creatures will see the PCWW stones and walk the other way,' Ella laughed.

'It's obvious they don't understand the way of life out here, Ella,' William said.

They were sitting in their usual chairs, each side of the fire place. The logs in the hearth smouldered and William placed a peat turf in the fire to keep it in until morning.

'It's nearly dark, Ella, let's to bed.'

'Tom went to sleep at once tonight, I'm glad all this upset isn't worrying him.'

Tomorrow was another day. A day nearer to their departure from their homeland.

William and Tom made a list of their outside possessions. One hundred sheep, one home cow and calf, three horses and Tom's pony, one pig, five ducks, thirty or so hens, a farm cart and many hand tools and implements, most of these passed down from Sam.

The Water Corporation issued the summons to all farmers still living in the Mewy valley in 1921. Every farmer had to leave his home and all agriculture must cease. Even the church authorities and the education board had a hand in the further destruction of the little community. Sheepstor Church was to be combined with the parish of Meavy and a new clergyman, Reverend Ernest Hughes, was to live with his family at Meavy Parsonage next to the Royal Oak Inn where Ella had once worked for the Tyackes. Sheepstor's school was to close down and all its pupils would have to walk daily to Meavy school next to the village green. Reverend Hugh Breton and his wife left Sheepstor village in great sadness for the incumbency of Dean Prior near Buckfastleigh on the other side of the moor.

One of the first duties of the vicar had been to marry William and Ella and strangely, one of his last was to conduct the burial of Charles Brooke, second white Rajah of Sarawak. With the war still in force when he died, permission had not been granted for his body to be, as he wished, taken by ship to Sarawak. He had wanted a stirring funeral to impress the natives who had idolised him but as the years passed by, and the third Rajah was installed, his family decided to bury him in Sheepstor next to the first Rajah in the month of June, two years after his death. The coffin was made of very fine grained Sarawak wood and, arriving the day before the burial, the body remained in the church over night. His widow Margaret, and the third Rajah Vyner Brooke and his wife Sylvia, attended the burial.

His tombstone was quarried, more appropriately than that of his uncle's, from the granite tor above the churchyard. The enormous grey granite boulder was dragged down the rocky hillside by William and men of the parish, using a sledge pulled by eleven horses.

It was also one of William's last accomplishments in the parish.

'It was a mighty difficult task, Ella,' he told her at the end of the day when the men had fixed the boulder over the grave, days after the Brookes had left the area. 'We had all taken our horses to pull the sledge but every man had to hold on to the rock over the bumpy ground. We eventually got it down to the wall but then we had to knock the wall down to drag it through to the grave.'

'Is it secure?' Ella asked him.

'Yes,' William explained. 'There was a crack on one side so we turned it over to rest on that side and the Crebers cut a very good edging around the rock. I've been helping to build up the wall again.'

If he had but known it, William had stood above the very spot where his father Will was buried. Such mysteries and secrets were held back from the living.

Park Cottage Inn was allowed to continue selling beer until the enlargement of the reservoir was completed. The moorland was now desolate, the valleys deathly and the people destitute.

It was not only the waters of the River Mew that filled the reservoir. Streams flowed into the river and in most of these valleys farmsteads had been built and fields cultivated. The principal streams were Double Waters near to the head of the river below Princetown, Hartor Brook, Stenlake, Riddypit Stream, Newleycombe Lake, Combeshead Brook, Deancombe Brook, Outhome Brook, Narrator Brook, Vinney Lake and Sheepstor Brook. All but the last emptied into the reservoir, meaning eviction for every farming family thereabouts.

Stenlake farm, in the upper reach of the Mew, was a long way from Burrator Dam but still the Gayden family received notice to quit. Like many farms on the moor, the house had been built next to the older farm building which had been a longhouse. The children there walked up over the moor and down to Walkhampton school. The farmhouse was positioned between the River Mew and the Devonport Leat which had once flowed speedily and silently towards the dock on the coast. Now it had been diverted into the reservoir, making a cascade down over rocks and passing beneath the road into the lake. Though the house was not far from the main Dousland to Princetown road on the moor, care was needed to avoid the marsh around the Stenlake stream.

Provisions were brought to the house once a week from the stores at Princetown as they had been to the former farmers, the Gill family. Frank Hodges was the delivery man at the stores and he timed his visit to Stenlake soon after midday in anticipation of hot apple pie and a mug of cider each week. Just one more person and business to deplore the clearing out of the farms and their families. Mr Gayden sold all his stock at Tavistock market and the family prepared to move out. Dorothy helped her mother to dispose of all the clothes and footwear they had accumulated over the years, conveniently disposing of them in large pits dug by Mr Gayden in the marsh nearby.

'That's one good thing about moving,' Mrs Gayden said to anyone she met. 'We've got rid of things we don't really need.'

It was the only good thing anyone else could think of as well.

Farmers in the Newleycombe valley likewise prepared to leave their homes. There were more crops grown in this valley as the land was a little easier to cultivate. Now the struggle to grow corn and root crops had come to nothing. Old Mrs Pearse at Kingsett had called all her nine children in from the moor by blowing a whistle. Her son and his wife did the same with their family and the children played on the same large beech tree that others down the generations had played on. John remembered fixing the swing on one of the branches. It was heartbreaking at sixty years of age to uproot from the family home, with all its memories and start again.

Kingsett was a long way up this valley and, like other farmers, the Pearses could not see how they impaired the purity of the water for people on the coast. Next to the house was a deep pit, a relic of the tinners, over which John Pearse had placed a safety cover. A ladder inside the pit enabled the family to store milk, cream and butter perfectly in the cool interior before taking it to sell at market. Farmers on the moor were enterprising and independent.

Deancombe valley was secretive, hidden and sheltered. Here too, farmers including the Shepherds prepared to leave their farms. All, that is, except one. Dickie Pengelly, as all his neighbours knew, was refusing to leave his farm at Combeshead near Outhome. He was a widower, aged eighty, and his son William, known to family and friends as Gilly, lived with him. Gilly worked out at Ditsworthy Warren and helped his father with his sheep but was at heart a rabbit man with no desire to run the farm.

'I shan't leave Combeshead,' Dickie said to William Shepherd out on the moor when they met riding out to see their sheep. 'Not until they carry me out in a box.'

He said the same to Mr Shillibeer and anyone else who called on him from the Corporation. Officials called on him, wrote letters and tried to reason with him but the old man refused to budge. Letters were destroyed unopened. After discussions they consented to leave him at Combeshead as long as he sold all his animals. Dickie sold some, gave others away and shot the rest.

Dickie's neighbours admired the old man. He was able to tell the Shepherds about Canada. Dickie had emigrated to Ontario when he was a young man, and Gilly had been born there in 1886.

Letters were written by Mr Breton to Devon County Education Committee. On 9 March 1923 the vicar wrote: '*If the school of Sheepstor is closed it will be entirely against the wishes of the Managers.*' To no avail, the school ceased at the end of the year. The teacher, Miss Devitte, requested to be excused from paying her last quarter's rent to cover her moving expenses, this was refused and she left the village.

37

TOM Shepherd was nine years old and for a few weeks he walked to Meavy school before the family sailed away to Canada. It was the month of May and the woodlands were again full of flowers and birds. He and his friends took the footpath to Meavy from Portland Lane, where the woods were a carpet of bluebells, collecting the Palmer children at Yeo farm. They returned home together after school by the path from the blacksmith's shop at Meavy which followed the River Mew up to Burrator Dam. Too young to appreciate that perhaps he might never see anywhere so enchanting again, Tom took the rocky woodland paths and scenery for granted.

Fred drove William, Ella and Tom to Horrabridge station in his horse and cart. So many tears had been shed by Ella with her parents Isaac and Alice Brown that she was tired and exhausted before the beginning of the sea voyage.

'I shall never see you again,' Alice Brown had sobbed.

'Don't, Mam. Lots who have gone abroad have come back again. Pengellys, Vanstones and Smales to name a few. I shall write you letters. You must get someone to write to me for you. Eileen Hughes at the Parsonage will write for you.'

'And what about Richard Moses,' William added. 'He's crossed the Atlantic Ocean six times.'

They were all reminded of Mr Moses, now seventy-three and living with his stepson and his family at Torr Farm in Buckland Monachorum. As a boy he went to Sheepstor school and worked with his grandfather for, like William, his parents had died. He had emigrated to America where he worked on a farm and made enough money to return to Sheepstor to marry the girl he loved on Dartmoor. She was Annie Bowden, and within weeks they were travelling back to America. After sixteen years they sold their farm and returned to Sheepstor to see their families. Once again they set sail for America but their little son Willy had died, followed shortly by Annie. Richard returned home alone. He married a widow with a young son and never crossed the Atlantic for a seventh time. Alice Brown was somewhat comforted by this knowledge.

Still, the little family looked forlorn on the platform at Horrabridge Station.

'Two and a half singles to Plymouth, please,' William had said to the man in the ticket office.

The big engine puffed into the station, Fred made his farewells, bags loaded into the guard's van and they were on their way.

At the docks they boarded the Canadian steamship *Metagama* which had begun its journey in Glasgow, calling at Plymouth en route to Vancouver. With dozens of other families embarking on a new life they felt less lonesome. William and Tom loved the crossing of the Atlantic but from the outset Ella had been sick and miserable. She stayed below deck in her bunk for most of the long voyage and there was nothing William or Tom could do to help her plight.

As Tom grew up he wanted to find out about his past but his parents genuinely could not help him. Unable to ask any other members of his family or friends, or visit graveyards to find his ancestors, he put his past behind him. With the love of his wife Beth, one of the pioneer women in British Columbia, the Second World War, hard work and the birth of his daughter Alice, life was too full for him to worry about life in a remote village on Dartmoor.

The raising of the two dams of Burrator and Sheepstor was well under way. The engineers, twenty-five years earlier, had anticipated the need for an increase in capacity in the future and with a large workforce of men, the task was comparatively easy. Fred Brown worked on raising the Sheepstor dam. His father could well manage without him in his journeying blacksmith's work as there were so few horses left in the area.

Park Cottage Inn, its eight-roomed house conveniently placed between the reservoir and the village, enjoyed a good trade again whilst the work was in progress and Josiah Nelder was a jovial innkeeper. Josiah's three daughters had to walk with their friends from the village to Meavy school every day. The two villages were integrating in many respects as both communities were diminishing. Houses were being built by the council next to Meavy Green to enable young families to rent the properties and stay in the village but in Sheepstor there was no such housing.

A railway platform was built on the GWR on the hill above the dam, named Burrator and Sheepstor Halt. Steps up to the platform and iron kissing-gates were placed on either side of the wooden structure. The train was useful to the workers who were able to afford the fare. Farmers and warreners who took animals to market at Tavistock or Plymouth found the station a great help. From the other direction, walkers and sightseers took pleasure in alighting at the station on the moor.

In December 1925 Meavy's old school closed down and the new school for Meavy and Sheepstor opened after the New Year. Men from both villages had laid the foundations for the new school near the smithy, working through the summer evenings after a long day's work in the fields and on the moor. Wives and mothers kept them supplied with pasties, and drinks materialised each evening.

The women of the two villages at this time formed a group affiliated to the Women's Institute, the WI, holding their first meeting in the old school in the New Year. Their husbands had met in the inns but this was the first time, apart from church services, that the women gathered together. Home life, children and cooking were the main topics discussed before a cup of tea was served and Sheepstor women walked home the few miles up by the river to their homes. Some afternoons the women went on the moor to gather flowers or mosses at the request of the Red Cross society.

Up at the dams work was nearly completed. News reached the workers that the TUC had called for a nationwide stoppage in British industry to support coal miners. For nine days in May industrial life was brought to a standstill, but not so in Sheepstor. Work did not cease at Burrator. The final stage at the dam was the removing of the spillway arches for the road to be heightened. For this purpose a suspension bridge was placed upstream from Burrator dam to allow entry into the village.

Motor cars and tractors were replacing the horses in Sheepstor but large notices at the bridge prohibited heavy vehicles. Perhaps because he was unable to read or did not realise the weight of his vehicle, Mr Lillicrap crossed the bridge with his steam traction engine pulling a threshing machine, stretching the cables on the bridge almost beyond repair. Such events caused major excitement in Sheepstor.

Young lads from Meavy and Dousland walked to Sheepstor after school to help with the hay harvest in the summer though the only fields left to harvest in the upper Mew valley were those of Burrator, belonging to the Nicolson family. In the autumn, the boys helped to collect in the bracken which had been cut by their fathers on the moor then piled it high on carts to be taken to farms off the moor for animal bedding. Piling the ferns at a great height, the boys then clambered on top for the ride home. Holding on to the high wooden sides of the cart they were always in good spirits as their fathers drove the shire horses down to the reservoir. Crossing the lake on the suspension bridge was a jolly jape.

It was dark by the time they were on their way home and as the bridge swayed beneath the weight of the animals and vehicle the boys could not help but be awestruck by the effect of the moon reflected in the lake, the five arches of the dam nearing completion and the silhouette of the dark tors rising behind them. The impression of this journey home never left the boys and collecting ferns at Sheepstor was a favourite annual event.

The towns of Plymouth, Devonport and Stonehouse had merged and work at the reservoir was essential for the burgeoning city. Hot, dry summers had also depleted the water storage. The enlarged lake looked even more beautiful, naturally filling the old river valley. The work was done, men finished work and moved away.

Fred Brown, on one of his visits to Tavistock Goosey Fair in October, met Eve. To his astonishment her name was Eve Shepherd. Neither she nor her family even knew of the existence of the Shepherds who had lived in the Deancombe valley. Fred and Eve were married in Tavistock Parish Church when the dam was completed. Alice Brown corresponded with her daughter Ella in Canada and was able to report on the Shepherd family's progress to the women of Sheepstor at the WI meetings. Eileen Hughes had left Meavy so Eve took on the role of writing to Ella for her mother-in-law.

At the official opening ceremony at Burrator, thousands of people gathered around the enlarged reservoir. More than a dozen motor buses were filled with invited guests and in convoy the visitors were driven around the perimeter road. Vinneylake farm, once secluded, was now on the edge of the road long since deserted by the Hamlyn family. The empty houses were going to rack and ruin with exposure to the Dartmoor weather and farm buildings were relics of their former glory. Mechanisation was just one more element changing the face of the countryside.

38

'Sheepstor, England

Dear Ella,

You will be surprised to hear from a stranger, but I am now your sister-in-law as Fred and I were married a few weeks back. What is more surprising is that I was Eve Shepherd and am now Eve Brown. Opposite to you who were a Brown and became a Shepherd. I am twenty-seven, much younger than Fred but we are very happy. Work has finished at Burrator so Fred is working for anyone who wants him in Sheepstor or Meavy. I can tell you that we are sleeping at Deancombe. No one knows and we shouldn't be there, but we haven't found a house yet. There's a baby on the way. Your mum and dad are old but quite well. All the best to you and William and Tom for Christmas, Eve.'

It was spring before a reply came from Canada to the home of Fred's parents.

'Yennadon, Canada

Dear Eve,

It was sure a surprise. William thinks you must be related to his grandfather from Outhome, across from Deancombe. Are you still there? William says you'll be thrown out if you're found, but Fred knows that. Tell mum we are fine and work hard. Tom is fifteen this year. William works for Mr Trethewey who is kind to us. He's in charge of his sheep. Love to Mum and Dad, Ella. PS When is the baby due?'

Eve had her baby at her mother's home in Tavistock but their makeshift home was still at Deancombe. There had once been two farms here and the newest building had a lintel bearing the date 1858 and the initials of Massey Lopes.

'Sheepstor, England

Dear Ella,

You will be sad to know your father passed away after Christmas. Your mother's not too well. Charlie's now one year old and John is two months. Park Cottage was pulled down by the water people. Your mother tells me to tell you we have a new vicar, Mr Green. He's old and not married. Hope this finds you well. Your mum sends her love, Eve.'

Letters took a long time to travel from Sheepstor to Maple Ridge in Canada and both women delayed in writing.

'Yennadon, Canada

Dear Eve,

Tell mum I'm so sorry about Dad and I wish I could pop in to see her. We are making a home for ourselves here, but the country is harsh. Tom is seventeen now. Love to Mum. Best wishes to you and Fred and the boys, Ella.'

One of the last letters between Eve and Ella, who had never met each other, was in 1932.

'Sheepstor, England

Dear Ella,

I am sad to tell you your mum passed away in the spring. Meavy church was full of people and Mr Green spoke kindly. The flowers were lovely. Just before Christmas, Dickie Pengelly, who refused to be turned out of Combeshead, died at the farm and was carried down the valley in his coffin, just as he wished. He was 90 years old. For the first time they got a horse and cart up to the farm and all his old friends from the valleys and village walked behind. Sheepstor church was packed. We moved into your mum's cottage at Meavy so there's no more hiding. Fred sends his best. We now have another son who we've called Tom. Hope you are not too bad in this depression. All the best, Eve.'

No more letters reached Meavy from Canada, but times were hard. Tom knew nothing of the letters from England.

Dickie Pengelly had emigrated to Canada nearly fifty years before he passed away at Combeshead. With his wife and two little daughters, Millie and Bertha, they had sailed and travelled by Canadian Pacific Railway to Ontario. William was born there, but following his wife's death, and left with a young family on his own, Dickie returned to the Pengelly family at Sheepstor. Dickie's sister Ann was married to Henry Creber at Mullicroft.

A photograph of the coffin being taken by cart over the moor, with an account of the funeral, appeared in the following week's newspapers. *Trek Across Moor, Farm Wagon As Hearse At Sheepstor Funeral, Moorland Farmer Stayed Until Carried Out,* read the headlines. There was a description of the cortege, the wagon decorated with ferns and the coffin surmounted by wreaths. Dickie's grown-up children who had never married, Millie, Bertha and Gilly, walked behind the farmers of the valleys. More than twenty men walked in front of the wagon in sombre mood on that December morning.

The bearers, who included farmers Shillibeer, Dark, Manning, Legassick and Northmore had to help the cart horse across the streams and boulders. As the company reached the new road around the reservoir more mourners, men in black coats and black bowler hats, followed the coffin as it wound slowly to the church under the shadow of the brooding tor. On this cold, bleak winter's day Sheepstor folk said farewell to the last farmer to farm and live in one of the most beautiful valleys in England.

Burrator House, still owned by the Lopes family, was now lived in by a relative and her husband, Captain the Honourable Erskine Nicolson. The land around the reservoir was chiefly owned by Plymouth Water Corporation. The vicarage, previously Brook Cottage, was now redundant and had been bought by Captain Hutchinson who renamed the house Greystones. Another house, Torrfields, was built up near to the tor by a surgeon, Mr Robinson. A couple of years later Captain Nicolson, who became Lord Carnock, built a house for his herdsman near the entrance to Burrator, naming it Brook Cottage to the confusion of the old-timers.

Farmers still managing the land around the village were Legassick, Manning,

Moses, Northmore, Ware and Watkins. Harold Watkins and his family had moved into West Hellingtown when they were forced to move out of Narrator. Ironically, and as all had observed, the Corporation could hardly prevent wild ponies, livestock and wild animals wandering onto the the land, whilst visitors to the beauty spot had picnics near the lake.

'What was it all for?' the Reverend H T Green asked his farming parishioners.

'You may well ask, sir, you may well ask. There's more uncleanness going on now than ever there was before that poor lot was turfed out,' Mrs Moses exclaimed.

An eagle was spied over Sheepstor, an unusual visitor to Dartmoor. Buzzards, soaring and calling like the larger birds plentiful over the moor, nested in the wooded valleys of Sheepstor. Foxes, rabbits and otters lived in peace in the deserted valleys and the moor attracted people who wanted to get away from the towns. Events that shook the nation in 1936 caused barely a ripple in Sheepstor.

'What a world we live in,' Mrs Northmore whispered to Mrs Ware, as they sat in companionable quietness in Ditsworthy kitchen. 'Good King George dies, his son reigns for less than a year and then marries an American lady twice married already.'

'Albert, Duke of York and his lovely wife will do well,' Mrs Ware predicted. 'It's been a turbulent year and no mistake.'

'Did you see the announcement of the death of Lady Brooke?'

'No, the second Rajah's wife, d'you mean?'

'Yes, she'd been living in Cornwall. Margaret Brooke knew all the famous people it seems.'

Less than three years after this, the country was at war again and this time it did affect Sheepstor. Soldiers were living and camping on the moor, American soldiers and airmen in every village. Low flying planes practised in the valleys, over the hills and tors, and followed lines of roads and rail tracks. One man in their midst, Peter the son of the Nicolsons at Burrator, never returned. He was killed on active service at sea.

One night in May 1941 a Junkers 88 German bomber flying over Burrator Lake crashed and landed in Lowery marsh. The villagers thought that Burrator dam had been the target. The plane caught fire and the four airmen were killed. They were buried in the churchyard of Sheepstor with full military honours three days later.

Sarawak was invaded by the Japanese whilst the third white Rajah, his wife and daughters were on holiday in Australia. His brother Bertram, and his son Anthony, wished to rule the Eastern country but to their displeasure, Vyner handed over Sarawak to the British Government. Following the cession, Anthony Brooke set out to visit the colony in response to the wishes of some Sarawak subjects. He was prevented by Colonial Office orders and forbidden to speak to the press. A member of the Brooke family was no longer welcome in Sarawak.

Mr Winston Churchill, Leader of the Opposition in the House of Commons, asked in Parliament why such a tyrannical declaration should be allowed. He was informed by the Colonial Secretary, Mr Creech Jones, that there was an urgent need in Sarawak to reconstruct the country and Mr Brooke's visit would confuse the people with another constitutional problem.

In both the British and Malayan press, articles continued to appear in support of Anthony Brooke. Originally the ban precluded Mr Brooke from entering Singapore unless he gave a pledge not to discuss the affairs of Sarawak. The colonial government were determined to achieve an end to Brooke rule, whatever the desires of the people at that time.

Riding out over the moor up on Eylesburrow, the moormen discussed the Brooke family.

'It's the end of the Brookes out there. The last Rajah received a tidy penny so I'm told from our government.'

'Aye, there's a rich source of minerals in the soil to be mined and there's a lot of oil around the coasts.'

'But with all their own troubles, the family still send a small amount of money to the church each year. I think they want to keep their connections with old Sheepstor.'

'The Brooke family and the Sarawak people seek a bond with Sheepstor.' Mrs Ware was describing the stained glass window by the door of the church to some schoolchildren.

'This memorial window was put in recently, in 1950. It commemorates all those who died in Sarawak during the war there, between 1941 and 1946. We have close connections with Borneo. The two saints are St Leonard and St Stephen, both Christian martyrs. At the base you see a wounded man against a background of Nipah palms.'

'What's that, Mrs Ware?'

'It's part of the scenery by the rivers in that country. The man is being comforted by our Lord and a Sarawak deer stands on the other side of the stream.'

'What are the butterflies for?'

'At the top is the Brookiana butterfly, named after Sir James Brooke and found in the jungle there and below is the Atlas moth, a beautiful large insect found in the tropical climate. Can you see the pitcher plant? That is also found in the jungles of Borneo. It never ceases to amaze me how our tiny village is linked with that foreign land.'

39

SHEEPSTOR was slumbering in a rapidly changing world. The air and scents of the moorland, the music of the running waters, the hills and granite tors, these remain unchanged. But after the war years, walkers and riders began to visit Dartmoor in their thousands and in 1951 the upland was designated one of the first National Parks in England and Wales. Walking in the valleys the sense of history enfolds each individual; on the hills the world is spread below and beyond and no one is ever alone for too many have been here before. Generations spanning four thousand years have walked on the hills, bearing their secrets to the grave.

Now the moorland was there to be explored, enjoyed and written about.

One of the country folk who had left Sheepstor before the raising of the dam wrote in his diary on his return thirty years later:

'All seems as it was in 1923, thank God. The same wild hills, clouds furling around the tors. Much rain made River Mew look almost its old self below the dam. The abandoned valleys are a sad sight.'

Those who wanted to get away from the bustle of town and city replaced the original country folk who found it increasingly difficult to live in Sheepstor with no transport, no school and no amenities. With funds to restore old properties in the village and private conveyances, foreigners, as the Dartmoor folk called anyone who was not born in their midst, settled into the peace and serenity of Sheepstor.

In the neighbouring villages of Meavy, Walkhampton and Yelverton housing estates were built after the war years but no houses were constructed in Sheepstor. Over the years stone structures replaced wooden ones including those put up by the Water Corporation near Park Cottage Inn. No further homes have been added to the tiny village.

The coronation of Elizabeth II in June 1953 drew crowds to see the display of public pageantry; news that the British team of climbers had reached the summit of Mount Everest arrived on the same day. Many watched the coronation on their new-fangled television sets, albeit through what seemed to be a snowstorm in London, but nevertheless an amazing thing. But still no one saw it in Sheepstor. Electricity had not found its way to this remote corner of the moor.

In Canada the same year, Esca Brooke Daykin died in Toronto, his lifelong wish to be recognised by the Brooke family died with him. For most of his married life he had made pleas to be recognised as the son of Rajah Charles Brooke. He wrote to Ranee Margaret in Cornwall and to her brother Harry de Windt. Edith Daykin's brother took the matter to the press and at one time both the Canadian and English newspapers carried the story.

Esca did not want to govern Sarawak, he wanted simply to be accepted as the eldest son in the Brooke dynasty. It came to nothing, the Brooke family disowned him. He wrote to King George VI and to the British Government, seeking compensation. The Colonial Office in London sent Edith Daykin the sum of £500; the matter was finalised. As a small boy nearly eighty years before, he had been sent to Sheepstor to be adopted and taken care of by the priest in the village. There was no claim made then to the world that he was the first-born son of Charles Brooke and none was countenanced at this time. Yet many Brooke officials, including Spenser St John, friend of the first Rajah, established a Bornean family like Charles Brooke. In his book, for which his uncle had written the Preface, Charles Brooke claimed that people of mixed European and Asian origin would become future rulers of Sarawak. He conveniently forgot Esca. The nearest his family came to their roots was when years later, in 1983, two of his daughters, themselves elderly, visited their father's birthplace, Simanggang and at last met their Malay cousins related to their grandmother, Tia.

Ten years were to pass before Esca's step-brother, the third white Rajah of Sarawak, died in London. His body was cremated and a memorial service held in a chapel at St Paul's Cathedral. Bertram, his brother, died two years after Vyner and the ashes of both these Brooke men, who gave so much of their lives to Sarawak, if so little to Esca, are buried next to the bodies of the two Rajahs in Sheepstor.

Eight thousand miles separate the Dartmoor parish of Sheepstor and the former independent State of Sarawak, now part of the Federation of Malaysia. In a ceremony in St Leonard's Church, the memory of the only white Rajahs the world has known was honoured by the dedication of two memorials, one hundred years after the death of the first Rajah. Lord Carnock, living in the Rajah's old home of Burrator, took part in the service in which the Sarawak anthem was sung.

The memorial tablets, describing a history of the Brooke family's association with Sarawak were given by Anthony Brooke who performed the unveiling. Placed at the west end of the church, one consists of a Portland stone tablet surmounted by the arms of the Rajah of Sarawak and bearing the names of the three Rajahs and of Bertram, the Tuan Muda, the young lord. The other, a bronze plaque, gives a brief history of their connection with the former state. They were dedicated by the Bishop of Exeter, and during the service a former bishop of Sarawak spoke of the links with the tiny village in which so many of the Brooke family were now assembled.

'It is for us,' Philip Jones said in his sermon, 'all who love Sarawak and the name and family of Brooke, to make the world know what these men proved; that true harmony between men of different race and colour can be forged and maintained. That is the paramount task of our time, and here in this place is our inspiration.'

'When you look north from the Astana garden in Kuching you see the cone of Santubong mountain straight before you, guarding the Sarawak river. When you turn to the west there is a long line of Matang and on its skyline the famous profile of the sleeping Rajah.'

'Here, looking down on all the sleeping Rajahs, is the curve and crag of Sheeps Tor. These men and those hills are all, and for ever, in the hand of God. As we go back to the world to work let us remember the words of the greatest poet of our day, Thomas Stearns Eliot: *"What the dead had no speech for, when living, they can tell you being dead. The communication of the dead is tongued with fire beyond the language of the living."*

'The men we honour today made a people into a harmonious and lively nation. They served God, but not in a conventional way, because the Brookes are not a conventional family.'

Within the past one hundred years, bonds between British Columbia and Sarawak were forged with Sheepstor by men seeking adventure or a new way of life. There were those who left the solitude of the moor to find excitement, and those who withdrew from the turmoil of life to find solitude in Sheepstor.

Influenced by the seasons and the farmer's year, along with the Christian church calendar, the country folk had no need to plan their life. From birth to death the farming community was secure, they had a job for life. Neighbouring farmers helped each other out through the year as many men were needed to fulfil tasks on the farm and there was a spirit of co-operation.

Sheepstor is visited quietly by famous personages today. The Princess Royal rode a horse up over Eylesburrow from Sheepstor to Princetown in recent years and Peter Brooke, former Northern Ireland Secretary, visited his family graves in the churchyard. Tight security with helicopters overhead and men and sniffer dogs on the ground appear incongruous in the pastoral setting. Prince Charles, as Duke of Cornwall, owns seventy thousand acres of Dartmoor. Farms on the moor form half of the Duchy estate which also includes the village of Princetown and the prison.

A rare traditional woven cloth from Sarawak, Puak Kumba, with native design, hangs in Sheepstor Church presented by a representative from Malaysia on a tourist trade visit to London in 1996. Meavy and Sheepstor schoolchildren established a pen-pal link with a school in Kuching. English letters were full of life on the moor, animals, pets and the contrasts of the seasons. In return the children were told there are no seasons in Sarawak, that pupils study two languages, Bahasa Malaysia and English and that racial groups, such as Malays, Chinese, Iban, Indian, Dyak and Bidayuh live together in peace and harmony. Dartmoor children learnt about the tropical sun, jungles and mountains. Letters and photographs from Meavy school appeared in the Sarawak *Sunday Tribune*. A typical letter from Kuching read:

'The weather here is hot, humid and wet. If you feel England is too cold you can always come and spend your holiday here. Besides the beautiful weather you can travel out of the city and see the Niah, Fairy and Mulu caves, the long houses, beaches, tropical wildlife parks and museums and taste our local foods and fruit. Tell us more about the Rajahs, we have not learned much about them. Please send us photographs.'

Meavy and Sheepstor children wrote about life on the moor, of tors, rivers, Pixies Cave, Devon beaches, pasties and clotted cream. They told their pen-pals of local historical happenings and the history of the Brooke family in Sheepstor. Teachers from Kuching schools told the English pupils about the special museum dedicated to the Brookes containing the Rajah's uniform and his sword in their city. The remoteness of Sheepstor, the place where the first white Rajah of Sarawak chose to be buried, followed by the other two Rajahs, continues to amaze visitors to the village.

40

THE Shepherd family had left Dartmoor, the valleys around Burrator were deserted, the Brooke family no longer ruled an Eastern country and the secrets of Esca Daykin had been obscured. Tourists visited Sheepstor and Burrator reservoir, to gaze upon the history and beauty of the area. Life went on. The few farming families out on the moor remembered life in the olden days, the newcomers took great pleasure in the peace and quiet they had sought.

Ditsworthy Warren was consigned to history, closed down with the arrival of the appalling infectious viral disease, myxomatosis in the 1950s which wiped out the rabbits in a cruel and terrifying manner, ending rabbit farming for good. The hilltop around Sheeps Tor, covered in ancient rabbit warrens, acquired more relics, of the time when rabbits had been farmed for food and sport, and of the time when every piece of land around Sheepstor was *used* by farmers, miners and stone-cutters.

Now farmers received grants for each animal, such as sheep or bullocks, that they grazed out on the moor and battles were fought by ramblers who believed it was their right to walk anywhere in the countryside. The remote and lonely country still provided some employment for those who were prepared to work hard and long in a beautiful but harsh environment. A few farms were still handed down from father to son as they had been for generations. Henry was one such farmer who rented a cottage in the village, leaving his son to manage the farm, but never relinquishing the work which was his life. Most sons of the present generation preferred other employment off the moor.

Working farms in the parish are now found only at Collytown, Yellowmead, Lambs Park and Yeo, a far-cry from the dozens of farmhouses where smoke always curled from the chimneys and children played around the doorways; where moormen on horseback drove their animals to pastures new and filled the granite church on a Sunday.

Sheepstor became a centre for walks out on the high moor, tourists and walkers leaving their cars in the village to return to after their day of exploration. Under Sheeps Tor, beyond the village, is an ancient prehistoric monument discovered by the Reverend Hugh Breton and friends when he was vicar of the parish. For thousands of years the stones had been concealed by turf and heather plants but after a prolonged drought in 1921 a few were revealed.

Mr William Manning of Yellowmead farm and the vicar re-erected the stones in their old socket holes with help from other farmers, discovering that the ancient monument consisted of four concentric circles. These circles probably encircled the burial place of a Bronze-age chieftain. One hundred and eighteen stones were discovered but it was obvious that many former stones that once stood here had been used in wall building by moormen down the ages. Mr Breton and friends found twenty-four stones in the outer circle which has a diameter of sixty-six feet.

Many of these moorland hillsides are covered in clearly defined tracks today, made by the thousands of walkers who come to enjoy such a sense of history, set among the splendid moorland scenery, looking out into Cornwall or towards Plymouth and the English Channel. The streams are crystal clear as they tumble through deep valleys over granite boulders, increasing in size as they collect the water flowing off the hillsides. Snow and storms still come in the winter and the east wind is a frequent visitor. But the moor, which once was the land for the worker, is now principally a playground.

The last train to come down the valley from Princetown was in 1956, the only sounds heard now being those made by traffic, aircraft, wildlife and the wind. The old village cross by the lychgate was placed there to commemorate the coronation of King George V and the paving around it in more recent years by Lord Carnock, formerly of Burrator House, in memory of his wife Lady Katherine. The cross at the church porch is in memory of the men of Sheepstor who died in the First World War, William Mortimore and Harry Blatchford and of Peter Nicolson who died, killed in action, in the Second World War.

Henry, the old-timer in the village, and Liz, recently moved into Sheepstor, were sitting on the seat outside the church gate in the evening sunshine.

'Electricity came to the village in 1965,' Henry told Liz. 'Burrator experimented with a generator powered by Sheepstor Brook above the falls in the ground but we weren't on the mains till then. Some farms had their own generators.'

'We are not on main sewerage.'

'No, each house has its own cesspit. Twasn't always so. Some cottagers took their lavatory bucket and threw the contents into Sheepstor Brook. I still saw that going on in the late fifties.'

'Oh dear. Not too good for the residents of Burrator House. Has there ever been a shop here?' Liz asked the old man, squinting into the failing sunlight.

'Oh, yes. Mrs Palmer opened one up in West Hellingtown, her husband was a farmer. She re-opened tea rooms in 1952 and two years later she opened the General Stores. She served villagers and visitors until she closed the shop in 1973. Nelson had a herd of Ayrshire cows and from the milk Mary made clotted cream. She sold some to shops and a dairy in Yelverton and served the rest to her visitors. Home-made scones and clotted cream, nothing like it,' Henry said licking his lips.

'How did they make the cream?'

'The milk went straight from the cow to a churn where the cream was separated off. Put into bowls the ream, that is the creamy milk, was slowly heated over pans of boiling water, not over-heating the milk mind you, and after many hours the thick crust was lifted off using a holed spoon. It was layered into basins. The milk left was fed to the calves.' The old man pushed his hat on the back of his head. 'Her grandparents had farmed at Narrator before the reservoir days, moving into Hellingtown when the Smale family left and sailed to

Canada in 1924. Several families emigrated at that time.'

'Did the family serve teas in the garden?'

'Yes, but there was a problem with wasps. Cos of the jam, you see. We had a cobblers shop, too. The husband of Mrs Evans the school teacher mended our shoes. Those of us who had some,' he added with a laugh. 'She always referred to her husband William as a bootmaker. Their daughter Maud married George Shillibeer, son of Amos, at the turn of the century. George and Amos were both caretakers of Burrator reservoir.'

'Whatever did you do in the evenings?' Liz wondered.

'Folk made their own entertainment and grew enough food for the family in the garden. We all shared it, we swapped potatoes with Mrs Dark, I remember, who made lovely bread.'

'Was there a pub?'

'Park Cottage Inn sold beer till 1928. We walked down to Meavy mill to get flour. Snow was more severe in them days, it used to be piled high over the hedges. We were often cut off from the rest of the world. But we never wanted for anything.'

'Oh, and there was a bull-baiting field, before my time that was,' Henry went on. 'In the field below the churchyard. It was a nasty cruel sport when the bull tossed little dogs out of the field. It was banned in about 1835 in our country but the ring is still in the middle of the field. Amos Shillibeer found it when he caught his plough share in the ring which was fixed to a granite boulder. The dogs were usually killed and women are supposed to have sat on the church wall to catch the poor dogs in their leather aprons. The ale house then stood where St Leonard's Room now stands.'

'And the warren out on the moor?' Liz asked.

'All gone now. The naval cadets from Britannia Royal Naval College stay there when they are training out over. Percy and Elizabeth Ware built the bungalow at the end of the track under Gutter Tor and lived there with their children. There wasn't room for two women in the Warren house, for sure,' he laughed. 'That's used by HMS Raleigh now and known as Gutter Tor Refuge. I remember when all the outlying farmsteads were lived in and people made a decent living.'

'I envy you your memories,' Liz said to the old man. 'That way of life has gone for ever.'

'Even the remains of the German airmen were taken from our churchyard to be buried in a German War graveyard up country.'

Liz asked the old man, 'Are there any memorials to these men?'

'Their names are on four different kneelers in the church, stitched by villagers and dedicated to their memory.'

'No new houses have been built here recently?'

'No, that's right. Glen Iris replaced a wooden place in 1985, that would be the last. Nelson Palmer had it built and named it from somewhere in New Zealand where one of his son's lives.'

'What about a school bus?'

'Oh yes, there were a lot of children round about in the sixties. A bus came to the village every school day. Back along I remember it took me and my father two days to take a load of hay to Okehampton with our horse and wagon, and two days to return. Life went at a slower pace in them days.'

Henry got up. 'It's getting dimsy, I'd better be getting off home 'afore I'm pixie led. Thanks for the chat, missus.'

'Thank you, Henry.' Smiling, Liz returned to her modern home in the village that was so old. Her life, she thought, with up-to-date appliances was more comfortable but not so colourful as in days gone by. Her house was built on the site of one of the wooden huts which had been erected by the Water Board during the construction of the two dams over a hundred years earlier.

These and others in Sheepstor were the people Emma Rose got to know and they talked to her freely as she sat in their kitchens drinking tea or coffee. Emma's obsession had dissipated as her picture became whole. She was fond of Sam and Sarah, they were real to her. Alone Emma grieved, wept and laughed with them. She wished she could have talked to Esca, but too late. The excitement of chasing documents, making notes and completing the painstaking task of carefully checking valuable information was at an end.

41

EMMA had pieced her story together as painstakingly as a jigsaw, day by day. To her joy, she at last understood why she looked the way she did. As the missing pieces from her picture fell into place, she felt happy and content here on Dartmoor. She had discovered more about herself during the three months in Devon than in all her life spent in Canada.

Dan was waiting in his Land Rover at the foot of the drive to Burrator House, ready to take Emma to the Deancombe valley. When he saw her heading towards him, he jumped out to open the passenger door. Emma crossed the cattle-grid and they greeted each other with a gentle kiss.

'Hi, Dan. Thanks for coming. I'm really excited. Hello Milly you old softie,' Emma said fondling Dan's black labrador dog. She was greeted in return by a rapidly wagging tail.

'You've got a bit more of your story to tell me, I hope, Emma. It's fascinating,' Dan said cheerily. 'Anyway, today we'll see where it all happened.'

It was early morning and Dan drove past the church, along by the flowing brook, past Collytown and Nattor farms to the end of the lane under Gutter Tor. Parking the Land Rover by the ford of Sheepstor Brook, they strode out across the moor.

'We'll go this way today. We may have time to go up on Eylesburrow. You told me it is part of the story.'

'Oh, it is. I want to go to the Deancombe valley first.'

With Milly running ahead, sniffing over the moor for scents of rabbits, the young man and woman trod over the rough grass and uneven moorland terrain towards the hidden valley.

The day was Friday, 4 August, a sunny day when the country was celebrating the hundredth birthday of Queen Elizabeth the Queen Mother.

'My great-great-great grandmother was still alive one hundred years ago today, Dan, when Elizabeth Bowes Lyon was born. Sarah Shepherd was sixty-three. Doesn't it make the generations seem near-at-hand?'

'You're really lucky to find your family so well-documented, Emma. It has been relatively easy to trace the generations in such a small parish.'

'Very much so. It's hard for me to believe,' Emma said. 'I have been in England for only three months yet I have discovered why I look as I do. Understanding why I am as I am, seemed to take on major importance to me after my husband left me.'

'You told me your grandfather who lives near you in Canada was born in the Deancombe valley.'

'Yes. He was born at the beginning of the First World War in a farm called Middleworth. The Water Corporation told the family to leave the farm and that is when they emigrated.'

'How old was he then?' Dan asked.

'Only a boy, but I'm more interested to see where the family lived one hundred and fifty years ago.'

'Don't worry, we shall see it all. You'll find Outhome very ruinous. You can make out where the door and windows were but the walls are all broken down and covered in moss.'

Standing at last on the threshold of Outhome, on the bank of the Deancombe Brook, made emotions well up for Emma. Dan thoughtfully left her alone and wandered about looking for anything that might have a relevance to the Shepherd family and their way of life here a century and a half before.

'Outhome cottage was almost certainly originally built as a tinner's dwelling, Emma. Look, let me show you the tinner's mill, right here, beside the brook next to the house.'

Dan pointed out the evidence of the late medieval mill, wheelpit, launder bank, leat and tail-race. He explained how it worked, crushing tin ore found in the brook.

'There are about twenty mortar stones around here, they were the large granite boulders placed beneath mechanical hammers for crushing tin-ore, resulting in two or more hollow cavities in the stone. One is built into the side of the wheel-pit, see? That indicates the wheel-pit was reconstructed at some-time. Your family may have been the ones who made the old tinner's house habitable. This tinner's mill is well-documented.'

'It will make Grandpa smile to know that the old mill is an English Heritage monument.'

'The farmer at Outhome disturbed the area around the tin mill. He built walls for his fields and planted trees amongst the ruins.'

They talked and laughed together.

Emma told Dan of her imaginings about the lives of the people that farmed this valley. There was Sam, small and reserved who kept his thoughts to himself; Sarah, happy and friendly before she was stricken with guilt; Will, a young Dartmoor man, impetuous and lonely who ended his life here; Annie, bright and loyal, with a knowledge that she didn't quite fit in the family; William, an orphan, doted on by his grandmother and his wife Ella, from the same mould as Sarah, innocent and trusting. Then there was Tom her grandfather, whom she knew and loved, taken away from these hills and valleys as a boy who now scarcely remembered his childhood here on the moor.

After their picnic lunch eaten in the ruins of Outhome, with Milly keeping her eyes on them for any falling crumbs, Emma talked over her family's labours and loves in this place. Walking uphill to the old mine on Eylesburrow they sensed a fellowship with each other, talking about their innermost reflections. Not only of the past and the present but way into the future.

Dan was able to show Emma the ruins of buildings, cottages, shafts and tin-workings. They imagined men working up here in all weathers, walking home long distances and returning in the mornings. He pointed out the last smelting house ever used on Dartmoor.

'The mine closed even before your ancestors Sam and Sarah married. It was a busy mine.'

'Sam worked here before he married, when he lived in Outhome with his parents.'

Dan smiled to hear Emma talk of Sam as though he might pop up any moment. It was real to her and she had become caught up with life on Dartmoor from Victorian times.

They lay back on the banks of a deep pit and Emma told Dan about Annie and Will.

'There is no evidence this truly happened, Emma. But it could be just as you describe. I've wished so often myself that stones could talk.'

As they walked back down the track to Dan's vehicle he told her that Outhome had been derelict before the building of the reservoir. There were families, though, who were forced to leave the area, the only job and home they had known because they lived within the water catchment area. You are going to tell me you know all this.'

Emma grinned at Dan. 'My great-grandparents were one of those families, as I've told you.'

'There is so much history out here, Emma. Tomorrow I am going to take you to Ditsworthy Warren and to the menhirs. These tall stones were put up as monuments to the dead four thousand years ago. I'm sure the Warren is part of your story but I doubt even you imagine how those Bronze Age people lived on the moor.'

'Now you are making fun of me, Dan.'

'Far from it, I'm only teasing you. I'm as fascinated in all your finds and visions.'

'It's just wonderful I have you to share it with me,' Emma declared. 'Each evening I find myself longing to tell you the next piece of the jigsaw.'

There was a lump in Emma's throat. She had experienced an obsession about finding out her family's past. The proverbial sleeping dog that her grandfather had spoken of was awake now. The truth could not hurt her Dartmoor ancestors and she was under no obligation to take the whole truth back to Canada. In this moorland solitude, away from the troubles of the world, she would leave many of her discoveries.

Dan believed that Emma possessed a sixth sense. He was aware her perception of the lives of the Shepherd family in Sheepstor coincided with well-documented lives of other families.

Emma stopped walking and looked at Dan.

'I feel responsible for rescuing the past from the mists of Dartmoor. Not only my belief in my own family but of all those who have walked on these moorland hills.'

'I think the same way, Emma. Rescuing the past from uncertainty has responsibilities as well as rewards for the historian. I've never had a friend to share my passion of Dartmoor with, not one as pretty as you, anyway.'

Emma felt the colour rise in her cheeks.

'I really value everything we share, Dan. I'm so glad you're coming to supper at Burrator this evening, I want to show you off to my kind hosts.' Milly came bounding back to see why they had stopped, looking at them expectantly.

At supper Emma told Dan and the Flints about the service in Sheepstor Church the previous Sunday. The four churches, now a united benefice, of Meavy, Sheepstor, Walkhampton and Yelverton, had held a team service of Holy Communion at Sheepstor.

'The little church was filled as I imagined it used to be years gone by,' Emma said. 'The bells pealed out and we sang hymns, but what was such a coincidence is that we sang the hymn "Faithful Shepherd, feed me in the pastures green". As a member of the Shepherd family I think it was meant for my family.'

'Emma has experienced so many situations whilst she's been on Dartmoor,' Dan said to Elizabeth and John Flint. 'One coincidence after another.'

'And,' Emma went on, 'I found myself sitting beneath the window dedicated to the Daykins which I hadn't noticed before. I know I have been guided these last months.'

Dan described some of Emma's telepathic experiences which continued to intrigue.

'Emma got talking to some people from Sarawak in the churchyard,' Dan said. 'They had come to visit the Rajahs' graves and Emma told them her ancestors came from their country and they have invited us to go and stay with them.'

'They were so hospitable, we might go one day,' Emma said smiling across at Dan.

42

SWEEPING up directly from the church is the massive tor which gave the village its name. Looking beyond, out to the moor, is Gutter Tor below which is the mire, the source of Sheepstor Brook. From here to Burrator is the peaceful Sheepstor valley. As Emma had read, *'A little winding rivulet, content to wash the foot of the haughty mountain.'*

Dan took many days off work in August and showed Emma all the places she had spoken of on this south-west edge of Dartmoor. They trod over the high moor, climbed tors and walked in the valleys. Emma found the moor mysterious, marvelling at how it never appeared the same from one hour to the next, seen from different places with changing colours. Dan had come to love everything about Emma, her sparkling personality, her beauty, her grace and her soft gentle voice. They shared the same interests, the same sense of humour and he felt sure they were meant to be together.

Emma found contentment and tranquility sitting by herself in the autumn sunshine in the north-east of the churchyard, where her family members were laid to rest. There was seclusion but not aloneness. She gazed again at the two gravestones of Charles Brittan's daughter and son, Betty and Charles, who had been buried in Sheepstor in their old age. The great old beech tree under which the Rajah was buried had long since been felled and Emma studied the gravestones all around her. Within the railings nearby, surrounding the Rajah's tomb, were memorials to the other white rulers of Sarawak.

In memory of Sir Charles Brooke, Second Rajah of Sarawak. Born 1828, died 1917.

His Highness Sir Charles Vyner Brooke. Born 1874, died 1963. Third and last Rajah of Sarawak.

Bertram Willes Dayrell Brooke, Tuan Muda of Sarawak, fourth in succession to the first Rajah. Born 1876 at Kuching, Sarawak, died 1965 at Weybridge, Surrey.

Outside the enclosure are memorial stones over the ashes of other family members.

Kathleen Mary Brooke, Ranee Muda of Sarawak 1907-1981.

Angela Brooke 1942-1986. Elder daughter of Kathleen and Anthony Brooke.

Anne, Lady Bryant daughter of Bertram Brooke 1910-1993.

JCVC Brooke 'Jimmy' son of Harry Brooke 1911-1995.

A young beech tree was spreading its branches over these tombs. In September, Emma travelled to Oxford to view the Brooke papers, especially the letters written by the first white Rajah when he lived at Burrator. She was amazed at the grandeur of Rhodes House where these archives are stored and its immaculately maintained gardens. She wandered happily round the colleges of the university and visited the Bodleian Library.

Emma had never seen a city so wonderful, so old or so beautiful. The letters in Sir James Brooke's own hand intrigued her. He had written pages to family and friends, and even wrote across the page on top of his own writing. She sat by an open window in a gracious panelled room with fragrances from the garden wafting in, reading of his contentment and peace in his Sheepstor home.

Brooke family letters and papers were also fascinating. The little book of paintings which Ranee Margaret worked on in Sarawak when she was a young wife was still as vivid and fresh as the day she reproduced the flowers of the jungle. Letters and newspaper cuttings about Esca Daykin, photographs, details of family feuds and conflicts were all at her disposal. Emma was mindful of the faded snapshot of William and Ella Shepherd in Tom's room. There was an obvious similarity between Tom's father and Esca Daykin.

Dan phoned faithfully every evening and Emma's absence confirmed in both their hearts that they were meant for each other. 'We must have been soulmates in another lifetime,' she told Dan as they whispered their goodnights one time. He was there to greet her on the platform at Plymouth station on her return from Oxford. They flung their arms round each other and kissed passionately, oblivious to the smiles of passengers on the departing train.

Despite her eagerness to be with Dan for ever, she refused to move into his cottage until she was his wife. She met his family and friends and was made to feel at ease by them all. Emma felt she had never been so relaxed and happy.

'But I have to return to Canada soon, Dan,' she said. 'I have found what I came to find, and more.'

'Marry me, Emma. We'll go to Canada together for our honeymoon.'

'You will always be my best friend, Dan, but I should love to be your wife and share the rest of my life with you.'

Emma thought about Sarah and Sam, Annie and Will, William and Ella all falling in love in this moorland village.

'It is your search for yourself and your family that brought us together, Emma. The bond is too strong to separate us. I promise I shall never let you go, not ever.'

Emma and Dan enjoyed walking to the summit of Sheeps Tor, looking down on the blue water of the reservoir. The steep climb over granite boulders in the autumn sunshine caused Emma to catch her breath. Bracken was turning brown and yellow gorse, still in flower, grew from the rocks. Men and women were rock climbing on the sheer face of the tor and when the couple reached the summit, the sound of the wind whispering through the grass and rushes filled their ears. Milly rushed around following scents and ponies and sheep grazed on the hillside. Below and around them, the patchwork of fields and the hills of Devon and Cornwall merged into the rolling landscape. Farms in the Sheepstor valley nestled below, sunlight glinting on houses in villages to the west. The English Channel at Plymouth Sound was like a gateway to the world beyond. Together they scrambled down to Pixies Cave and carefully dropped down into the opening.

'This has become smaller since I have known it,' Dan said. 'It is hard to find, but a genuine niche in Sheepstor's history.'

Dan and Emma walked once again up the Deancombe valley together in the autumn sunshine with Milly confidently leading the way.

'Dartmoor is so special, Dan, it's one vast, open-air museum where we can roam and explore. Time and weather are eroding the old farm buildings, though, I fear.'

'Yes, and sadly not everyone takes care at these sites. Each time we visit I find something I've not seen before. The moormen in those farms used the granite all around them, left for our generation to see and speculate about.'

'I realise wood and thatch have disappeared but granite relics like gate-posts, feeding troughs, bridges and walls remain. Do you sense the hard-working happy folk here, Dan?'

'I do indeed, work was tough in all weathers. It must have been a thriving community. Farmers were enterprising and made use of tinning remains. Tin was a valuable metal and signs of man's efforts to extract it exist in almost every Dartmoor valley.'

'This valley has a special atmosphere, it is so ancient. I shall try to convey the beauty to my family in Canada.'

'Life on Dartmoor has never been easy, Emma. Who knows if farmers would still be in the valleys if the Plymouth Corporation had not impounded the water at Burrator. The way of life has changed and probably the uninterrupted occupation of hundreds of years might have come to an end anyway by now.'

The couple sat under the ruins of Combeshead farm, eating their picnic, observing animals and birds as well as riders, walkers and runners, crossing the brook and moving across the moor. In the autumn sunshine by the sparkling brook, with the gentle breeze stirring the bracken, Dan and Emma sat and bade farewell to the moorland for a while. Emma was sure that Milly, who lay by her side, was aware that they were leaving her with Dan's parents for the next month.

'One of the old moormen told me that when he was a boy he and his friends placed cabbages on top of the chimneys,' Dan told Emma. 'They thought it was great fun when it sent the occupants running outside as the room filled with smoke.'

'They must have climbed on to the roof from the trees. Highly dangerous with a thatched roof, I should think,' Emma smiled.

'Youthful exuberance never changes,' Dan laughed, giving Emma a hug.

Milly, wet from lying in the brook, got up and licked them both as they laughed together.

Walking to the summit of nearby Down Tor, from where there is a magnificent view, Emma and Dan looked down on the familiar moorland, feeling at one with their surroundings.

'What a wonderful view, Dan. See the patterns of the old fields in the Deancombe valley.'

'There is so much clitter beneath the tor, Emma, all those scattered rocks, it was once a more elevated tor. I have counted twenty three other tors to be seen from here.'

Dan named most of the countless hills for Emma and pointed out Bronze Age remains on the hillsides below. Clouds were scudding across the sky casting moving shadows on the moor. Emma realised how little time a person passed in a lifetime, compared with this land which had altered so little in thousands of years.

'Come on, Milly,' Emma called, 'we're going home.'

43

EMMA and Dan Worthy were aboard their flight to Canada, her father and mother waiting eagerly at Vancouver airport to meet them. They would spend a month in Maple Ridge for their honeymoon and then return to Dartmoor to settle down and make their home together. They were going to look up Prowse family members in Yennadon, Emma's home district, and travel to Toronto in their quest to find any members of the Daykin family. One day, perhaps, they might visit Malaysia.

What was Emma to tell Tom? Should she relate to her grandfather all she had discovered in England about his background? Should she tell him that his father had been born out of wedlock and that his grandparents had been brought up together believing that they were brother and sister?

Should she tell him that his father had been conceived on a Dartmoor hillside amongst the ruins of an ancient tin mine? That his grandfather came from an old farming family on the Dartmoor hills but his grandmother was born into a high class Malay family? That his grandmother was lost by her family in deep snow on the moor and left for dead as the foreigners returned to Borneo?

The final blow would be to tell Tom that his grandfather had committed suicide not even knowing that the baby who became Tom's father had been conceived. That his grandmother broken-hearted died a few days after his father's birth and that his father had never known either of his parents.

No. She would tell him about the Deancombe valley, the ruins of Outhome Farm cottage, Sheepstor village and St Leonard's Church. She would describe Burrator House and tell him of the involvement of the Brooke family and the connection with Sarawak. Emma would tell him she had visited his birthplace, Middleworth Farm, the ruins of which were being preserved by Dartmoor National Park.

She would relate to him her visits to all the derelict farmsteads with Dan, all those in the River Meavy watershed and how not only the Shepherd family, but the occupiers of all the farms had been served notices to quit.

Without telling him the complete truth she might guide him to consider that his grandfather had married a Sarawak lady staying with the Brookes at Burrator. Emma would truthfully enlighten her grandfather that the story of his grandparents and of his father's birth was one of the greatest love stories on earth.

No reference to suicide. No alluding to illegitimacy. No touching on abandonment. No mention of scandal, sadness or tragedy.

There were many positive facts she would relate to the old man. Of her visit to Yennadon House in Dousland. Meeting with members of the Prowse family at Yelverton. The discovery that the aunt of Ernest Prowse who had been Mayor of Vernon near Vancouver, had married the Rector of Meavy who had conducted services in Sheepstor at the time when his grandparents worshipped in the church.

Talking to a Prowse descendant called Mary, in Yelverton, over a welcome cup of tea, Emma learned that Mary's grandmother, Adeline Mary Prowse, was the sister of Ernest who had emigrated to British Columbia and named the district of Yennadon. Mary had traced the Prowse family tree and was hoping to visit the family in the Yennadon district of Maple Ridge. Emma was shown photographs and newspaper cuttings of the Prowse family in her home district – including Ernest, Jessie and Bonnie. Emma promised to look up family members for Mary when she returned home. So many Marys and Williams in Emma's story.

She would tell her grandfather that the first-born son of the second white Rajah of Sarawak, born in the Far East, was transported at the age of six years to the curate of Sheepstor, to be adopted by him and his wife. That like Tom's own father, this man was the son of a Malay woman and an Englishman. Not only that, but he had been taken to live in Canada from Sheepstor as a young boy as Tom had been. In Toronto, as a man, Esca tried to make sense of his birth, of his identity, just as Tom had done. The similarities would interest Tom, especially when Emma told him how alike he was to the photographs she had seen of Esca Daykin in an Oxford library.

It was from Annie, Tom's grandmother that Emma originated, the baby born of Sarawakian parents, and she who had contributed so greatly to the way Emma, her mother and grandfather appeared. His mother had been a member of the Brown family from Meavy and Emma had met many of that family on her frequent visits to the village. Their spirits, like those of Emma, were in the countryside. All sent their best wishes to Tom.

Fred and Ella Brown's children, although younger than Tom Shepherd, had passed away but their grandchildren were Emma's age and pleased to talk to her and show her photographs of their families. Emma had never experienced being part of a large family that could trace its roots back for generations and she felt it comforting. Everyone in Sheepstor and Meavy knew someone related to the Browns whose ancestors had been the village blacksmiths.

Emma had so much to report to Tom about the changes on Dartmoor since he had left for Canada as a child in 1923; of the beauty of Burrator Reservoir and the deserted valleys in the Mewy valley. She would tell him how Dartmoor, the high moor and its border country, had become one of England's first designated National Parks; how the three parishes of Sheepstor, Meavy and Walkhampton were now one parish and united under the title of Burrator. She would be able to acquaint him with recent changes in the area, the arboretum, boats on the lake for fishing and the numerous visitors to Sheepstor.

Emma would delight in describing the wonderful offers of hospitality she received in the tiny village. Notwithstanding visitors, sightseers and tourists, the village was still far away from the world and what is known in this world as progress. The moorland solitude has changed with easier access and communications but a holy peace still pervades Sheepstor and materialistic influences seem far away. The hills, the streams and rivers are the same, only man has disrupted the peace with contentions and disputes. These pass with generations and all that is worthwhile remains, leaving enough evidence for folk with imagination and a sense of history to frame a picture.

'Do you think Tom remembers his great-grandmother Sarah?' Dan enquired one day.

Emma was thoughtful. 'No, he has never spoken of her. I know now that he was only three years old when she died. I will tell him of her great love for him.'

44

EMMA could not help indulging in a little more nostalgia, musing about life on Dartmoor in Victorian times even here, high in the sky above the Atlantic. Dan was longing to talk to old Tom about things he was able to recall about living in the Deancombe valley. Remembering that Tom had told her he walked to Meavy school in his last year at Sheepstor, she and Dan had walked that way several times. Through the pathfield gate on the left bank of Sheepstor Brook in Portland Lane, they had walked across fields passing Burrator grounds and through woods passing Yeo Farm and the old farm building now modernised as a family house.

The lane had led them past Marchants Cross where they followed the road to Meavy, crossing the River Meavy on stepping-stones, once always known as the River Mew. Dan had told her the history of this way where monks, trading between the abbeys of Buckland Monachorum, Tavistock and Buckfast, had ridden across the moor in all weathers guided by the tall granite crosses. And he had taken her on a long walk on high Dartmoor to experience part of the Abbots Way; she had been overawed by the remoteness of the walk and of the hardships these men had endured centuries ago.

Passing the existing school, where young children were running about making happy and merry noises in the playground, they had walked along the old country lane between Devon hedges to the village green. Picturesque and the centre of the village, the green was surrounded by St Peter's Church, the Royal Oak Inn, the ancient oak tree of a thousand years still bearing leaves, and the old school.

Here Emma's grandfather had attended lessons, before the new Meavy and Sheepstor school was built, during his last few months in England. She imagined the one candlelit room and him playing out on the green at lunchtimes. Emma took some photographs of the building, now Meavy Parish Hall, and of the green. This should surely bring back her grandfather's memory of his schooldays. The scene was wonderful to Emma, truly English, and so old.

Sitting under the eaves of the old inn, and regarding the old school across the green, Emma told Dan the only story Tom had ever told her about this school.

'A lorry was delivering bottles of beer and lemonade to the pub and right outside the school it turned so sharply that all the wooden crates and their contents fell off the lorry smashing on the road. The children all rushed out of the schoolroom and, to the teacher's consternation, picked up the marbles that were rolling around everywhere.'

'That's when marbles were inserted into bottles before they were filled, to seal them I suppose,' Dan observed.

'It made an impression on Grandpa, anyhow,' Emma beamed.

Checking her watch to see how long they had before landing, Emma said,

'What did you think of that account in the *Western Morning News* this morning, Dan, that claims historians are preparing to rewrite the history books in Canada? It reckons that Sir Francis Drake first discovered the coast of British Columbia in 1579. Isn't it amazing?' Emma thought of this as another link between her home and Dartmoor.

'Samuel Bawlf in Canada claims that Drake explored vast parts of British Columbia while searching for a western entrance to the Northwest Passage,' Dan said.

'Why did Drake not make these findings known?'

'To keep the discoveries secret from the Spanish who were trying to topple Queen Elizabeth I from the throne,' Dan explained.

'At school *we* learned that James Cook and George Vancouver discovered our province two hundred years after this date.'

'Well, this research, that claims Drake discovered Vancouver, is disputed by an Englishman.'

'It would be marvellous though, to consider that Drake sailed to our coast of Canada before he returned to Dartmoor and engineered the leat from Sheepstor in 1585.'

So many coincidences, so many links.

Emma closed her eyes and put her head back on the plane seat. She was returning to Canada with pictures and scenes in her memory never to be taken from her, the truth about her ancestry and with the man who was to be her future. Emma had found herself and she had found Dan. If she and Dan had children they would be able to read her story of the Shepherd family, of Sheepstor, Sarawak and Canada.

Suddenly she wanted to hug her grandfather. Tom had reached the eve of his life and she longed to give him contentment. Emma knew it would be enough for him to see the peace and joy in her life which she had found in an isolated moorland valley. Tom and Dan would like each other, she knew. Two countrymen from Dartmoor with so much to talk about notwithstanding their age difference.

The marriage of Dan and Emma had taken place at Tavistock Registry Office, where John Sauls had signed his name when he registered each of the births of his three children at Burrator in the mid-nineteenth century. At the blessing of their marriage vows in Sheepstor church, six bells pealed from the tower and the organist accompanied the hymn.

It was in this peaceful ancient building where Sam and Sarah had made their vows to each other. Baptisms and burials of members of the family she had come to characterise in her mind happened here. Emma had looked at the old granite octagonal font where Will and Annie were baptised, and William and her grandfather Thomas Frederick Shepherd. Sarah was present on all these occasions and her burial was the final entry of the Shepherd family in the church registers.

'I know you are thinking of the past, Emma. It is wonderful that we have dedicated ourselves to each other where so many of your family occasions took place,' Dan whispered to her. 'We can now look forward together.'

'I feel a sense of security, Dan, that I've never known.'

'Not one of your family could have looked as radiant as you are today,' replied Dan, struggling to find words to express his deep admiration for his wife. They anticipated their future together with mutual pleasure.

Emma had thought of Tom in singing their chosen hymn.

'Lord of all kindliness, Lord of all grace,
Your hands swift to welcome, your arms to embrace.

That was how her grandfather had always been to her.

'Be there at our homing and give us we pray
Your love in our hearts, Lord, at the eve of the day'.

As the plane landed Emma squeezed Dan's hand.

'I do love you, Dan.'

'Not as much as I love you, Emmie.'

The world was far away and at that moment they existed only for each other. Emma hugged to herself one last secret thought. Could Annie's actual father have been a Brooke? Tom did look so like photographs of Esca.

EMMA'S FAMILY TREE

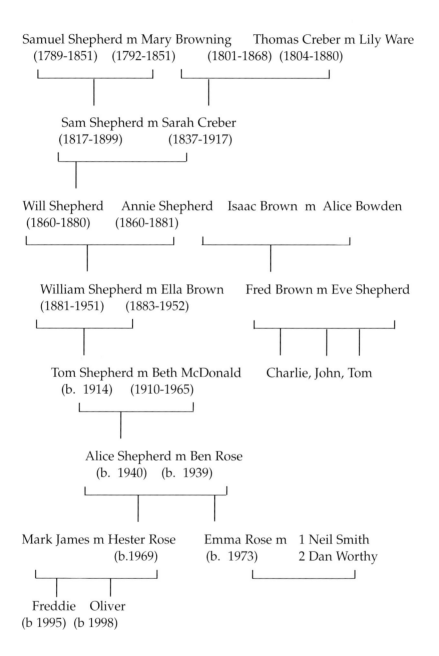

Samuel Shepherd m Mary Browning   Thomas Creber m Lily Ware
(1789-1851)   (1792-1851)   (1801-1868) (1804-1880)

Sam Shepherd m Sarah Creber
(1817-1899)   (1837-1917)

Will Shepherd   Annie Shepherd Isaac Brown m Alice Bowden
(1860-1880)   (1860-1881)

William Shepherd m Ella Brown   Fred Brown m Eve Shepherd
(1881-1951)   (1883-1952)

Tom Shepherd m Beth McDonald   Charlie, John, Tom
(b. 1914)   (1910-1965)

Alice Shepherd m Ben Rose
(b. 1940)   (b. 1939)

Mark James m Hester Rose   Emma Rose m 1 Neil Smith
         (b.1969)   (b. 1973)   2 Dan Worthy

Freddie   Oliver
(b 1995) (b 1998)

BIBLIOGRAPHY

Baring-Gould, Sabine (1912) *Sheepstor*, Hoyten & Co, Plymouth

Breton, Hugh (1912) *Beautiful Dartmoor*, Hoyten & Co, Plymouth

Breton, Hugh (1932) *The Forest of Dartmoor*, Hoyten & Co, Plymouth

Brooke, Margaret (1913) *My Life in Sarawak*, OUP, Singapore

Brooke, Margaret (1934) *Good Morning and Good Night*, Constable & Co Ltd, Great Britain

Brooke, Sylvia (1990) *Queen of the Headhunters*, OUP, Singapore

Brown, Mike (2000) *Dartmoor 2000*, Forest Publishing, Devon

Collier, William (1896) *Harry Terrell – a Dartmoor Philosopher*, William Brendon & Son, Plymouth

Hahn, Emily (1953) *James Brooke of Sarawak*, Arthur Barker Ltd

Healey, Edna (1978) *Lady Unknown*, Sidgwick & Jackson, London

Hemery, Eric (1983) *High Dartmoor*, Robert Hale, London

Hemery, Eric (1983) *Walking the Dartmoor Railroads*, David & Charles, Newton Abbot

Hemery, Pauline (1999) *The Book of Meavy*, Halsgrove, Devon

Jacob, Gertrude (1876) *The Rajah of Sarawak vols 1 & 2*, Macmillan, London

James, Trevor (1999) *"There's one away": Escapes from Dartmoor Prison*, Orchard Publications, Devon

Kingdon, Anthony (1979) *The Princetown Branch*, Oxford Publishing

Lee, Sidney, editor (1912) *Dictionary of National Biography 1901-1911*, OUP, London

Lo, Joan (1986) *Glimpses From Sarawak's Past*, AGAS SDN BHD, Kuching

Maxwell, Herbert (1897) *Sixty years a Queen*, Harmsworth, London

Nickols, Sheila, editor (1972) *Maple Ridge: A History of Settlement*, Canadian Federation of University Women, B.C.

Payne, Robert (1960) *The White Rajahs of Sarawak*, OUP, London

Pybus, Cassandra (1996) *White Rajah: a Dynastic Intrigue*, University of Queensland Press, Australia

Runciman, Steven (1960) *The White Rajahs*, Cambridge Uni Press Rutter, Owen, editor (1935) *Letters from Rajah Brooke to Baroness Burdett-Coutts*, Hutchinson & Co, London

Stanbrook, Mary (1991) *Old Dartmoor Schools Remembered*, Quay Publications, Brixham

St John, Spenser (1899) *Rajah Brooke*, Fisher Unwin, London

BBC TV documentary – A journey to Sarawak with Joanna Lumley 1991: Executive Producer: Lavinia Walker A Warner Sisters Production

Newspaper cuttings – *Western Morning News, Western Evening Herald, West Devon Mercury, Plymouth, Devonport and Stonehouse Herald, Sarawak Tribune, Church Times, The Malayan Tribune, The Illustrated London News*

Magazine articles, *The West Country Magazine*, Personal letters, SPG leaflet, *Sarawak Fever* – a paper written by Bob Reece